A Nameless Grace

ISBN 978-1-291-00915-6

Forthcoming in the *Far Horizons* series;

The Good of the City

The Farthest Horizon

For Jake

She could hear her brother before he even got through the door. "Rose! *Rose!* Put down whatever you're fiddling with, and come and help me with these figures."

Rose sighed, and closed her book, slipping in the embroidered bookmark her mother had given her as a birthday present. "Coming, Charles."

She set the book down beside her chair, and walked through to join her eldest brother in the room that served as his office.

"What's up?" she asked, leaning over his shoulder to look at the computer screen.

"I can't get these cashflow forecasts to come out how I want them."

Rose looked at the spreadsheet for a few moments, then tapped the screen with a fingernail. "There's your problem. That formula should be absolute, not relative."

Charles glanced up at her, smiling wryly. "I don't know how you kids do it."

She frowned. "Charles, in case you've forgotten I turned eighteen last month."

"Sorry, kitten. Thanks for the help – I don't know where we'd be without you. Tell you what – why don't I take you out for dinner tomorrow, seeing as we didn't get to go out on your birthday."

Rose smiled. "Thanks, Charles, that'd be lovely."

She straightened. "Now, are you sure you're going to be OK with the rest of this?"

Charles nodded. "Think I've cracked it now."

Rose walked back into the lounge, and she was about to pick up her book again when her mobile rang. She picked it up, glancing at the display. "Hi, Paul. Don't tell me, you need a favour. I've just finished bailing Charles out of a conundrum."

The voice at the end of the phone was apologetic. "Sorry, kitten, I could use some help. A client is visiting, and I've promised him a tour of the business tomorrow afternoon, but I have to get these production schedules sorted out."

"OK," said Rose, "I can manage that."

His relief was obvious. "I owe you one, Rose. Reception, one o'clock tomorrow?"

"I'll be there." She ended the call, and sat down. Somehow the book she'd been reading had momentarily lost its appeal, and Rose suppressed a flash of irritation at her brothers. The fact that the business was expanding so rapidly could only be a good thing, but she always seemed to be the one who filled in the gaps.

Rose shook her head. Her book would be there later, and she could log on to the literature forum and see how her friends were getting on with it.

She glanced at her watch. Not long till dinnertime; she might as well go and see if her mother needed any help in the kitchen.

She found her mother preparing vegetables, and sat down opposite her at the kitchen table. Rose picked up a handful of peas, and with the ease of long practice began to shell them.

"What are you making, Mum?"

"Just a casserole, darling. I got some of your favourite ice cream for dessert."

Rose grinned. "Thanks, Mum."

She remembered her conversation with Charles. "I won't be in for dinner tomorrow. Charles is taking me out – I think he feels guilty for having to work late on my birthday."

She finished shelling the peas. "There you go."

"Thanks, dear. Dinner will be about fifteen minutes – tell Charles?"

"OK."

Rose went back through to the study. "Dinner won't be long."

Charles nodded, his eyes fixed on the figures on the screen. "Call me when it's on the table."

Rose climbed the stairs to her bedroom, sitting down at her dressing table to brush her hair. As usual, she looked critically at her reflection in the mirror. She'd always thought her black hair and dark eyes were her best feature, although her eyebrows were perhaps a little too thick. In contrast to the rest of her colouring, her skin was pale, and not for the first time she wished she had the chance to spend more time outdoors as she'd done as a child. Riding, spending time at the beach, just walking with her friends in the countryside nearby.

Her mother's voice from downstairs interrupted her reverie. "Dinner's ready, darling."

Rose quickly caught her hair up in her favourite silver clasp, and went down the stairs, putting her head round the study door to remind Charles to come to the table.

They sat down and started to eat. "So who's this client that's coming to visit?" Rose asked.

Charles glanced up. "Actually I've never met him. His name's David Stuart – he's been a customer of ours for about two years, and he's considering moving all of his business to us this time around."

Rose nodded. "Paul's asked me to give him a tour tomorrow."

"Great. Make sure he sees the main production line, we have a run of his product on there at the moment. I particularly want him to see the quality control process."

Their mother interrupted gently. "I think that's enough business talk for now. Rose, how are you getting on with your book?"

Rose smiled wryly. "It's really interesting, when I get a chance to think about it. After dinner I'll go on the forum and see what the others have posted so far."

She put her fork down. "Didn't you say something about ice cream?"

"Of course, dear."

"I'll have mine later," said Charles, getting up. "I need to have these figures finished tonight."

Rose and her mother sat for a while with their ice cream. "Shall I take Charles a cup of coffee?" offered Rose.

"Thanks, darling."

Charles nodded absently as Rose set the steaming mug on the desk. "Are you sure you don't need any more help?" she asked.

"No, I'm fine."

Rose went back up to her room and flipped open the laptop, logging on to the discussion forum where she spent most of her time online. She noticed some new posts with the title "Happy ever after?" and rolled her eyes. Obviously some of her friends were rehashing the periodic discussion on meeting the man of their dreams, riding away with him into the sunset. Some hope.

She clicked onto the next thread, and started to look through her friends' responses to the book they'd decided to read together...

***

The next morning Rose helped her mother with the shopping, and they got back to the house in time for lunch.

"Getting something from the salad bar was a really great idea, Mum," Rose grinned.

"Have some more, dear. You have a busy afternoon, and I don't want you being too hungry before you get to dinner – you know what Charles is like, he's bound to be at least a bit late."

Rose took another sausage roll, then piled her plate again with lettuce and tiny tomatoes. "Good point."

After lunch she went upstairs to change, putting on the smart skirt and jacket she always wore when she visited the factory.

She drove the few minutes to the business park, grinning as she pulled into the space reserved for Charles. He was seeing the accountants, but if he came back that afternoon he could take his chances in the main car park or walk from the overflow.

Rose walked into reception and nodded at the girl behind the desk. "Hi, Beth. I'm supposed to meet David Stuart?"

Beth nodded. "His office called to say he's running about ten minutes late. Can I get you a coffee?"

"That'd be lovely." Rose reflected that maybe there were a few advantages to being involved in the family business, after all.

She sat down on one of the well-upholstered sofas, and sipped the coffee Beth put down on the table beside her. Several people walked through the reception area as she waited, all of them giving her a smile or a friendly nod as they passed.

Rose glanced up as the door opened. A tall man in an immaculately tailored suit entered, walking up to the reception desk. He signed his name in the book, and Beth pointed him towards Rose.

"Mr Stuart," said Rose more confidently than she felt, getting to her feet as he approached and stretching out her hand. "I'm Rose Middleton. My brother has asked me to take care of you today."

He smiled, shaking her hand firmly. "Please, call me David. Paul did let me know he wasn't able to be here this afternoon, but he assured me that you'd be able to answer any questions I might have about the production process."

Inwardly Rose felt a trace of satisfaction at the confidence Paul had shown in her, but she kept her manner businesslike as she replied. "Can I offer you a coffee before we start?"

He shook his head. "No, thanks – I'd like to get straight on if that's OK. Perhaps afterwards."

Rose led him through a door, and down the corridor that led to the main production area. "Fortunately, given the processes we use here, you won't need any specific protective equipment, but if I can ask you to stay behind the yellow lines, and be aware that there may be automated vehicles moving around."

He nodded, seeming impressed by her care to observe proper procedure.

They made their way through the production areas, and Rose pointed. "There's the line we're currently running for you."

David watched as the components moved past on the conveyor belt. "And quality control?"

"Through here. I'll ask the shift leader to take you through the process."

They walked into another area where white-coated technicians were standing at benches of equipment. "Peter, this is David Stuart," introduced Rose. "Peter's our senior quality control analyst for this shift."

Peter nodded. "As you can see, we have samples straight from today's batch here. Each one goes through a series of tests to ensure it complies with the specification, then a percentage are tested to destruction. The rest are tagged, then stored so that we can check back with a unit from the same run if you have any problems in the field."

"I see," said David thoughtfully. "What's the average failure rate?"

Peter grinned. "Since we finished qualifying the production equipment after the prototype run, none."

David blinked. "Impressive."

He turned to Rose. "Well, I think I've seen what I need to. How about that coffee?"

Rose nodded. "Thanks, Peter," she called over her shoulder as she led David back towards the reception area.

"Let's go to the staff restaurant," she suggested. "They do some quite decent Danish pastries, if you fancy one with your coffee."

When they got to the restaurant, Rose picked up a tray, and David followed her along the counter. "The cinnamon whirl looks good," he pointed.

"Two of those then, Sally," confirmed Rose. "How do you have your coffee, David?"

"I'd love a cappuccino, two sugars."

Rose nodded. "That and a double espresso, Sally, thanks."

"I'll carry the tray," offered David, and Rose picked a table with a view over the landscaped area behind the factory.

They sat down, and David sipped his coffee. "I'm impressed," he said. "Our other supplier rejects about half a percent of their production at test, and we've had at least two units fail in the field so far."

"We've invested a lot in the equipment," said Rose. "Paul and Charles took a big gamble, but I think you've seen how it's paid off."

David nodded. "Well, Rose, I'll report back to our board, but on today's showing, I think it's very likely we'll move the rest of our production to yourselves."

He looked at her thoughtfully. "You're obviously very much involved in the business, but – forgive me if this is too personal a question – do you have other plans?"

Rose smiled. "It's OK. Actually, I'd love to study — maybe a degree in English — but Charles and Paul really depend on me at the moment to help out here."

She considered telling David about the assistance she'd given Charles with his spreadsheet, but decided she'd have to know him better before she'd trust him with that kind of insight.

The thought of getting to know David better tugged briefly at her mind, and she had to push it aside to concentrate on his next words. "Well, thanks for the coffee, Rose. If you can tell Paul I'll be in touch when I've spoken to the board."

They walked back through to the reception area, and Rose stood by the desk as David signed out, then shook his hand. "Bye, then." He walked out to the car park, glancing over his shoulder as the door closed behind him, and Rose watched as he drove off.

"Good meeting?" asked Beth.

"Definitely," confirmed Rose. "Well, I'd better get going. Thanks for the coffee, Beth."

Behind the reception desk, Beth watched with a thoughtful expression as Rose returned to her car. She had an inkling that David Stuart would be back, and not just because of a zero percent production failure rate. If she was any judge, a certain pair of dark eyes might have something to do with it...

**

When she arrived home, Rose finally managed to get a couple of hours without interruptions to spend with her book, and the next time she glanced at her watch it was past five o'clock.

She went through to the kitchen. "I'm going to start getting ready, Mum. If Charles calls, can you tell him we can leave any time after seven?"

"Of course, dear."

Rose went upstairs and got into the shower, turning the temperature up and enjoying the feel of the water on her skin. She decided to shave her legs, and as she used the razor, trying not to nick herself, she caught herself imagining not an evening out with her brother, but dinner with someone tall, handsome, attentive... Ouch!

She rinsed the tiny cut, telling herself it was her own fault for not paying more attention. Somehow the face of her imagined dinner partner bore a strong resemblance to David Stuart...

Rose shook her head, rinsing off the foam from her legs and getting out of the shower. She wrapped her hair in a towel, then pulled on her old dressing gown to go through to her room.

She looked through her wardrobe, and chose a simple black cocktail dress. She finished drying, brushing her hair out straight, then dressed. The earrings Paul had bought her for her birthday, and she was ready.

She walked down the stairs to the kitchen. "Did Charles call?"

Her mother smiled. "He did. And he's leaving the office on time."

Rose raised her eyebrows. "Wonders will never cease."

As if on cue, the front door opened and Charles came in. He nodded to his mother, then seemed to notice Rose for the first time. "I'm impressed."

He glanced at the clock. "Shall we get going?"

They walked to his car, and Rose got into the passenger seat, while Charles slid behind the wheel.

"Where did you book?" asked Rose.

"There's a new place, out of town, think it's a converted barn. It gets good reviews."

Rose settled more comfortably into her seat, and after a few minutes Charles said, "Here we are."

He turned in through the open gates, and parked the car. Rose got out, glancing at the neat paths and carefully-tended shrubs, then walked with Charles to the door. Inside there was a small bar area, and an arch leading through to the restaurant itself.

The maitre'd approached. "Good evening, sir, miss. Do you have a reservation?"

Charles nodded. "Name of Middleton – for half past seven."

"Very good, sir. Please, have a seat in the bar, and your table will be ready shortly."

"What would you like to drink, Rose?" Charles asked.

She thought for a moment. "I think I'd like a rum and Coke, please, lots of ice. Look, there's a seat over there."

Charles went to the bar, and Rose sat down, glancing round at the panelled walls and the engravings of local scenes.

"Here you are," Charles said, returning with their drinks.

He sat down opposite her. "How did you get on with David Stuart today?"

Rose pursed her lips. "You're not going to talk business all night, are you?"

He shook his head. "I promise. I just wanted to know what his reaction was."

"He was very impressed. I think he'll move all of his production to us, but he has to discuss it with his board first."

Charles nodded. "Excellent. We already have the tooling in place, and once Paul gets the production schedules sorted out –"

"You promised," chided Rose, holding up a finger in mock warning.

He grinned. "OK, I surrender."

The maitre'd returned. "Your table is ready, if you'll follow me."

They went through into the restaurant, and Rose sat down, imagining what it would be like to have someone hold her chair for her.

The maitre'd handed them menus. "Your waiter will be with you shortly."

Rose opened her menu and looked at the starters. "Paté on wholemeal toast sounds nice."

Charles nodded. "How about the main course?"

"Mm, I think I'd like the venison."

The waiter approached, and Charles gave their order, then turned back to Rose.

"So, any boyfriends on the horizon?"

She snorted, just managing to avoid the last sip of her drink going down the wrong way. "OK, Charles. Two things — one, that's my business, and two, when am I supposed to meet these boyfriends when you have me helping you two out in the office every other minute?"

He held up his hands. "OK, Rose, I'm sorry — really. What do you want to talk about?"

She subsided. "I really enjoyed this afternoon." Unaccountably she felt herself colouring. "When I got back from the factory, I mean. I managed to get quite a way into my book."

Charles clearly hadn't noticed her momentary embarrassment. "Tell me again what it's about."

"Well," began Rose, "it's set in medieval times. The idea is that a young woman joins the intelligence corps of the king's army during a war, then gradually gets drawn into the use of magic…"

At the mention of magic, she could see Charles switching off. "Hasn't all that wizard stuff been done to death? Harry Potter?"

Rose took a deep breath. "It's true that a lot of what's written these days is pretty derivative — Tolkien really started the whole genre — and most writers really struggle not to be formulaic. But I like this one, it seems… I don't know, it seems to really point to something…"

She tailed off, and Charles looked at her, the expression on his face a mixture of concern and helplessness. "Rose… I know this stuff is really important to you, I'm sorry I don't really understand it. But I promise, when we get on top of things with the business, we'll get someone in…"

Rose nodded, reaching across the table to put her hand on his for a moment. "I know what you're doing with the business is for all of us. I don't mind helping, really I don't."

She took a deep breath as she saw the waiter approaching. "Here are our starters."

The waiter put a plate down in front of her, and she concentrated on buttering bread, spreading the paté, taking a bite. "This is good."

Charles nodded. "The soup's really good too."

They ate in silence for a while, then Charles said, "I almost forgot one bit of news. Lily called, she's coming home for half term."

At the mention of her younger sister, Rose smiled. "That's fantastic – it feels like ages since she was here for my party. We can go out shopping…"

Charles rolled his eyes. "Leave some time for me and Paul – we have a treat planned for her already."

"I will," promised Rose.

They finished their starters, and the waiter brought the next course. "The cranberries in the sauce really go well with the venison," said Rose.

Charles looked unconvinced. "I think I'm happy with steak, as things go."

"Sure you don't want to try a little bit?"

He shook his head, and Rose shrugged. "More for me."

Finally Charles put down his fork. "That was good. Do you think you'll want dessert?"

Rose grinned. "I could manage a little something."

Charles caught the waiter's attention and asked him to bring the dessert trolley. Rose's eyes lit up when she saw the dark chocolate mousse.

"Definitely some of that for me," she pointed.

The waiter passed her one of the small bowls. "Cream, miss?"

"No, thank you."

"Would you like coffee, Rose?" asked Charles.

"Please."

"Two coffees, then," Charles told the waiter.

Rose sampled her mousse. "This is amazing."

The waiter returned with their coffee, and Rose sipped hers. "Thanks for a lovely meal, Charles."

When they'd finished, Charles paid the bill, and they walked back to the car. "So, what's on the cards tomorrow?" asked Rose.

"Nothing much –" Charles started to say, then glanced at Rose, obviously recalling something he'd forgotten. "Damn. Sorry, Rose, is there any chance you can cover reception for Beth tomorrow morning? She has a family funeral. I'm really sorry."

Rose put her hand on her brother's shoulder, smiling. "It's fine, Charles, really. As long as Beth's back in time for me to meet Lily at the station."

"Thanks," said Charles, looking relieved.

When they reached the house, it was dark. "Mum must have gone to bed," said Rose. "Think I'll do the same if I have to be at the factory first thing."

She leaned over to kiss Charles on the cheek. "Night, then. And thanks again for dinner."

***

Rose arrived at the factory just before eight, this time resisting the temptation to park in Charles's space, and put the coffee machine on. She switched on the computer, pulling up the office diary. There were no visitors scheduled for the morning, so she poured herself a cup of coffee and logged on to her literature forum to catch up on the discussions.

Rose was concentrating on a paragraph about archetypes when the desk phone rang. She picked up the handset. "Good morning, Middleton Sons, how can I help you?"

There was a pause at the end of the line. "Ah, this is David Stuart from Lewis's."

He hesitated again. "Rose, is that you?"

She grinned broadly, even though she knew he couldn't see her expression. "Hi, David, yes. Good to hear you again."

His voice still held surprise. "I didn't think they'd have you manning the phones as well – is there anything there you *don't* do over there?"

"Beth has the morning off — a family matter," explained Rose. "So I'm covering."

She thought she detected a hint of reluctance in David's voice as he returned to business matters. "Ah, I could do with speaking to Paul, if he's available."

"Sure — I saw him arrive about ten minutes ago. I'll put you through."

Rose pressed the shortcut key for Paul's office. "I have David Stuart on the line," she said.

"Great — put him on."

She switched back to David's line. "OK, David, just transferring you now."

"Thanks, Rose," he said.

She put the call through, and sat back. Was it just wishful thinking, or had she detected something more than just politeness in his words to her?

She noticed that their call had finished, and a few moments later Paul came out of his office. "Good news from Lewis's?" Rose asked.

"Very good. David has confirmed that they'll be moving the rest of their production to us as soon as their other supplier has finished the current batch."

"That's great news," said Rose.

Paul nodded. "It's a good job I got those production schedules sorted."

He looked thoughtful. "David did have one condition – well, he phrased it as a favour."

"What's that?"

"He asked if all the contract and service review meetings could be held over here, rather than at their offices."

Rose shrugged. "Maybe he wants to be close to the production line, so that you can go down and take a look straight away if there's any question about the product."

She grinned. "Or maybe the coffee and pastries over here are better."

Paul nodded. "Anyway, it's not a problem. He'll be coming over on Monday to sign the contract. Twelve, we said."

"I'll put it in the diary," promised Rose.

The rest of the morning was uneventful, and Beth returned just after one. "Hi, Rose. Everything OK?"

"Fine," confirmed Rose. "You?"

Beth nodded. "It was a lovely service, actually. The vicar said some things that really made me think."

Rose paused for a moment. "Well, I'll leave you to it. I'll get some lunch, then I'm picking Lily up from the station."

Beth smiled. "Say hi to her from me."

"Will do."

Rose walked down to the staff restaurant and got a jacket potato and salad. Without consciously thinking about it, she found herself sitting at the same table she and David had shared the previous day, and she realised she was looking forward to Monday.

She finished her lunch and took her tray to the rack, then walked back to the car park. The station was a few minutes' drive away, and she concentrated on making her way through the Friday afternoon traffic.

When she reached the station, she parked in a short stay space and walked over the bridge to the platform. The display showed the train as on time, and she found a spot on a bench.

The train pulled in, and Rose stood up, scanning the opening doors. Finally she caught sight of her sister's distinctive school uniform, and wove her way through the stream of commuters towards her.

Lily's face lit up when she saw her sister approaching, and the two hugged, oblivious to the bustle around them. "How are you?" asked Rose.

"Really great. I'm enjoying all my subjects, and the sport. The exams are a bit scary, though."

Rose nodded. "Well, no need to think about that for the next couple of days. I thought we'd go shopping tomorrow, and Paul and Charles have got something planned for you – a surprise, they haven't even told me."

Lily grinned. "Cool!"

Rose glanced around. "Looks like the rush is over. Come on, let's get to the car."

They walked back over the bridge, and Lily threw her bag into the back seat. "Can't wait till I can learn to drive too."

When they reached the house, their mother was waiting. "Hi, darling," she said, hugging Lily. "I've made coffee, and there's some home-made cake."

They sat down at the kitchen table. "Can we ring for pizza later?" suggested Rose. "It'll save cooking, and if Charles and Paul are late, they can always warm theirs up in the oven."

"Yay!" said Lily. "Pizza!"

"Of course, dears."

Lily finished her cake. "Come on, Rose, let's go upstairs, I've got loads to tell you."

"OK," Rose grinned. "We'll come down in a bit, Mum."

They went up to their room, and Lily sprawled on the bed while Rose sat on the edge.

"So what's new, angel?"

Lily smiled mischievously. "I got kissed last week."

Rose started to speak, then reminded herself that her little sister was fifteen, after all. "Wow. Tell me everything."

"Well, there's this boy, I've seen him looking at me. So one lunchtime he's sitting by himself, everyone else is playing some game so they're not paying any attention. I go and sit next to him. 'Hi, I'm Lily.'

"He looks up. 'I'm Jack. I've seen you in Mrs Allan's class.'

"I grin. 'I know – I saw you looking at me.'

"He looks embarrassed. 'I think your hair's really great. My sister has blonde hair, but it's not as long as yours.'

"'You can touch it if you like.'

"He stretches out his hand hesitantly and strokes my hair. I lean a little bit toward him, and somehow our lips touch. Then the bell rings for the end of break and I have to dash."

She smiled, remembering. "I liked it."

Rose touched her sister's hand. "That's sweet."

She sighed. "But Lily – be careful. Some of the older boys won't settle for just a kiss."

Lily nodded. "Don't worry, Rose."

From downstairs they heard the sound of the front door. Lily pouted. "Now I won't get to hear what you've been up to."

"Tell you tonight," promised Rose.

They went downstairs to find Paul and Charles in the hall. Paul ruffled Lily's hair. "Hi, angel."

She grinned. "Rose tells me you two have something planned."

Charles flashed Rose a look. "It was supposed to be a surprise."

Rose shrugged. "I didn't tell her where you're going – I don't know myself."

He subsided. "OK."

"Can we phone for the pizza now?" asked Lily. "I'm starving."

"Sure," said Rose. She glanced at Charles. "Credit card please."

Charles reached inside his jacket, handing her a black card.

"So what does everyone want?" Rose asked.

"Charles and I will have our usual," said Paul. "Come on, Charles, let's go in the kitchen and mix some drinks."

Rose glanced at Lily. "I think I know what you and Mum want – I'll ask for extra jalapenos."

Lily nodded. "Can I have some cheesy garlic bread too?"

"Of course – after all, Charles is paying."

Lily giggled. "Pity we can't phone for something else while we've got his card – can you imagine the look on his face if a Porsche turned up outside or something."

Rose raised her eyebrows. "Just kidding," said Lily quickly.

Rose took out her mobile and dialled, giving their order. "OK, half an hour."

They went through into the lounge as their mother came in with a tray of glasses. Paul and Charles followed with pitchers, and Lily glanced at them with interest. "Can I try it?"

Charles glanced at his mother. "Sure, dear," she said. "Just one glass, though."

Paul poured, and everyone took a glass. "How about a toast?" said Paul.

Rose nodded. "So… 'Better a simple meal with peace, than a house full of feasting with strife.'"

The doorbell rang. "Talking of food," said Rose, getting up to answer.

She came back in carrying a stack of boxes. "OK, we have two with extra jalapenos – Mum and Lily. Charles, Paul, here are yours, bacon and mushroom."

She opened her own box. "Can't beat spicy beef and pepperoni."

"Mm," said Lily. "This is better than school food."

"How's it going?" asked Charles.

Lily looked across at Rose, grinning. "Oh, the usual."

"Your exams are soon, aren't they?" said Paul.

Lily looked crestfallen. "Thanks for reminding me – not."

"You'll be OK," said Rose. "Tell you what, we can spend a bit of time looking over your stuff this week."

She grinned, nudging Lily. "After shopping, that is."

They finished their pizza, and Rose took the empty boxes out to the kitchen. When she returned, Lily was flicking through the DVD's under the TV set.

"Can we watch this one?" she said, holding up a film.

Charles glanced at his watch. "Paul and I should go through the figures from this afternoon."

"You'll watch with us, won't you, Mum?" Lily asked.

"Of course, dear."

Lily slid the disc into the player and curled up on the sofa next to Rose. The music started, and they watched the view pan over the skyline of New York, zooming in on a tall office building...

As the credits rolled, Lily yawned. "Think it's time for bed. Night, Mum."

"Night, dears."

Lily and Rose climbed the stairs to their room and got ready for bed. Rose smiled as Lily put on her Disney nightshirt.

Rose pulled the covers over them and turned out the light. Lily snuggled into her pillow, and said, "Your turn to tell, Rose."

"Well," said Rose, "actually I think there is someone who likes me."

"Cool. What's his name?" asked Lily.

"David – he's quite senior at one of the companies we make products for."

"You mean he's *old?*"

Rose laughed. "Hardly, angel. Probably in his mid-twenties."

"Like I said, old," declared Lily firmly. She thought for a moment. "Have you kissed him?"

Rose shook her head. "But I wouldn't mind…"

"So when are you going to see him again?"

"Monday – he's coming to the office for a meeting. But Lily – he probably doesn't even remember I exist. Just because we had coffee once…"

Lily thought for a moment. "You know what? I bet he does remember you. I bet he's looking forward to Monday, and he's going to ask you out."

Rose sighed. "It'd be lovely if you were right. But I'm not getting my hopes up."

She turned onto her side. "Anyway, it's time we got some sleep – big day tomorrow."

Lily smiled. "I get to go shopping, and then I find out what my surprise is."

"You bet. G'night, angel."

"Night."

***

Rose was woken by the early morning light streaming in, promising a glorious day. Lily was still sleeping, her blonde hair spread across the pillow.

"Wake up, sleepyhead," said Rose softly. "I think I can hear Mum making breakfast."

Lily stirred, turning over, and opened her eyes. "I had a really nice dream."

She swung her legs out of bed and stood up, stretching. "Mm, you're right, I smell bacon."

The two girls went down the stairs and into the kitchen. "Hi, Mum."

"Morning, dears. Breakfast is just ready."

She put two plates on the table and they sat down. Lily cut her toast into soldiers and dipped them into the yolk of her fried egg. "Just right, Mum."

When they'd finished breakfast, Rose helped wash up while Lily went upstairs to shower, returning in jeans and a t-shirt, her hair in a ponytail. "Your turn, Rose."

When Rose came back down, Lily was sitting in the lounge, Rose's laptop in front of her.

"Your friends have some interesting ideas," she said.

Rose blinked. "Didn't know you were into literature."

Lily nodded. "Actually, our new English teacher is really cool. Is there anything on here about Jane Austen?"

"I'll find something for you later," promised Rose. "Now, you ready to shop?"

"You bet!"

They drove into town and parked in the multi-storey. Lily got a ticket from the machine and put it on the dashboard, then Rose locked the car.

"Where first?" asked Rose.

"Well," grinned Lily, "you're going to need some new stuff if things get off the ground with David."

Rose shook her head, smiling. "Might not happen."

"So you and I can go out somewhere one evening and you'll have something new to wear."

Rose couldn't help being carried along by her irrepressible sister, and as they walked down the shopping precinct, Lily pointed. "I've always wanted to look in there – they have some lovely things."

They went inside, and Lily ran her fingers along a rack of silk dresses. "Aren't these gorgeous?"

Rose couldn't help but agree. "Look, this one's in your size."

Lily unhooked the hanger. "Great – I'll try it on."

They walked to the changing rooms, and Lily slipped into one of the cubicles. When she emerged in the dress, she'd taken her hair out of its ponytail and she used one hand to pile it on top of her head. "What do you think?"

"You look fantastic," said Rose.

Lily smiled. "I like it too." She looked at her sister hopefully. "Can we get it?"

Rose grinned. "Of course – I kept hold of my birthday money so I could treat us both."

Lily hugged her. "You're the best."

Rose kissed the top of her sister's head. "So now you have to pick out something for me."

Lily went back into the cubicle and changed, draping the dress carefully over her arm. "Let's pay for this – there's another place that I want to look for yours."

They walked on down the precinct, Lily's dress in a bag, and she pointed. "There."

Rose looked. "Gosh, that looks like an expensive place."

Lily pointed to the window. "They have a sale on."

They went into the shop, and Lily started at one end of the rack with the sale tickets. "No... no... maybe... aha!"

She pulled a dress from the rack. "What do you think? It's in your size."

Rose looked unsure. "Isn't the neckline a little low?"

Lily rolled her eyes. "Try it on. You can always wear something underneath."

"OK," Rose decided. She took the dress to the changing rooms, and emerged a few minutes later, glancing around to make sure only Lily was in sight.

"You look great," Lily gave her verdict.

"Well… All right. But I'll try it out on Charles and Paul first – I know they'll tell me if they think it's too much."

Lily beamed. "Come on then."

Rose changed back, and they paid for the dress. "Now let's look for shoes," urged Lily.

"Slow down," laughed Rose. "We have all morning. How about we go and get a coffee?"

"OK," conceded Lily. They walked to the coffee shop, and Rose ordered her usual espresso and Lily's favourite caramel macchiato.

"I don't know how you drink that stuff, it's all sugar – you won't even taste the coffee," teased Rose.

Lily licked foam from her upper lip. "I like it. So, what else do we need after shoes?"

"I wouldn't mind having a look at the perfume counter in that big department store."

"Cool," said Lily. "I can look at the makeup."

They finished their coffee, and walked on to the shoe shop.

"What do you think?" asked Lily, trying on a pair of platforms.

"Are they in again?" laughed Rose. "Maybe for a Sixties party or something."

Lily looked down the next aisle. "Here, Rose, this is what you need."

Rose raised her eyebrows. "You'd practically need oxygen with some of those heels."

Lily grinned. "Well, try some – maybe with just a couple of inches? Here, these ought to do."

Rose slipped on the shoes, and tried a few steps. "Actually that's not too bad."

"And with that dress, you'll look fabulous," enthused Lily.

"We'll see," said Rose. "OK, I'll take these."

They paid for the shoes, and Lily said, "Shall I drop the bags back at the car, so we're not carrying them around?"

"Sure." Rose handed her sister the key. "I'll meet you at the perfume counter."

When Lily found her, Rose was looking bemused at the selection of different fragrances. "Hard to know where to start."

Lily grinned. "Well, these ones here are the same make as Gran wears, so probably rule those out. And those in the middle are all those new ones with the stupid adverts – you know, guys in sailor outfits and stuff."

She picked up a sampler. "Try this one – I've heard some of the girls in the year above me talking about it."

Rose took the bottle and tentatively dabbed her wrist. "What do you think?"

Lily sniffed. "Hmm, it's OK. Here, try this other one."

She took Rose's other wrist and sprayed a little of the scent. "Wow, I really like that. It's not too heavy – like flowers or something. It suits you."

Rose nodded. "I think you're right. Thanks, Lily."

She caught the eye of the assistant. "We'd like this one, please."

When they'd made their purchase, Lily pointed to another section of the counter. "There's the makeup."

They spent a few minutes looking at the different shades, and Rose said, "Tell you what – next time we go out, I'll make you up with some of my stuff, and you can decide what works."

Lily grinned. "That'd be cool."

Rose glanced at her watch. "How about some lunch? Then we can have a look at the bookshop before we go home."

"Great."

Rose looked at the list of departments on the nearby sign. "They have a restaurant here – shall we try it?"

"OK."

They took the lift to the top floor, and found the restaurant. "This looks posh," said Lily, glancing at the potted palms. "I do like the Art Deco style."

"There's a table by the fountain," Rose pointed.

They sat down and leafed through the menu. "The paninis sound good," said Lily. "And look, they do milkshakes – I'd love a vanilla one."

A waitress in a lace-edged apron approached. "What can I get you?"

"I'd like a ham and cheese panini," said Rose. She glanced at Lily, getting a nod. "Two of those, please. And one chocolate and one vanilla milkshake."

The waitress wrote on her pad. "I'll just get your milkshakes. The paninis will be about ten minutes?"

"No problem," smiled Rose.

"So what books are you looking for this afternoon?" Lily asked when the waitress had gone.

Rose smiled. "That's not always how it works – I might not even know a book exists till I see it in the shop."

"OK," said Lily thoughtfully.

"But they'll have lots that you'll recognise," Rose assured her. "And I think there's a section with study guides so you could pick something to help you with your exams."

Lily nodded. "Good point."

The waitress brought their milkshakes, and Lily stirred hers with her straw. "Brrr!" she said, taking a sip.

She glanced at Rose. "So, what do you think my treat is?"

Rose raised her eyebrows. "I really don't know. Paul and Charles aren't exactly the most imaginative, are they. But you never know, they might surprise you."

She sucked on her straw. "What would you like it to be?"

Lily grinned. "You mean realistically, or if I could have anything I wanted?"

"Anything."

"Wow. Well, it'd be nice to travel, so how about we get to fly by private jet."

"We?" queried Rose.

"You'd have to come with me, of course," said Lily.

"So then what?"

"We land on some Caribbean island, and get taken to a hotel. One of those that has little chalets just off the beach, with a balcony facing the sea. There's fresh fruit, and just along the beach there's a bar in a shack, with a guy with dreadlocks serving."

Rose nodded. "I've got the picture in my head now. What else?"

"Well, of course the waves are fantastic, and some hunky guy surfs in and carries his board up to the bar and offers to buy us a drink."

Rose chuckled. "Look, here comes our food. Just in time – who knows where that story would have ended up. But I love the idea of a holiday in the sun."

The waitress set their plates down on the table. "Enjoy your meal."

Lily took a mouthful of her panini. "This is fantastic."

Rose nodded. "And loads of salad too. We can tell Mum about this place."

Lily looked across at her. "So what would your ideal surprise trip be?"

Rose felt herself unaccountably blushing. "I suppose lots of couples have their honeymoon in the Caribbean, so it could start out like yours. But I wouldn't need some guy to surf in, he'd already be with me."

"Good point," said Lily. "Well, might be sooner than you think."

"I don't know," laughed Rose, "are you still setting me up with David?"

"Anything's possible," Lily said, her expression earnest.

"Well, you'll be the first to know," promised Rose.

They finished their meal, and Rose walked to the till to pay. When she returned, Lily was looking at her mobile.

"One of my friends just texted me," she said. "Her parents took her skiing for half term. Some people have all the luck."

"Well, when Charles and Paul have the business really established, maybe we can run to the occasional ski trip."

"I suppose."

"Anyway," said Rose briskly, "let's take a look at the bookshop, shall we."

They made their way out of the department store and walked along the precinct to the end, where the older part of the town centre began. The bookshop was in a narrow alley, with an old-fashioned sign hanging outside.

A bell rang as they opened the door, and the proprietor looked up. "Welcome," he said. "Are you looking for anything in particular?"

"We'd just like to browse for a while," said Rose, "but if you can show us where you keep the study guides?"

"Up one floor and to the left. Most of it's on English literature, if that's what you're looking for."

"Perfect," said Lily.

They climbed the narrow stairs, passing books shelved in odd corners. Rose resisted the temptation to stop at the first interesting volume she saw, and they reached the section they'd been aiming for.

"OK," said Lily. "This one is on the syllabus, and that one. Oh, and here's one that was optional reading, but I really liked it – can we get it anyway?"

"Slow down," smiled Rose. "Here, make a pile on the end here – nobody's going to move them."

Lily opened one of the guides and was soon engrossed, while Rose looked further along at a shelf of second-hand books, the lettering on the spines faded and harder to read.

"Don't you get a crick in your neck doing that?" asked Lily, watching Rose scan along the rows of books with her head on one side.

"A bit," said Rose, "but it's worth it. Oh, look, this one looks like a first edition."

"Is it valuable?" asked Lily.

"Not especially – they printed a lot of this particular title. But I always check inside, in case it's signed by the author or something. That would make it a lot more special."

Lily nodded. "I'll remember."

Rose moved further along, and Lily turned back to the book she was holding.

A little while later she glanced at her watch. "Hey, Rose, it's nearly three. We should probably get back."

Rose reappeared with a small stack of books in her arms. "Well reminded, Lily. I could lose myself in here for hours."

She glanced at the end of the shelf. "Have you got yours?"

Lily picked up her pile. "I think these are all the ones I need."

They made their way back down the stairs, piling their selections on the counter. The proprietor carefully wrote each title in a ledger, then rang up the sale.

Lily grinned at her sister. "This beats getting them new."

The proprietor glanced up with a smile. "And there's something reassuring about books that have already been enjoyed – loved, even."

They left the shop and walked back towards the car park, a bag of books in each hand. "That's the only downside," said Lily. "These are heavy."

Rose nodded. "I'll remember to park closer next time."

When they reached the car, Rose slid the bags of books behind her seat. "That way they won't slide about."

She started the engine. "Right, let's see what those brothers of ours have cooked up for you."

When they reached the house, Paul's car was already outside. He came out of the lounge to meet them. "Perfect timing – I know you two will need a little while to get ready."

Rose looked confused. "I thought it was Lily's surprise."

Paul grinned. "That's the first surprise – this treat is for both of you."

Lily glanced across at her sister, beaming. "Yay!"

"You don't get to find out everything all at once," cautioned Paul. "But the first thing you need to know is that this evening is formal dress – the more sophisticated, the better."

Rose pretended to scowl at him. "Good job we went shopping, seeing as you didn't give us any warning."

"And ruin the surprise?" he grinned.

"Come on, Lily," said Rose. "We'd better get started."

They took their bags upstairs, and Rose hung both dresses carefully on the back of the bedroom door. "You want to shower, Lily?"

"I'd quite like a bath, actually. We're not in a rush, are we?"

Rose shook her head. "Take your time."

Lily went into the bathroom and started the water running. She opened the bathroom cupboard, looking along the row of bottles. "Goody, there's still some of my favourite bath oil left."

The fragrance drifted from the bathroom as Lily sank into the water, and Rose sat down in front of the dressing table to trim her fingernails. She ran through in her mind some possibilities for the evening's surprise – the ballet? An opera?

She imagined Lily and herself on the dance floor, each with a partner leading them in a waltz… or perhaps a foxtrot?

Rose shook her head. "Probably we're just going out to that same restaurant again," she told herself.

"Did you say something?" asked Lily, coming back into the room with her hair wrapped in a towel.

"Nothing," said Rose. "Just trying to stop my imagination getting away with me."

Lily grinned. "I know what you mean."

She started to towel her hair dry. "You're going to wear your new dress, right?"

Rose nodded. "And I'll do your hair like you wanted."

Lily started to dress, then paused. "Do you think Mum might lend me something from her jewellery box? A pendant or something?"

"I'm sure," said Rose. "Let's ask her if we can have a look once we're nearly ready."

Lily slipped on her new dress, and looked at herself in the mirror as she turned. "This was a good choice."

Rose nodded. "My turn in the bathroom, then I'll start on your hair and makeup."

She quickly showered, then pulled on her dressing gown and went back into the bedroom. "OK. Hair first, then I can concentrate on your face."

Lily watched in the mirror as Rose used pins to secure her hair, letting just a few strands frame her face. "That looks amazing."

Rose started to apply Lily's makeup, emphasising her fair eyebrows with a touch of pencil, and dusting her eyelids lightly with a pastel blue shade that sparkled just a little.

"You don't really need any more colour in your cheeks," she said. "Wish I didn't look quite so pale."

Lily glanced in the mirror. "How about lipstick?"

"Here, try this one."

Lily carefully applied the lipstick. "Wow, that's quite dramatic."

Rose nodded. "You'll definitely turn a few heads."

She opened a drawer. "I think I'll wear this under my dress."

Lily glanced up. "OK. You'd look fine anyway, but if you'd feel more comfortable…"

"Can you zip me up?" asked Rose.

Lily helped her with the zip. "What are you going to do with your hair?"

"Just my silver clasp, I think. And I've got my earrings."

Rose sat down at the dressing table, starting to apply her makeup. "Is that enough blusher, Lily?"

Lily nodded. "It's fine. Don't forget your perfume."

Rose retrieved the bottle and dabbed scent at her wrists and throat. "I'm glad we got this one."

She stood up. "I think I'm ready."

"Shoes?" prompted Lily, smiling.

"Oops." Rose sat down on the bed to slip on the shoes she'd bought, then got to her feet again.

"Wow," said Lily, "that really makes a difference. I can't wait to see Paul's expression when he realises you're practically looking him in the eye."

"Let's go down, then," grinned Rose.

They walked into the lounge, finding Paul and Charles already in their evening suits. Paul's reaction didn't disappoint, and Lily exchanged a glance with Rose. "Told you," she whispered.

"So," said Charles. "The car will be here in a minute."

"Still not letting on?" queried Lily.

He shook his head. "You'll see when you get there."

There was a knock on the door, and Rose opened it to find a uniformed driver.

"Is your party ready, miss?" he asked.

Rose nodded, and went back inside. "The car's here."

She remembered her conversation with her sister. "Mum, did you find anything for Lily?"

"She has Gran's pearl necklace with the pendant," her mother assured her. "Now, don't keep the driver waiting – have a really good time, all of you."

"We will," assured Charles.

They walked to the car, and Lily said, "Charles, you can take the front seat."

Rose raised her eyebrows as Paul held the door for her and Lily to get in, then slid in beside them on the wide seat. "I could get used to this old-fashioned courtesy."

The car pulled away, and they were soon on the road out of town. As the road climbed up onto the moors, Lily looked around. "There are some amazing clouds, Rose."

After a few miles the road descended into a small town, its architecture evoking a bygone era. "Getting warmer," said Paul, smiling.

The car pulled up outside a large stone building with domed towers and a carriage circle outside the wide entrance.

"This is the Opera House, isn't it?" said Rose.

Charles nodded. "Entertainment first, then supper afterwards."

"Brilliant," said Lily. "But what's the entertainment?"

Paul grinned. "We might as well tell you – we'll get programmes as we go in anyway. Tonight's production is Jane Austen – Pride and Prejudice, though not quite as you might imagine it."

Rose beamed. "Fantastic – I've always wanted to see it produced live."

She turned to Lily. "Is that OK?"

Lily grinned. "Are you kidding? Arranged marriages, underage elopement with a wicked seducer, society balls, and the gorgeous Mr Darcy – lead me to it!"

Rose chuckled. "When you put it that way… You seem pretty up on the plot."

Lily rolled her eyes. "It's one of my texts, silly – didn't you see the study guide in the pile."

She hugged Charles, then Paul. "This is a perfect treat – it's fun, it helps with school, I get to dress up, and dinner out afterwards too. Thanks so much, you guys…"

Paul grinned. "Glad you're pleased. Come on, let's go in."

They walked up the broad stone steps, and Charles bought programmes for them. Paul handed their tickets to an usher, who looked up attentively.

"Mr Middleton, sir, of course. If your party would like to follow me…"

He led them up the stairs, but instead of directing them to one of the large doors into the auditorium, he turned down a side corridor. "This way, please."

On one side of the corridor were smaller doors, and he opened the first one. "Please, make yourselves comfortable. I'll return shortly to take your orders for drinks."

"Wow," said Lily. "A whole box to ourselves. This just keeps getting better."

She sat down on the small sofa at the front of the box. "Come on, Rose, this is ours."

Rose joined her, and the two men took armchairs either side. There was a knock on the door, and the usher entered.

"What can I get you to drink?"

"Can I suggest a pitcher of Pimm's?" Paul said, glancing round.

There were nods of agreement. "OK," said Paul. "And a glass of lemonade, please."

At his last words Lily looked crestfallen, but he glanced at her and put his finger to his lips. She looked puzzled, but didn't speak.

"Very good, sir."

The usher returned after a few moments with a tray. "I'll come back at the start of the interval in case you need anything else."

When the door had closed behind him, Paul walked over to the tray and picked up the lemonade, carefully pouring it into the top of the jug.

Lily grinned. "Thanks, Paul. I'll only have the one glass, anyway."

They sipped at their drinks, and after a couple of minutes the bell rang to prompt everyone to take their seats. The small orchestra began to play, and the lights dimmed.

Rose felt Lily's hand slip into hers, and Lily glanced across at her, smiling. The curtain rose on the Bennets' living room, and Rose had to make an effort not to whisper the dialogue to herself under her breath as the play began.

On the odd occasion when Rose took her eyes off the stage, she saw that Lily was entranced, following every word, and she was almost sure she heard her sister gasp at Elizabeth's final line in the first act – "You are, Mr Darcy, the last man in the world whom I could ever be prevailed on to marry."

The curtain fell, and the lights brightened. Lily turned to Rose. "This is brilliant. I get it so much more now than just reading it."

"Does anyone want another drink?" asked Paul.

"No thanks," replied Lily.

Rose shook her head. "Let's stretch our legs a bit, Lily."

They went out into the corridor. "I think the loos are back towards the stairs," Lily said.

As they returned, the bell went for the end of the interval, and they resumed their seats. Again Lily slipped her hand into her sister's, and Rose felt Lily's fingers tighten on hers as the events of the second act unfolded – Darcy's explanation of his antipathy to Wickham, Elizabeth's shock at learning of Lady Catherine's plans for Darcy to be engaged to her daughter, Lydia's elopement.

The girls suppressed their giggles at Elizabeth's conversation with Catherine de Bourgh. "I love this bit," whispered Lily.

Finally the play wound up to its climax, and as the actors took their bows, Rose was certain she saw the glint of tears in her sister's eyes. She squeezed Lily's hand as she released it, and Lily smiled.

"Right," said Charles. "Ready for some supper?"

Lily nodded. "Definitely."

"The theatre has a private restaurant," explained Paul, "so we don't even need to go outside."

They walked back down the stairs, and as the rest of the audience dispersed they followed a trickle of people through into an ornately-decorated dining room.

The maitre'd approached. "Mr Middleton – your table is ready, sir. This way, please."

When they were seated, the sommelier brought the wine list. Paul glanced at Lily. "Seeing as this is such a special night, I think champagne is in order."

"Very good, sir."

The sommelier brought a bottle, opening it expertly and pouring. Lily picked up her glass and sipped, then sneezed. "The bubbles go up my nose," she protested with a smile.

Rose chuckled. "Wait till it's stopped fizzing a bit."

Their waiter approached. "Are you ready to order?"

Rose glanced at the menu. "Just a salad for me, please."

"Me too," said Lily.

Paul and Charles ordered omelettes, and the waiter left.

"It was a different world in those days, wasn't it," said Lily, her thoughts drifting back to the play.

"Better, or worse?" asked Paul.

Lily looked thoughtful. "I think the point of the book was that society had a lot of expectations, and you couldn't always go against them – except by incurring a scandal, as Wickham did. But Elizabeth succeeded, she got the man who was meant for her."

She paused. "I don't know if I believe that or not – that there's really just one person who's meant for each of us. Destined?"

Charles shrugged. "This is all a bit deep for me."

Their food arrived, and the conversation lapsed for a while as they ate. Finally Lily put down her knife and fork. "That was really good."

"Dessert?" asked Paul.

"If there's ice cream," grinned Lily.

Paul caught the waiter's eye. "What's available for dessert?"

"We have cheesecake with raspberry coulis, chocolate torte, or fruit salad. Or your choice of ice cream."

"Vanilla ice cream for me, please," said Lily. "Rose?"

"Fruit salad for me."

"I'll try the cheesecake," said Charles. Paul nodded. "And chocolate torte for me, please."

The waiter left, and Lily grinned. "That means I get to try a bit of everything."

Paul rolled his eyes. "I might have known."

Their desserts arrived, and Lily claimed a tiny bite from everyone else's plate before concentrating on her ice cream.

"This fruit salad is pretty exotic," said Rose. "Apples of course, grapes, but then there's pomegranate, and I'm almost sure they've added a little honey."

They finished their meal, and Paul said, "Would anyone like coffee to finish with?"

"Please," said Rose.

"Me too," added Lily. "They ought to bring a bowl of those brown sugar lumps."

She grinned. "I like eating one or two of those by themselves," she added guiltily.

Paul called the waiter over and ordered the coffee. When it arrived, each saucer had two foil-wrapped chocolates, and Lily's eyes lit up.

Rose picked up one of her chocolates, putting it on Lily's saucer. "I only want one."

Lily smiled. "Thanks, Rose."

Paul watched as Lily dropped three lumps of sugar into her cup, adding cream and stirring till the sugar had dissolved. "There's that sweet tooth again. Do you remember when we used to visit the sweet shop when you were little?"

Lily nodded. "I could never decide what to buy, I spent ages working out different ways of spending my pocket money."

Rose sipped her black coffee, blowing on the surface to cool it. "And I just bought a tiny bar of dark chocolate – it was really expensive, but it was worth it."

They lingered over their coffee for a while, then Paul glanced at his watch. "I'd better give the driver a call."

Charles went to pay the bill while Paul phoned, and Lily turned to Rose. "This has been brilliant – let's think of a surprise for those two sometime soon."

Rose nodded. "At the end of term?"

"Great idea."

Paul returned to the table. "He'll only be five minutes, so he'll probably be there when we get outside."

Charles rejoined them as they walked from the restaurant back to the entrance, and Lily spotted the driver waiting for them. "There's the car."

As they drove back towards the city lights, Lily said, "Charles, Paul – thanks for a lovely evening, this really was a treat."

"No problem, angel," said Paul. "We should do this more often."

The car dropped them off at home, and the girls hugged Paul and Charles. "Night, then. And thanks again."

Rose followed Lily up to their room, and glanced wistfully in the mirror. "I feel like Cinderella at the end of the ball. I don't really want to take this off."

Lily nodded. "But we've already said we'll do it again. Here, let me help you with the zip."

When they were finally in bed, Lily said, "Rose?"

"Hmm?"

"Are you getting up in the morning? You know, for church."

"Sure. The service isn't till eleven, so we can sleep in till nine, have a quick shower and a couple of slices of toast, and still be there in plenty of time."

"Cool."

Rose leaned over to kiss her sister on the cheek. "Night, angel."

"G'night…"

***

After breakfast the next day, Lily and Rose walked the short distance from the house to the old Norman church. "Shall we go up in the balcony?" asked Rose.

Lily nodded. "I like it – I can see who's here, then I can find my friends when the service has finished."

The organ started to play, and Lily picked up a hymn book, opening it and holding it so that Rose could see.

At the end of the hymn, they sat down, and the white-haired vicar announced the Bible reading. A young woman walked to the lectern and began to read:

"I will sing for the one I love, a song about his vineyard. My loved one had a vineyard on a fertile hillside. He dug it up and cleared it of stones and planted it with the choicest vines. He built a watchtower in it and cut out a winepress as well. Then he looked for a crop of good grapes, but it yielded only bad fruit."

She sat down again, and the vicar climbed into the pulpit and began to speak.

"I wonder if anything like this has ever happened to you. Someone you care for has an idea in mind, something they're deeply committed to. You watch as they do everything right – preparation, materials, hard work. They look forward to the reward that they have every right to expect, and then... Nothing. It doesn't happen.

"How do you feel for them? Wouldn't you share their disappointment, want to ask why? Maybe you would ask God why, even wonder if it was your fault, if you'd done something wrong, if you could have helped more.

"I want to talk to you about Jacob, and the hard work he put in..."

Rose glanced across at Lily, and smiled. The expression of concentration on her sister's face was indistinguishable from the one she'd worn as she watched the play the previous evening, and Rose guessed that Lily was absorbed in imagining the story as the vicar spoke.

He drew his message to a close, and they stood to sing a final hymn. The vicar gave the blessing, and Lily looked around. "There's Anne – I really want to catch up with her. I'll see you in a bit."

She clattered down the stairs, and Rose followed more slowly, making her way to get a cup of coffee.

She looked around, but didn't see any of the people she was particularly close to, so she stood with her back against one of the pillars, sipping her drink and just watching the various conversations.

Lily reappeared after a few minutes, smiling. "I'm glad I talked to Anne. She's having a really good time at college."

"Great," said Rose. "Are you about ready to go?"

A young girl came by carrying a tray, and Rose put her empty mug down. "Thanks, Steph."

They walked to the door, shaking hands with the vicar on the way out. The sun was shining as they made their way back down the path between the carefully-tended flower beds, and Lily turned her face upwards, closing her eyes. "What a gorgeous day. Shall we go out for a walk after lunch?"

"I'd like that," said Rose.

When they arrived home, Paul and Charles were up, and their mother had lunch ready. "Would anyone like to go for a walk with us after lunch?" Rose asked.

"Sorry, kitten," said Paul. "Charles and I have to go through some figures for the meeting with David Stuart tomorrow."

At the mention of David's name, Rose felt a strange sensation, and Lily caught her eye, smiling.

"Sorry, dears, I have the ironing to get through," said their mother. "But you two go out, enjoy the sunshine."

They sat down to eat, and Lily concentrated as she poured gravy into her Yorkshire puddings, the tip of her tongue sticking out of the side of her mouth. "This is great, Mum."

"Leave some room," her mother smiled. "There's apple crumble for dessert."

When they'd finished eating, Paul glanced at Charles. "Think it's our turn to help clear up."

Lily grinned. "Come on, Rose. Let's get going."

"Anywhere particular you want to go?" asked Rose as they walked out to the hall.

"How about up toward the moors," suggested Lily. "We can walk up to those big rocks, there's a fabulous view."

They got into Rose's car and headed in the same direction as they'd taken the previous night. As the rocks came into view, Rose turned off the main road. "I remember there's a spot down here where we can park."

She stopped the car at the end of the track. "Here we are."

They squeezed through a gap in the wall, and started to climb towards the rocky outcrop. "It's a little spooky," said Lily. "I wouldn't like to be here on a dark night."

When they reached the rocks, Lily scrambled up to the flat top of a large boulder. "Come on, Rose," she urged. "The stone's really warm, we can sit up here for a while."

Rose joined her more cautiously, and looked out over the valley. "I'm glad you suggested this place."

They sat for a while without speaking, then Lily said, "Rose?"

"Hmm?"

"What did you think of this morning? You know, what Reverend Ashton was talking about."

Rose thought for a moment. "I enjoyed hearing about Jacob – the vicar really has a way of imagining how things were, how the people involved must have been feeling."

She paused. "I had a strange sensation that somehow the story could be about me. I don't really know what that means..."

Lily nodded. "I understand. It felt a bit like when we were at the play, I was trying to decide which of the Bennet sisters I'm most like."

Rose looked at her quizzically. "Doesn't everyone imagine themselves as Elizabeth?"

Lily shook her head. "I think I'd prefer to be Jane."

The two girls carried on discussing the different characters. Then Lily glanced up. "Rose, did you feel a spot of rain?"

"Definitely. Come on, let's dash back to the car before it really starts to throw it down."

They reached the car just in time, and sat for a moment catching their breath. "Home?" asked Rose.

"Yes," decided Lily. "I'm sure Mum will make us some tea – maybe she'll even bake some of those scones we like so much..."

***

The next morning as Lily and Rose were having breakfast, Paul put his head around the door. "I'm off now – Rose, you'll be there in plenty of time for the meeting, won't you?"

Rose nodded. "Don't worry."

The front door closed, and she turned to Lily. "Ready for a bit of revision?"

Lily took a deep breath. "OK."

They spent the morning going through Lily's exam schedule, making a revision timetable for the rest of the week. Halfway through, their mother brought them coffee and cake, smiling as she put the tray down and returning to the kitchen without speaking.

"There," said Rose finally. "I think we can cover what you need, and there's plenty of time left for going into town, or for you to have some friends round if you like."

She glanced at her watch. "Time I got going. How about you help Mum with lunch? I'll get something to eat at the factory, so it'll be just the two of you."

"OK," said Lily. She gave Rose a knowing smile. "Hope it goes OK."

When Rose arrived at the factory, Paul was waiting for her. "I've got all the contracts and schedules prepared – I don't think there'll be any snags."

They went into the conference room, where Beth was just putting out glasses and a jug of water.

"Thanks, Beth, this looks perfect," said Rose. Beth smiled, and closed the door behind her as she headed back to the reception desk.

Paul sat down at the top of the table, and Rose took a seat facing the door. The phone rang, and Paul picked it up. "Thanks, Beth."

He turned to Rose. "David's here."

The door opened, and Beth showed David into the room. He shook hands with Paul, then with Rose, meeting her eyes as he sat down opposite her.

"Who'd like water?" offered Rose.

"Not for me, thanks, Rose," said Paul absently, checking through the papers he'd brought

David nodded. "Please."

Rose reached for his glass, filling it from the jug. She held it out to him with both hands, and he took a sip, then put it down.

"So," said Paul. "I've prepared our standard manufacturing contract, and the schedules are all in line with your forecasts. We do have some additional capacity if you find you have extra demand."

He paused. "It may be a little early in our discussions to bring this in, but we were already thinking of investing in another line, with the same equipment we're using for your production. If you'd be interested in taking a share in the investment, we'd look to offer you a significantly reduced cost per unit, and preferential access."

David raised his eyebrows. "I see."

He glanced at Rose. "That's a very attractive proposition, I'll have to give it some thought."

He cleared his throat, turning back to Paul. "Let's go over the contract as it stands, to make sure there aren't any loose ends."

Paul nodded. "Rose, could you take notes please." He handed David a copy of the contract, and they started to run down the document paragraph by paragraph.

"This all seems to be exactly as we discussed," said David finally, turning over the last page. He reached inside his jacket, taking out a pen.

"Not often you see anyone using a fountain pen these days," said Rose.

David smiled. "Just a little quirk of mine – I prefer them."

She watched as he added a flowing signature to the document, then pushed it across the table to Paul.

Paul scribbled his signature. "All done," he said, holding out his hand.

David shook Paul's hand, and nodded to Rose. He picked up his glass. "Here's to the start of a great partnership."

Paul glanced at his watch. "Just one o'clock. Can we offer you some lunch, David?"

"That'd be great. After those Danish pastries last week, I'm sure the rest of the menu will have something to tempt me."

They walked to the staff restaurant, and Paul nodded to Sally. "What's the special today?"

Sally smiled. "We have quite a treat today. The chef's made dolma – minced lamb wrapped in vine leaves."

"Sounds amazing," said Paul. "I'll definitely try that."

Rose nodded. "Me too."

"Well," said David, "I don't want to be wondering what I missed. Count me in."

"Since we have something to celebrate, shall we have some wine?" asked Paul. "Sally keeps some stashed away for just this sort of occasion."

"Great idea," said David.

Sally went out to fetch the wine, then served their meals. David picked up his tray and walked straight towards the same table he and Rose had occupied the previous week.

They sat down, and Paul poured for them all. "Cheers."

They tapped their glasses together and drank. "I do like Shiraz," said David. "All those spicy overtones."

Rose took a bite of her dolma. "Mm, this is delicious."

When they'd finished eating, Rose glanced across at Paul. "Shall I get us some coffee?"

He shook his head, getting up. "Not for me. I have another meeting. But you two go ahead if you like."

David nodded. "Thanks, Paul."

As Paul walked away, Rose smiled at David. "Coffee, then?"

"Please. I don't think I could manage the pastry, though."

"Yours is cappuccino, isn't it?" asked Rose.

David nodded. "Well remembered."

Rose walked to the counter, returning with two cups. She watched as David spooned sugar into his coffee, stirring.

He glanced up. "I'm glad we got a few minutes to ourselves. There's something I'd like to ask you."

Rose felt her heart begin to beat faster. "The contract's OK, isn't it?"

David smiled. "Not business. I wondered if you'd like to have dinner with me tonight."

Rose sensed herself blushing, and she was sure David must notice that suddenly her confident exterior had melted away.

"That's... I'd love to," she managed.

He broke into a broad grin. "Wonderful. Shall I pick you up from home, say six?"

Rose felt an unaccountable hesitation. "Can I meet you back here?"

David nodded. "Sure."

He picked up his cup, finishing his coffee. "I'm afraid I have to get back to the office. I'll see you tonight, then."

Rose watched him go, then reached for her bag. She noticed that her fingers were trembling a little as she took out her phone and dialled.

"Hi, Lily. Guess what?"

Her sister's voice held amusement as she replied. "I think... you have a date."

Rose shook her head disbelievingly. "You were right. I think David does like me."

"What's not to like?" teased Lily. "Are you coming home, then?"

"I'll see you in a few minutes."

Rose drove home, parking next to Charles's car in the drive. Lily opened the door, and hugged her. "Well done."

Rose hesitated. "Lily?"

"Hmm?"

"Could you do something for me?"

"Anything, you know that."

"I'm not going to tell Paul and Charles that it's David I'm going out with."

Lily looked puzzled. "Why not?"

"I don't want them looking for a business angle, you know what they're like."

Lily nodded. "OK."

They went back into the house, and Rose walked through to the kitchen. "Hi, Mum."

"Hello, dear. Everything OK?"

"Fine, Mum."

Rose paused. "I won't be in for dinner. I've been invited out."

"That's no problem, dear."

Rose found Lily in the lounge, and her sister glanced up, smiling. "Let's go upstairs and talk."

They went into their room and Lily closed the door, then sprawled on the bed. "Tell me everything."

Rose recounted the afternoon's events. "I'm sure I must have looked really stupid."

Lily made a dismissive sound. "I bet he liked that you felt shy."

She got up from the bed. "So, we'd better work out what you're going to wear. How about your new dress?"

"That'd be –" Rose began to reply, then stopped. "Don't know why, but I think I want to wear something else."

"OK," said Lily, already riffling through Rose's wardrobe. "What about the dress you wore when we went out for your birthday? The black one with the embroidery."

"Great idea."

Lily grinned. "And I could do something with your hair – you haven't tried that heated styler that Aunty Jane bought you yet."

"I suppose I'd better do my legs again," said Rose. "I always seem to nick myself, though."

"I have some cream," said Lily. "I'll do it for you, it's really easy. Come on."

They went into the bathroom, and Lily showed her sister how to use the cream. "I wish I'd thought of this ages ago," said Rose.

While they were waiting for the cream to work, there was a tap on the door. "Hope you two aren't going to be all afternoon in there," came Charles's voice.

Lily rolled her eyes. "We won't be long."

"OK," they heard Charles grumble as he went down the stairs.

"Right," said Lily. "Now you just shower it off."

She slipped out of the door, closing it behind her, and Rose got into the shower. She directed the spray at her legs, and watched the cream disappear.

She washed her hair, then pulled on her dressing gown and went back to the bedroom to find Lily leafing through one of her study guides.

"Oops, sorry, angel," Rose said. "We were supposed to be studying this afternoon, weren't we."

Lily grinned. "I'll just do more tomorrow. Getting you ready for your date is way more important right now."

She took out her hair dryer. "Your hair needs to be nearly dry but not quite."

Rose sat while Lily directed the dryer over her hair, and finally Lily said. "There, that'll do."

She opened a drawer and took out the hair styler, plugging it in. "One of my friends went to a ball last term, and I thought her hair was really amazing. I'll see if I can get yours the same. You're not allowed to look until it's finished."

Rose turned, facing away from the mirror, and Lily sat on the end of the bed, starting to use the styler on her hair. "Do you think he'll kiss you?" she asked.

Rose blinked. "Should I give him the chance? It's only the first date."

Lily grinned. "So you're expecting there to be more?"

"Hey, that's not what I meant," said Rose, but she couldn't help smiling at the thought.

"Earth to Rose," teased Lily after a few moments. "Turn this way a little?"

Rose shifted position, and Lily continued to apply the styler to her hair. Finally she set it down, pulling out the plug. "There."

Rose looked in the mirror. Her usually-straight hair had been transformed into soft waves. "Wow, Lily, that's amazing."

Her sister smiled triumphantly. "I thought I could do it. Now, how about you get dressed, and I'll do your face."

Rose dressed, starting to feel a growing sense of anticipation. She sat down in front of the mirror again, and held as still as she could while Lily deftly applied her makeup. "OK, how does that look?"

"I really like it," said Rose. "I don't think it's too much, but I definitely look different."

"One last thing, then – your new perfume."

Rose applied the scent to her wrists, then her neck. "If he does kiss me, he'll remember this fragrance, that's for sure."

She stood up. "Gosh, is that the time? I'd better get going. What shoes shall I wear?"

"The ones with the heels, of course," smiled Lily.

Rose walked downstairs with Lily following her, meeting Charles in the hall. "What's the occasion?" he asked.

"I have a date," she said, trying to sound offhand.

He raised his eyebrows. "Don't I recall you telling me you didn't have time for boyfriends?"

Rose smiled wryly. "I think what I said was, you and Paul keep me too busy to find one. As you can see, I managed anyway."

Charles nodded. "Well, enjoy yourself. But, Rose –"

"Hmm?"

"Do be careful."

"I will," Rose promised. She looked into the kitchen. "Don't wait up, Mum."

"OK, dear."

Rose opened the front door, then turned to look back over her shoulder. "Bye, Lily. I'll try not to wake you when I come in."

She got into her car and started the engine, glancing at her reflection in the mirror. "Well, here goes."

When she reached the factory, the building was dark, and she pulled into a space, then got out of her car to wait. After a few moments, she saw David's car approaching, and he drew up beside her, getting out.

"You look fantastic," he said.

On impulse Rose leaned over and kissed him on the cheek. "Thanks."

When she stepped back, she looked at David's face, trying to read his changed expression. He seemed to pull himself back to the present, and he walked round to open the passenger door for her. "Hop in."

He closed the door for her, then walked round and took his own seat, starting the engine. "I hope you don't mind, I booked somewhere for us to eat – I wanted to make sure of getting a table."

"That's fine," Rose assured him.

As they drove, Rose realised they were travelling in the same direction that Charles had taken her the previous week, and after a few minutes David pulled into the car park of the barn restaurant. "Here we are."

She glanced across at him. "I hope I haven't spoilt the surprise – I have been here before."

He shook his head. "I'd heard good things about this place. But if you want to go somewhere else, I can cancel the reservation?"

"No, not at all. I really enjoyed myself the last time we came."

She grinned. "You might get an odd look from the maitre'd, though – I'm not sure he knows Charles is my brother."

David got out to open Rose's door, holding out his hand to help her out of the car. They walked towards the restaurant, and he opened the door for her to enter ahead of him.

If the maitre'd had any thoughts, he kept them to himself when David confirmed their reservation, and he showed them straight to their table. David held Rose's chair for her, and she smoothed her dress as she sat down.

"What can I get you to drink?" asked the maitre'd.

Rose glanced across at David. "I'd quite like to try a cocktail, if that's OK."

"Of course," he smiled.

Rose thought for a moment, then turned to the maitre'd. "There's one called a 'Dark and Stormy'?"

He nodded. "No problem."

"And I'll have a glass of white wine, please," added David.

The maitre'd left to get their drinks, and David grinned at Rose. "Is that how you'd describe yourself, dark and stormy?"

She shook her head. "Hardly stormy. I'm the one who has to keep cool when Paul and Charles are rushing all over the place."

David nodded. "How come you got so involved in the business? I'd have thought you'd be itching to get away from home to study."

For a moment Rose looked sad. "The firm was just a traditional engineering company when Dad was alive, turning out small runs of parts for local manufacturing firms. Dad had a heart attack – massive, there was nothing they could do – and Charles and Paul took over. They decided to modernise, but there was just so much to do, and they couldn't afford to take on extra people in the office…"

David reached across the table to touch her hand briefly. "I'm sorry about your father."

A waiter brought their drinks, and Rose managed a smile as she lifted her glass. "Here's to happier times."

"Happier times," echoed David.

He opened the menu. "Seeing as you've been before, what do you recommend?"

"The venison's really good," said Rose, hiding her surprise at being asked her opinion.

"Then I'll give it a try," said David. "Have you found something you'd like?"

Rose ran her finger down the page. "I think I'll have pasta for a change."

David caught the waiter's attention, and they gave him their orders.

"So how about you?" Rose asked. "You seem to have worked your way up the ladder quite quickly."

She glanced across at David, hoping she hadn't made it sound like a criticism. But he just nodded thoughtfully. "Partly I'm good at what I do, but also I've had some good breaks, been in the right place at the right time. And there are a few people who've helped me, given me chances."

He smiled. "I'm sure there's more still to come."

Their starters arrived, and David said, "How's the melon?"

"Lovely," said Rose. "I think there's a drop of kirsch on it. Want to try a piece?"

David grinned, and reached across with his fork, spearing a chunk and putting it in his mouth. "Mm, see what you mean. Do you want to try the paté?"

Rose nodded, and he held out a piece of toast. "'Scuse fingers."

She leaned forward and took the offered morsel with her teeth, raising her eyebrows and cupping her hand under her mouth in case it dropped.

"This is good," she said round a mouthful of toast. "Though I have a confession."

"What's that?" asked David, smiling.

"I had the paté last time, so I should have let you keep all of yours."

He leaned back in his chair and laughed out loud. "You got me there. But I don't mind, really."

They finished their starters and the waiter took their plates. "So what do you like to do when your brothers aren't running you ragged?" asked David.

"It does have its compensations," said Rose. "They're pretty good at treating me and my sister in return for all the help."

She smiled. "Last weekend they surprised us with a trip to the theatre."

David suddenly looked embarrassed. "Ah, actually I already knew about that one."

Rose blinked. "How?"

"I was there. I saw you in the interval, but you didn't notice me."

It was Rose's turn to laugh. "Sorry! Lily and I were so absorbed in the play, you could probably have been wearing a flashing sign and we would still have walked past you."

She grinned. "I knew there was a reason why I didn't wear the same dress tonight."

David shook his head. "I've never been that sure about feminine intuition, but now I'm beginning to wonder."

"So," said Rose with a mischievous smile. "Which one are you? Bingley or Darcy?"

David grimaced playfully. "Nice but dim, or standoffish with a good heart? That's a tough one."

He looked up at Rose. "I don't think I'm either of those, but hopefully I'm someone you can trust, have fun with, get to know better?"

Rose didn't speak, but nodded, hoping her face didn't betray too strongly the emotion his words had stirred in her.

He gave her a few moments, then said in a lighter tone, "So what about you and Lily? Elizabeth and Jane?"

"OK," said Rose smiling, "now you're scaring me. That's exactly what Lily said this afternoon when we were out."

David grinned. "Maybe it's true. Intelligent, independent, playful. Beautiful."

Rose looked down, and David said, "I'm sorry. I've embarrassed you, I didn't mean to do that."

She shook her head. "Don't worry."

Their waiter approached, clearing his throat. "Are you ready for your next course?"

David nodded, and the waiter put plates in front of them. Rose sampled her pasta. "This is good."

"The venison's great, too," said David.

He started to speak again. "Do you –" and at the same time Rose said, "What –"

They both stopped. "Go ahead," said David.

Rose smiled. "I was going to ask about your parents."

"They live in India. They'd been over there quite a few times, and when Dad took early retirement they decided to move there permanently."

"Wow," said Rose. "So you're on your own over here?"

David shook his head. "My younger sister's still here – she's at boarding school down South."

"I'd love to meet her," said Rose.

David nodded. "She'll be back at the end of term."

Rose felt a thrill at his ready acknowledgement that their date could develop into a more permanent connection.

David glanced at her empty glass. "Would you like another drink?"

"Mm, please. White wine?"

He signalled the waiter. "A glass of white wine for the lady, please."

When the waiter had gone, Rose grinned. "I'm not used to being called a lady."

David smiled. "Nothing wrong with a bit of old-fashioned courtesy."

The waiter brought Rose's wine, and she sipped. "I'm having a lovely evening – thanks, David."

They finished eating, and David glanced at Rose. "Dessert?"

"Well, maybe…" she grinned. "The chocolate mousse is pretty good."

David called the waiter over. "What desserts do you have?"

"There's a lemon tart, meringue with strawberries, and pears in red wine… oh, and chocolate mousse."

Rose didn't hesitate. "Chocolate mousse, please."

"And for me too," confirmed David. "Coffee, Rose?"

She nodded. "Two coffees, then, please," added David.

As the waiter left, David grinned at Rose. "I was watching your face – you were beginning to think there wasn't any mousse, weren't you."

"Am I really that easy to read?" she sighed.

"Don't worry – I won't take advantage."

Their desserts arrived, and Rose took a spoonful of the dark mousse, then sipped her coffee. "Mm, it's good."

Finally she put down her spoon. "Perfect. Thanks so much, David."

He smiled. "I've really enjoyed myself too. Let me go and settle the bill, then we can make our way back?"

David got up from the table, taking out his wallet, and Rose was left alone with her thoughts for a few moments. Lily's question came back into her mind – Do you think he'll kiss you?

Rose made a decision. If David looked as if he was going to kiss her, she would let him. She hoped he would…

David returned to the table. "Ready?"

Rose got to her feet, and took David's offered arm. She nodded to the maitre'd as they passed, and leaned a little into David's shoulder, feeling as though things couldn't possibly get any better.

She reluctantly took her arm from his as he opened the car door for her, and they set off towards the lights of the town.

When they reached the factory, David stopped the engine and again walked round to open the door for Rose. He stepped back a little as she got out of the car, but she was still conscious of his nearness.

"Well, goodnight then," she said. She hadn't meant her voice to drop – it must have been her nervousness – but David leaned in a little closer to catch her words. As he moved nearer, Rose unconsciously turned her face upwards slightly and lifted her eyes to meet his. She saw him search her face for any hesitation, then... his lips met hers, just for a moment, and he moved back, his eyes still on her face.

He paused, as if fixing the moment in his memory. "Goodnight, Rose. I'll wait till you're safely on your way."

He leaned against his car and watched as she walked to hers. She opened the door, starting the engine, and looked back, smiling, as she drove away.

When she got home, she closed the front door behind her, and took off her shoes, doing her best to climb the stairs silently.

She pushed the bedroom door open, and stopped, surprised. The lamp on Lily's side of the bed was shining, and her sister looked up as she entered. "What time do you call this," she teased.

Rose sat down on the bed. "I had the best time, Lily."

"And?" Lily insisted gently.

Rose grinned. "I got kissed."

Lily sat up to hug her. "That's brilliant!"

Rose nodded. "He was really thoughtful, we had a wonderful evening."

"When are you seeing him again?"

"We didn't set anything up," Rose shrugged.

"You are impossible!" laughed Lily. "Do you even have his number?"

"I'm sure he'll be in touch," said Rose confidently. "Now, can you give me a hand getting this makeup off?"

***

Rose didn't have to wait long. As she was checking through some invoices at the office the next morning, Beth came in, grinning broadly.

"There's a delivery for you at reception."

Rose followed her back to the reception area, and stopped, her mouth open. On the desk stood a basket, and rising from it the elegant stems of orchids, their creamy flowers seeming almost too perfect to be real.

As Rose looked more closely, she saw an envelope tucked into the edge of the basket. She carefully opened the flap, taking out a simple white card and reading:

"Thanks for last night. I thought you might prefer these to your namesake."

The card was signed 'David' and at the bottom was a phone number. Rose tucked the card into a pocket, and glanced up at Beth.

"I think I can guess who sent those," Beth said, smiling.

Rose hesitated. "Can I ask you a favour, Beth? Don't let on to Paul and Charles that you know? I want this to keep this separate from work."

Beth nodded. "I understand. My lips are sealed."

Rose picked up the flowers. "I'll take these home. If Paul or Charles asks, I'll be back after lunch to finish the invoices."

She lowered the basket carefully onto the passenger seat of her car, and drove home. Lily opened the door as she pulled into the drive. "I thought you weren't coming back till later? I'm getting on OK with my revision."

Rose lifted the basket from the car, and Lily's eyes widened. "Wow. Now I get it."

They went inside, and Rose set the flowers in the middle of the dining table. "There. That'll make a nice centrepiece."

She took the card from her pocket. "I'd better give David a call, he'll be wondering if the florist has delivered yet."

Lily nodded. "Tell him hi from me."

Rose climbed the stairs, closing the bedroom door behind her. She took her phone from her pocket, and added David's number to her phonebook. The small action seemed strangely significant, and she smiled to herself as she pressed the key to save the entry.

She took a deep breath and dialled. The phone barely had time to ring before David answered. "Hello?"

"David, it's Rose. Thanks so much for the flowers, they're gorgeous."

She could tell he was smiling. "I'm glad you liked them."

Rose took a deep breath. "When can I see you again?"

The answer came without hesitation. "I'm free tonight. What would you like to do?"

"Dinner was lovely, but could we do something a little more relaxed? See a film, have pizza?"

"Of course." He thought for a moment. "Do you mind if I get the tickets for us? Then it'll be a surprise."

"I'd like that," Rose assured him. "Shall I meet you at the pizza place?"

"OK. Six o'clock suit?"

"Sure."

"See you later, then."

Rose ended the call, and sat for a moment, hardly able to believe that she'd be with David for a second evening in a row.

She went downstairs to the kitchen. "I'm out again tonight, Mum. Hope that's OK – I promise I'll be in tomorrow."

"That's fine, dear. It's nice to see you getting out a little."

Rose went back into the lounge, and Lily looked up. "You OK?"

Rose nodded vigorously. "Pizza tonight, and a film."

"Yay!" said Lily. "I think he really likes you."

After lunch, Rose changed, putting on her favourite jeans and a t-shirt, and picking up her leather jacket. She drove to the factory, and winked at Beth as she passed. Even the invoices didn't seem so tedious, and when she glanced at her watch it was half past five.

As she walked out towards reception, Beth was just shutting down her computer, and Rose said, "Are you going towards town?"

Beth nodded. "I have to get a few bits of shopping for my Mum."

"Great – we can walk down together."

They made their way down the main road towards the pedestrian precinct. As they approached the cinema complex, a tall figure emerged from the entrance. "Hi, you two."

"Hi, David," said Rose. It seemed the most natural thing in the world for her to put her arms round him, and for him to kiss her briefly.

"Well, I'd better get going," smiled Beth. "Otherwise Mum's cat will be complaining. Have a good evening, you two."

"See you in the morning," said Rose. Beth nodded, and headed off in the direction of the supermarket.

"Shall we go in?" said David. "You look great, by the way. I like the jacket."

They walked into the cinema complex, stopping at the pizza place. "Doesn't look too full," said Rose. "What time's the film?"

"We have plenty of time," reassured David.

They went in and were seated, and Rose glanced at the menu. "Want to share a large pizza, and get some salad?"

David nodded. "You pick."

Rose raised her eyebrows. "Can you cope with spicy hot, extra jalapenos?"

"Bring it on," grinned David. "Good job they have free refills on the lemonade, though."

They ordered, then went up to the salad bar with their bowls. Rose took small tomatoes, potato salad, pasta, and drizzled French dressing over her bowl.

David grinned. "I see you and I have quite different tastes in some things." He quickly filled his bowl with sliced cucumber, grated carrot, and shredded lettuce, and poured thousand island dressing over the top.

They went back to their table, and Rose picked up a tomato. "Want to try one?"

David nodded, and took it from her fingers with his lips.

Rose smiled. "So how was your day?"

"Great, actually. We've finally taken delivery of the last batch of components from our other supplier, and we're doing a hundred percent quality check because of the problems we've had. Any of theirs that give our customers a problem, we're automatically replacing with a new unit from your production line."

Rose nodded. "Sounds like good customer service."

"We're doing our best to make sure our customers come back to us next time. Anyway, how about your day?"

"Well, there was one surprise," Rose said, her eyes sparkling. "How did you know I liked orchids?"

"Just a lucky guess."

"So I took the flowers home – they look lovely on the dining room table – and the rest of the day was paperwork, pretty routine really."

"Well," said David, "hopefully the film I picked will give you an opportunity for a little escapism."

Their pizza arrived, and David lifted a slice onto Rose's plate, then took one for himself. He pretended to eye it apprehensively. "Well, here goes."

He took a bite and chewed thoughtfully. "Actually this is pretty good. I think you've converted me."

"Didn't you eat lots of spicy junk food while you were at college?" asked Rose. "Kebabs from street vans, that kind of thing."

David shook his head. "I shared a house with some friends and we were really organised with the cooking, so the food was pretty good. And uni was a bit of a slog, there wasn't a lot of time for late nights and kebabs afterwards.

"The nearest we got to this sort of thing was a bowl of chilli at the pub round the corner from the department, when we had a couple of hours between morning lectures and an afternoon lab session."

He grinned. "An English degree would probably be a little less intense."

Rose didn't miss the fact that he'd remembered their very first conversation. "Lots of reading, though."

They finished their pizza, and David glanced at his watch. "We have time for dessert, if you'd like."

Rose shook her head. "Buy us some popcorn?"

"Of course."

David drank the last of his lemonade, and went to pay the bill. When he returned, he said, "Close your eyes and hold out your hand."

Rose obeyed, mystified, and felt him drop something into her palm.

She opened her eyes. "Oh, Smarties!"

David gave a conspiratorial smile. "I picked up a few from the ice cream machine. They won't mind – and anyway, next time we come in here I'll buy you ice cream."

Rose felt a warm glow at his certainty that they'd be having pizza again soon. She held out her hand. "Want some?"

David took a couple. "You have the rest."

They walked to the cinema concourse, and Rose glanced at the posters. "I'd like to see that one," she said. "You don't often get to see decent fantasy films."

"It wouldn't have anything to do with the fact that it's got Sean Bean in, would it?" teased David.

They queued for popcorn, then made their way to the door where an usher was taking tickets.

"Screen five," the usher said as she handed David the ticket stubs back.

He glanced at Rose. "Do you know yet?"

She shook her head, smiling. "I made sure not to look at the displays."

They went into the auditorium. "Where do you prefer to sit?" asked David.

"Let's go all the way up to the back," replied Rose.

As they sat down, the lights dimmed, and the trailers started to roll. "We usually give them marks out of ten," Rose whispered.

"Me too," grinned David.

The first trailer was for a horror film with plenty of screaming and running, and Rose glanced at David. "I'd give that about a two."

He nodded. "Definitely."

The next film was a romantic comedy, and David said, "I could give that an eight, actually."

"I'd go as far as a nine," Rose replied. "So you'd be OK to see that one?"

"Sure."

The trailers finished, and after the obligatory advert for hot dogs and Coke, the certificate screen for the main feature flashed up.

"Bride and Prejudice," read Rose. "Must have something to do with Jane Austen."

David grinned. "You'll see."

The film started, and Rose watched the chaos of Indian street life with fascination. As the various characters were introduced, she flashed David a smile. "I get it. This is going to be great!"

She reached for David's hand, twining her fingers in his and leaning closer to him in her seat. As the plot unfolded, she couldn't help but be drawn in, laughing at Mr Kholi's hapless attempts to romance Lalita.

Rose gripped David's hand as Will Darcy and Lalita searched for Lakhi, and David distinctly heard a whispered 'Yes!' as Darcy finally gave Wickham a solid punch to the jaw.

As the credits rolled, Rose turned to David. "That was brilliant – I didn't even know they'd done that."

They waited until the lights came back up and the rest of the audience had dispersed, then made their way slowly towards the exit. "Is that where your parents are?" asked Rose.

David shook his head. "They're much further east, the other side of Nepal. It's a beautiful place, very lush, in the foothills of the Himalayas."

Rose opened her mouth to speak, then held back. She was sure there'd be time later to say how much she'd look forward to visiting the place he was describing.

They reached the street, and David said, "Would you like a coffee or something?"

Rose glanced across the precinct. "I fancy a milkshake, if that's OK?"

"Of course."

They went into McDonalds, and waited their turn to be served. "What flavour?" asked David.

"Guess," Rose teased.

"I'm going to say... chocolate," he said decisively.

"Spot on," Rose laughed. "Am I really that predictable?"

"Never," said David seriously.

They got their drinks – David chose vanilla – and sat down. Rose stirred her milkshake with the straw, then sucked. "Ooh, that's cold."

She looked across at David. "This has been another lovely evening – thank you so much."

David smiled. "So, I'm afraid I'm a bit tied up for the rest of the week – I have to catch up on some work – but I have a suggestion."

"Whatever it is, the answer's yes," grinned Rose.

David raised his eyebrows. "I'll hold you to that. Actually, I was going to suggest that you come to my place on Saturday – I have a project I think you might enjoy helping me with."

He paused. "You could bring Lily if you like – she has to go back to school next week, doesn't she? I don't want you to miss out on your time with her."

Rose felt tears prick at her eyes. "That's really thoughtful. I'm sure she'd love to come."

"Settled, then." He grinned. "Wear clothes you don't mind getting wrecked."

They finished their milkshakes, and David said reluctantly, "Well, better get you home. I guess you left your car at the office? I'll walk you up there, if you don't mind dropping me back at the multi-storey."

They made their way back to the office, and Rose unlocked her car. They got in, and David glanced at her as he fastened his seatbelt. "Don't worry, I'm not too bad as a passenger."

He was true to his word, seeming relaxed as Rose drove round the ring road. She pulled in to the side street by the multi-storey car park and stopped the engine.

"I'll see you on Saturday, then," she said.

David nodded. "Can't wait."

He unfastened his seat belt, then turned towards Rose again. "Night, then."

"Do I get a kiss?" she asked, trying to keep her voice casual.

In answer he leaned toward her, slipping his arm round her shoulder and pulling her to him. This time she closed her eyes as their lips met, and she couldn't help but breathe in deeply, catching the fragrance of his aftershave. For a moment she sensed him wanting to prolong the kiss, but he pulled away reluctantly.

"Night, my love. Sleep well." Then he was gone.

Rose sat still, her heart beating faster, hardly trusting her memory of his parting words, somehow feeling completely at peace while at the same time her emotions turned cartwheels.

Finally she took a deep breath, and started the engine.

**

When Rose came down the next morning, Lily was by herself in the kitchen, finishing breakfast. She glanced up, smiling. "I didn't hear you come in last night. How did it go?"

Rose smiled. "I had a fantastic evening. And I have a surprise for you."

Lily blinked. "For me?"

"I'm going to David's place on Saturday – and you're invited."

"Are you OK with that?" Lily enquired.

"Of course," grinned Rose. "I think it's sweet that he wants to spend time with you as well."

She fetched herself cereal and sat down. "Are you studying again today?"

Lily nodded. "Have you got time to help me?"

"I have to go into the office for an hour or so, but then we can have the rest of the day," promised Rose.

She finished her breakfast, and picked up her keys from the hall table as she passed. "See you in a bit."

Rose drove to the factory, and was soon absorbed in her task, making sure that the firm's insurance certificates were up to date.

She glanced up as Beth came into the office. "Hi, Beth. Don't tell me there are more flowers?"

Beth shook her head. "But this came for you." She held out an envelope with Rose's name handwritten on it.

Rose opened the envelope, taking out the card inside. A piece of paper fell out, and she picked it up, unfolding the single sheet. Inside was a carefully-sketched map, with directions to David's house.

She opened the card, reading the inscription. "Thanks for another great evening. See you and Lily anytime after ten on Saturday. David."

Rose smiled. "Thanks, Beth. I'm done here, so I'll get going – I promised to help Lily with her revision today."

Beth nodded. "See you tomorrow, then."

When Rose got home, Lily was sprawled on the sofa with her notes. Rose showed her David's card and the map. "Can't wait," smiled Lily.

They spent the day concentrating on Lily's English revision, and Rose talked to her sister about the film David had taken her to see. "It was a really different perspective on Jane Austen. I'll get it for us on DVD when it comes out."

At four o'clock their mother arrived back. "Are you two still at it?" she smiled. "Don't wear yourselves out."

Lily set her books aside. "Come on, Rose. Let's give Mum a hand with dinner."

By the time Charles and Paul came home, there was a delicious aroma emanating from the kitchen. "Smells like your famous stew, Mum," grinned Paul.

"Actually the girls did most of it," she replied. "Come in and sit down, it's ready."

As they ate, Paul said, "Lily, is there anything you need for when you go back to school? Charles and I could take you out on Saturday."

Lily glanced up. "I'd love to, but I'm busy on Saturday. I'm going to D–" She caught herself. "I'm going to Rose's boyfriend's house with her."

Charles raised his eyebrows. "OK. When do the rest of us get to meet this mysterious boyfriend, Rose?"

"Soon," she assured him.

For the rest of the week Rose divided her time between paperwork for the business, and helping Lily to revise. When Friday afternoon came, she closed the book she'd been using to test Lily on her maths, and smiled at her sister. "OK, that's it – no more studying."

Lily grinned. "Thanks, Rose. I feel much better about the exams now."

Charles treated them to pizza for tea again, and afterwards the two girls went out into the garden to sit on the stone bench by the apple tree.

"So, what do you think David's project is?" asked Lily.

Rose considered for a moment. "Actually, we've hardly talked about what he likes to do when he's not working – apart from going to the theatre."

"And taking girls out for dinner, and pizza, and to the cinema," Lily pointed out.

"Well, only one girl as far as I know," grinned Rose. "But no, I have no idea what David's project is, except that it's going to be messy. Perhaps he's one of these experimental artists and we're going to throw paint around."

"Or he's mad about gardening and he wants us to dig over his flower bed," Lily teased.

They did their best to outdo one another with increasingly ridiculous suggestions until they were helpless with laughter. "OK," Rose said finally. "Whichever of us was closest gets to ask David any question they like tomorrow, and he has to answer it."

Lily grinned. "I already know what I'm going to ask."

"Go on."

She shook her head. "It's a surprise."

Rose rolled her eyes. "OK, then. But remember the idea is to keep him, not scare him away."

"I won't," promised Lily. "Come on, let's go back inside, it's getting chilly."

***

The next morning after breakfast, Rose went into the garage and started looking in the old chest of drawers that stood by the door. "Hey, Lily," she called. "I've found the stuff we used to wear when we were helping Mum with the decorating."

Lily came out. "Isn't that the colour that we used in your bedroom?" she said, pointing at a splash of paint across the jeans Rose was holding up.

"Think you're right," grinned Rose. "Come on, let's go up and put this stuff on."

When they came down, Charles looked at them with a baffled expression. "That wouldn't have been my first choice of outfits to impress a boyfriend."

"Good job you don't have a boyfriend to impress, then," riposted Lily, sticking her tongue out at him.

"Very funny. Anyway, try not to get into any trouble," he cautioned.

"We'll be fine, Charles," Rose assured him.

She unlocked the car, and handed the map over to Lily. "The directions look straightforward enough – head out of town, turn left here, it's a couple of miles down this road, then keep an eye out for a drive on the right."

As they got closer, Rose slowed down, and Lily pointed. "That must be it."

"Wow," said Rose.

A pair of wrought-iron gates stood open, a broad drive leading up between neatly-clipped rhododendron bushes. At the end of the drive was a gravelled area obviously intended for parking, and beyond that a small lake. On one side of the lake, a short path led to a Georgian-style house with distinctive turreted chimneys.

Rose guided the car up the drive, stopping at the edge of the lake, and they got out.

"Morning, you two," they heard David's voice from behind them.

They turned to see him emerging from the door of a low brick building, wiping his hands on a cloth. He wore dark overalls with smears of grease, and Lily grinned at Rose. "Well, there's a big clue. Looks like I might win."

"Maybe," Rose replied. "Don't count your chickens."

David walked up to them and kissed Rose. "I've been looking forward to seeing you all week. And I'm glad you could come, Lily."

Lily smiled. "I had to find out for myself what's so special about you – Rose has been different ever since you asked her out to dinner."

Rose tried not to look embarrassed. "You'll get used to Lily – she says things just how she sees them."

David grinned. "I don't see a problem with that. Would you two like a coffee or something before we get started?"

"That'd be lovely," said Rose.

David nodded. "Have a seat." He indicated a wooden table by the water.

They sat down while David walked across to the house, disappearing for a while. When he reappeared, he was carrying a tray. "I know how Rose takes her coffee, but I wasn't sure what you'd want, Lily."

He set the tray down on the table. "So I brought whipped cream and a couple of bottles of syrup – hazelnut, caramel?"

Lily's eyes lit up. "OK – I'm starting to get it, Rose."

David pressed down the plunger on the cafetiere, and poured three mugs. Rose took hers, sipping at the hot, dark brew. "Mm, it's good."

Lily took the caramel syrup and topped up her mug, then spooned on cream. She lifted her mug and drank, leaving a trace of cream on her top lip. "Mmm."

Rose caught Lily's eye. "Ah, Lily…" She pantomimed wiping her mouth.

"Oops." Lily ran her tongue quickly over her lips. "Thanks, Rose."

Rose looked around. "This is an amazing place you have, David."

He smiled. "Glad you like it. My family lived here from when I was a child, and I have the place to myself now, except when Poppy's here."

Rose smiled. "Your sister?"

David nodded. "I can't wait for you to meet her."

He glanced at their mugs. "More coffee?"

Rose looked over at Lily, who shook her head. "No thanks – but later?"

"Of course. So, do you want to see my project?"

Rose nodded. "We've been guessing madly all week."

David smiled. "I hope you're not disappointed. I can't quite manage anything as exciting as a time machine."

He stood, and the girls followed him back to the building from which he'd first appeared.

"Here goes," said David, pulling the sliding door aside.

Lily gasped. "Oh!"

"It's... beautiful," said Rose, stepping forward to look more closely.

Inside the garage, gleaming in the sunshine streaming in through the door, stood a long, low shape, its distinctive silver emblem standing proudly above the grille.

"Can I?" asked Rose.

"Of course."

Rose gently trailed her fingertips over the bonnet, then turned back to David. "Are you restoring it?"

He nodded. "I've been working on it for a couple of years. From a mechanical point of view it's practically finished, but... I don't really have the touch for the interior – the upholstery and such."

He indicated the dash. "I have the wood for the inlay – I daren't tell you how much it was for the original walnut – and I was hoping you two would help me out with the fine work."

Rose ran her fingers over the steering wheel, the controls. "We'd love to, wouldn't we, Lily?"

Her sister seemed to pull herself back to the present. "Definitely."

"Thanks so much," said David. "Let me show you."

He led them to a neatly-arranged workbench. "See, here's the inlay, and this is the pattern. I've got a saw with a really fine blade, and craft knives, and glass paper – should be everything you'll need."

Rose pulled a stool up to the workbench. "Right. Come on, Lily, you can do the measurements and I'll saw. Then when we've got the pieces, we can both trim them, and try them against the pattern."

"Sounds like you've got this sorted," grinned David. "I need to do some more work on the engine – give me a shout if you need anything."

He moved over to the front of the car and lifted the bonnet, while Lily used a soft pencil to draw faint lines on the gleaming wood.

"OK, Rose," she said hesitantly. "I think that's marked up now."

Rose glanced at the plan, then at the piece of wood in Lily's hand. "Looks right to me."

She carefully fastened the wood into a vice, and picked up the saw. She set the blade against the edge of the wood, and began to cut, bending down every so often to blow dust away from Lily's pencil lines.

"Nearly there," she said, not taking her eyes from what she was doing. "Can you hold this end, Lily, so it doesn't fall?"

Lily nodded, and Rose moved the saw more slowly. "There."

She unfastened the vice, and laid the piece on the pattern. Lily leaned over her shoulder to look. "I think that's spot on."

Rose let out the breath she'd been holding. "OK. Put it on that side, and let's do the next one."

They were deep in concentration when David walked back over to the bench. "Gosh, you two, when you get going on something, you really focus. I think it's time we had some lunch."

"Just let me finish this last cut," said Rose. "There."

She straightened, pushing her hair back from her face. "So, what's for lunch?"

David grinned. "Take a seat by the lake, and I'll go and get it."

The girls went back to the table by the edge of the water, and David reappeared after a few moments with a laden tray. "So, we have smoked salmon and cream cheese on brown bread, and a few salad things."

He put the tray down. "And I thought we could treat ourselves to a glass of wine."

Lily glanced at Rose, who nodded, smiling. "That'd be lovely."

David poured the wine, and Lily took a bite of the salmon. She closed her eyes. "This is heavenly."

As they ate, Rose looked out over the lake. "Oh, there are ducks. See, Lily, they have little ones."

She took the crust from a piece of bread, and tossed it into the water. The ducks swam over, and Lily quickly pulled small pieces from another slice of bread and added to their treat.

When lunch was finished, David said, "Would you like me to give you a bit of a tour before we go back to work? It's just the right time of year to see the garden at its best."

They set off along the path which led round the edge of the lake, Rose beside David, Lily walking behind them. Lily smiled as Rose's hand crept into David's, and she held back on the teasing comment she was tempted to make.

The path took them past the front door, then across a stretch of lawn to a summer house, almost a cottage. "It's nice to sleep out here when the weather's warm," said David.

They carried on, reaching the opposite shore of the lake. The path led into woodland, and David pointed out some of the trees. "We have quite a lot of firs – this one's a Korean variety, it has really distinctive cones."

"What's this big one?" asked Lily.

David glanced across. "That's one of my favourites – a cedar. Take a deep breath, you'll smell it."

Lily breathed in. "Mmm, I see what you mean."

The path ran through a stone arch covered with honeysuckle, and they found themselves opposite the house again. "Shall we get back to work?" asked Rose.

Lily nodded. "We still have to smooth off the edges of all the pieces we cut this morning."

They resumed their seats at the workbench, and Rose said, "Here, Lily, wrap the glass paper round this block – that way the edge will be flat."

Lily picked up one of the pieces, and started to carefully rub down one edge, running her thumb over the surface to check its smoothness. "OK, I think that's done."

She took another piece. "I think this one goes next to it – I'll do that edge next, and we can see how closely they fit."

Rose nodded. "If we lay the pieces out on this other table, we can arrange them in the places where they'll go when they're finished."

The pattern built up piece by piece, and finally Rose stood, stretching. "That's the last one."

She glanced across to where David was carefully adjusting a complex-looking mechanism. "David?"

"Yes, my love?"

Again Rose felt her heart leap at his words, but she did her best to keep her voice steady. "Come and have a look."

David walked over to the table. "Wow. I didn't expect you to get that far today."

He reached out a hand to pick up one of the pieces, running a finger along the edges. "Smooth as silk."

He looked at the car thoughtfully. "I think we could put these in place. See, the inlay goes on the face of that panel there, in front of the driver's seat."

"If you give me the pattern, I'll squeeze into the space and stick them on," offered Rose.

Lily picked up a tube from the workbench. "Is this the glue?"

David nodded. "Let's go for it, then."

Rose twisted, managing to get herself into position close to the panel. "We should start at the top corner, I think."

Lily carefully applied glue to the first piece, and handed it to her sister. "There," said Rose, positioning it carefully and holding it in place with her thumb while the glue took hold.

Methodically they fitted the other pieces into position, until Lily handed Rose the last one. "Gosh," said Rose, pressing it gently into place, "that is such a perfect fit."

She moved back from the panel. "Ouch. I think I need some help getting out of this corner."

She took David's hand, leaning her weight on his arm as she turned, getting to her feet. She finished the movement standing close to him, face to face, and for a moment neither of them moved.

Lily wondered if she was going to have to remind them that she was still there, but Rose smiled, squeezing David's fingers then reluctantly taking her hand from his.

He took a deep breath. "Let's see how it looks." He took a soft cloth, and dabbing on a little beeswax, buffed the surface of the completed inlay.

"Oh, wow," breathed Rose. The wood glowed softly in the golden light of the late afternoon sun, its different tones and the contrasting directions of the grain making it appear almost alive.

David was visibly moved. "Thanks, you two. It's more beautiful than I imagined."

Lily spoke hesitantly. "How close is it to being finished? The whole restoration, I mean."

"Almost there," David replied. "I wish I could take you out in it today, but there are just a few things that still need doing. I need three or four more weekends on it."

Rose looked thoughtful. "If I help, maybe we can get it done for when Lily comes back at the end of term."

"And Poppy will be here too," said David. "That'd be perfect – the four of us could drive out for a picnic."

He glanced at his watch. "Speaking of food, I think it's time for dinner. Let's go inside, I've set the dining table."

Rose looked at her paint-splashed clothes. "I'm not really dressed for it."

"Doesn't matter," smiled David. "You look wonderful just the way you are."

They walked across to the house, and David showed them into a wide entrance hall with stairs leading up to a landing.

"You'll probably want to freshen up," he said. "There's a bathroom just across the landing there."

He headed for the kitchen, and the two girls climbed the stairs. Rose splashed her face, then took a brush from her bag and ran it quickly through her hair. "That feels better."

Lily nodded. "Rose?"

"Hmm?"

"He really loves you."

"I think you're right," said Rose, her eyes taking on a softer look.

Lily grinned. "Come on. Let's see what he pulls out of the hat for dinner."

They went back down the stairs, following the sounds of activity until they reached the kitchen, where David was carefully stirring a small pan.

"Nearly ready," he said. "Go through and sit down, and I'll bring everything through in a minute."

He indicated a doorway, and Lily followed Rose into the dining room, finding the table laid with a crisp white cloth. Silverware and wine glasses were at each place, and in the centre stood a crystal vase with a single rose.

Lily sat down, and Rose glanced at the place settings. "I think I'm opposite you, and David has the seat at the head of the table, nearest the kitchen."

She took her seat, and a few moments later David appeared carrying a large soup tureen, which he put down in the middle of the table.

"Home-made mushroom soup," he said. He took a bowl and carefully ladled soup into it, putting it down in front of Rose. "Do start."

He served Lily, then himself, and sat down, picking up his spoon. He glanced at Rose. "How is it?"

"Great. Did you put a little cream in it?"

David grinned. "My not-so-secret ingredient."

When they'd finished their soup, David went back out into the kitchen, returning with a tray. He set two covered dishes on the table, then put the empty tray aside.

"That smells amazing," said Rose.

David lifted the lid. "Chicken supreme, and the other bowl is rice."

The girls helped themselves, and Rose said, "The rice seems different — fragrant somehow."

David nodded. "It's basmati, with just a pinch or two of spices — my parents bring them back when they come to visit. I save them for special occasions, and this is certainly one of those."

Lily glanced at Rose. "I think I won our bet."

Rose rolled her eyes. "Go on then."

David gave her a puzzled grin. "Go on, tell me."

Rose smiled wryly. "Lily bet me that whichever of us got closest to guessing what your surprise was today, could ask you any question and you'd have to answer it."

David chuckled. "I don't suppose I get any say in this, do I."

Lily shook her head firmly. "I guessed that you were building something and needed us to help. Rose thought you might be working on a painting."

David shook his head. "I think you're right, you were the closest. So what's the question?"

"How many girlfriends have you had before?" asked Lily without hesitating.

Rose looked at David as though to ask him what she could do with her sister. But he just nodded. "Fair question."

"Actually, only three," he said. "Ann was the first – she was the daughter of a couple my parents knew out in India. Missionaries, actually. She came over to do her A-levels, and I met her at school."

He looked wistful. "She was great – living overseas had given her such a different perspective, she was always surprising me. But when she went back the first summer, she got together with someone she'd gone out with before. They're married now, I occasionally hear from them."

"Then there was Lynn – she was a redhead, gorgeous. I met her at university, we had a great time, going to balls and such like. When we finished studying and I moved back here, somehow it just didn't work out, us being so far apart."

David paused. "The last girl I went out with was Nicola. That didn't end well – she was very insecure, always afraid I was going to leave her. Of course the more she clung, the more I felt like I did want to get away, and eventually I had to break things off."

He took a deep breath. "Well, now you know all my secrets."

Lily looked thoughtful. "I can see there's more to this going-out thing than I'd realised."

David reached out to touch her hand. "I really hope you get to go out with someone nice – so you know what it's like to have someone show you respect, listen to you, find out what you want."

Lily nodded, still pensive. Then she brightened. "Anyway, now you have Rose. So it's all OK."

David smiled, glancing at Rose. "It's true, Lily, I'm really enjoying getting to know your sister. But a lot of it's up to her – how she feels."

He stood up, and Rose couldn't decide whether she was glad they were moving on from that part of the conversation, or disappointed that her unsubtle sister wouldn't have more opportunity to get David to put his feelings into words.

"Now, what about some dessert? It's just ice cream, but I have some wafers. There's chocolate or vanilla."

"Vanilla, please," said Lily.

"Chocolate for you, Rose?"

She nodded. "Please."

David went out to the kitchen, returning with bowls of ice cream and a packet of wafers. "Would you both like coffee? I can make some more whipped cream."

"Mm, please," said Lily round a mouthful of vanilla ice cream.

"We can take our coffee into the lounge," said David. "I'll light a fire – it's cooler now the sun's gone down."

He finished his ice cream, then went out to put the kettle on. Soon the aroma of the coffee mingled with a hint of wood smoke, and David came back into the dining room. "OK, come on through."

Lily went first, sprawling on the rug in front of the fire, and Rose took a seat on the sofa. David joined her, and she curled her legs under her and leaned against him, his arm around her shoulders.

David passed Rose her coffee, and she took a sip, then put her cup back down on the low table. "David?"

"Hmm?"

"Would you like to come to church with me and Lily tomorrow morning? It's only a short service, and everyone's really friendly."

David smiled. "Of course. I'd really like that."

Rose closed her eyes, resting her head on his shoulder, the firelight seeming to impart an otherworldly glow to her face.

After a few minutes she lifted her head and sighed. "I don't want to move, but I suppose we should be getting back."

Lily got to her feet. "Are the car keys in your handbag?"

Rose gave her sister a confused look. "Yes, but...?"

Lily grinned. "I just want to give you two a couple of minutes by yourselves, dummy."

She retrieved the keys from Rose's bag. "It's been a wonderful day – thanks so much, David."

He nodded. "See you tomorrow, Lily."

She closed the door as she left, and David smiled. "She's very thoughtful."

Rose nodded. Then she lifted her head to look into his eyes, her expression serious but somehow at the same time expectant. "Hold me?"

David turned, taking her into his arms, and she felt an indescribable sense of contentment, of being secure, overwhelming even the thrill of being so close to him.

She felt a moment of disappointment as he reluctantly pulled back to look at her. "I think our couple of minutes is up."

David stood, then helped her to her feet, and they walked out to the car. Lily was sitting in the passenger seat, humming along to the radio, and she smiled as David opened the door for Rose to get in.

Rose wound down the window. "See you at church, just before ten?"

David nodded. "Sleep well, my love."

He smiled at Lily, and she lifted a hand in farewell as Rose started the engine and they moved off.

***

The next morning at breakfast, Rose was uncharacteristically jittery, and Charles asked in an irritated voice, "What's up with you?"

"I–" began Rose, and stopped, looking at Lily with a helpless expression.

"Rose's boyfriend is coming to church this morning, and she's anxious about what he'll make of it."

Charles nodded dismissively. "Perhaps I should come along to size up this mysterious boyfriend."

Rose suppressed a wince. "Of course, if you want to, Charles."

He shook his head. "I have things to do."

Rose glanced at the clock. "We should be going – I'd like to get there before him."

As they walked down the road, Lily said, "I can't believe I have to go back this afternoon."

Rose gave her a guilty look. "I hope I haven't neglected you this week, with work and then going out with David."

"Are you kidding? I got all my revision done, and there was the play last weekend, and then yesterday. I just wish I could stick around to see what happens next with you two."

"I'll text you every day," promised Rose.

They reached the church, and Rose stopped, surprised to see David waiting for them at the gate into the churchyard.

"I didn't want to be late, and I thought it'd be easier if we all went in together," he explained.

Rose nodded. "OK."

She paused for a moment, then took his hand. "No point in leaving people guessing," she said with a smile.

They walked to the church door, and the vicar nodded at Rose as they passed. Rose turned towards the stairs to the balcony, then changed her mind.

"Let's sit near the front," she said.

They found seats, David between the two girls, just as the organ started to play.

David picked up a hymn book. "I know this one," he said, opening the book and holding it so they could see the words. As the hymn began, Rose glanced at David in surprise. His voice was a tuneful baritone, and he sang with enthusiasm.

The hymn finished, and they sat down. The vicar walked to the front and gave a few notices, then opened the heavy Bible on the lectern. "Could we have our reading please."

A young woman walked to the lectern, running her finger down the text to find her place, then starting to read.

"While Jacob was still talking with them, Rachel came with her father's sheep, for she was a shepherd. When Jacob saw Rachel daughter of his uncle Laban, and Laban's sheep, he went over and rolled the stone away from the mouth of the well and watered his uncle's sheep. Then Jacob kissed Rachel and began to weep aloud. He had told Rachel that he was a relative of her father and a son of Rebekah. So she ran and told her father."

David was following the reading in the pew Bible, and Rose noticed that as the young woman returned to her seat, he read on, turning the pages.

The vicar walked to the pulpit and glanced down at his notes. "I want to go back and talk about Jacob again this week…"

As he finished his message and gave out the number of the final hymn, Rose looked across at David. He returned her glance, the expression on his face thoughtful. They stood to sing, and Rose relaxed into the familiar words, David's voice at her side now somehow reassuring.

The vicar gave the blessing, and people started to move towards the back to get their coffee. "Can I get you two a drink?" offered David.

Rose smiled quizzically. "Thought I was supposed to be making you feel at home here, not the other way round."

David raised his eyebrows. "But then, I hear Jacob ended up watering Rachel's sheep."

Lily punched him playfully in the arm. "Hey, what are you saying."

David went to the serving hatch, returning with two mugs of coffee. "Here you go. I picked up a couple of biscuits, too."

Lily took her mug. "You have the biscuits, Rose. I'm going to have a quick chat with Anne, if that's OK."

She waved at her friend, heading across the church towards her, and Rose turned to David. "Is there anything you wanted to ask? About the service, or what the vicar said, I mean."

He shook his head. "But it's given me a lot to think about."

Lily returned, smiling. "Anne says hi."

She glanced at her watch. "Oops, shouldn't we get going? Mum said she'd make lunch for one o'clock."

Rose nodded. "Wish you were coming with us, David," she said.

He smiled. "Don't worry. And anyway, I'll see you tomorrow. I'm coming over to the office to talk to Charles and Paul about their proposal for me to take a share in the new investment."

They made their way out of the church, stopping at the gate out of the churchyard. David turned to Lily. "I hope the rest of the term goes OK."

She smiled. "Thanks. I'll see you when I get back – and I can't wait to meet Poppy."

She leaned across and kissed him on the cheek, then glanced at Rose. "I'll walk up the hill slowly – catch me up?"

Lily set off, not looking back, and David grinned. "She's very thoughtful – I think we're a bit conspicuous here, though, to be honest."

Rose nodded. "But nobody can object to the sort of kiss I'd give my brothers, can they."

She leaned over and kissed him as Lily had done, but her lips lingered on his cheek for a moment, and she whispered, "See you tomorrow, darling."

She glanced back as she walked up the hill, then increased her pace until she drew alongside her sister. When they reached the house, Charles opened the door, frowning. "I wondered where you'd got to – lunch is ready."

They went in and sat down, and their mother started to serve. "Would you say grace for us, Charles?"

Charles cleared his throat. "For what we are about to receive, may the Lord make us truly thankful. Amen."

The rest of the family echoed the Amen, and Paul passed Rose the plate containing slices of roast beef. She smiled her thanks, and served herself and Lily before passing the plate back.

When lunch was finished, Lily pushed back her chair with a sigh. "I'd better get my stuff together – my train's in about forty minutes."

"I'll come and give you a hand," said Rose, and the two went upstairs. Lily began to put her notes and books into her bag. "Thanks so much for helping me this week, Rose."

"No problem." Rose felt tears prick at her eyes. "I'm so glad you were here, that you've had a chance to get to know David already."

"Are you going to be OK?" Lily asked. "Nobody knowing it's him, I mean."

Rose nodded. "I'm in no rush to tell them – this way, they can't interfere. Actually, in some ways it'll be fun – I'm looking forward to the meeting tomorrow."

Lily grinned. "I'd like to be a fly on the wall."

She fastened her bag. "OK, I'm ready."

They went down the stairs, and Lily went into the kitchen to give her mother a hug. "I'll write you a letter at the end of the week," she promised.

Paul and Charles were waiting in the hall. "Good luck in your exams," said Paul, hugging Lily.

"Don't get distracted," warned Charles. "Boys, or anything like that."

"No, Charles," promised Lily dutifully.

They drove to the station, and Lily slid down the carriage window to lean out. "It's only six weeks to the end of term," she said.

Rose nodded. She reached up to squeeze Lily's hand. "Take care, angel. Text me when you get there."

She watched the train out of sight, then walked slowly back to her car. When she arrived home, Paul was in front of the computer, and Rose put her head round the door. "Do you need me at the office tomorrow?"

He turned. "David Stuart is coming over for a meeting – you remember we talked about him investing in the production facilities."

"OK – I'll come and take notes. Think I'll go upstairs now – I need to catch up on my online forum, I've hardly looked at it while Lily's been here."

Paul grinned. "Of course, your mysterious boyfriend would have nothing to do with that."

Rose smiled knowingly. "Of course not."

***

The next day Rose was at the office early for the meeting, and David gave her a quick hug when he arrived. Beth had already quizzed Rose about her weekend over their first coffee of the day, and she grinned at David as he signed the visitor's book.

Just before twelve, Paul emerged from his office. "Ah, David, you're already here. Shall we go through?"

They went into the conference room, and again Rose poured water for David. Their fingers touched as she handed him the glass, and she looked up, her eyes revealing the amusement she was carefully keeping out of her expression.

Paul finished leafing through the documents in front of him. "So, David, I take it you've examined the proposal."

David nodded. "It all seems very straightforward. Capital investment of this figure here, in return for the same value of ordinary shares in Middleton Sons, dividends to be paid quarterly based on the share price on the day."

He took out his fountain pen, signing above his typed name. Rose looked at the flowing signature, imagining how hers might look with David's surname in place of her own...

"Rose?" she heard Paul's voice, obviously expecting an answer to a question she hadn't heard.

She pulled herself back to the present. "Sorry."

"Could you make a couple of copies, and ask Beth to file one and send the other over to Lewis's?"

"Of course, no problem."

Paul stood. "Will you stay for lunch, David?"

Rose felt a pang of disappointment as he shook his head. "Sorry, I have another appointment."

Paul nodded. "OK, no problem. I'll call the contractors this afternoon and make sure they can plan the installation of the new equipment."

He turned to Rose. "You'll see David out?"

"Of course."

"Well," said Paul, "thanks again, David. I'm sure this is the start of a great relationship."

Rose pressed her hand over her mouth, feigning a coughing fit to hide her laughter. David handed her his glass, and she nodded her thanks, sipping.

"Are you all right, Rose?" asked Paul anxiously.

"I'm fine," she managed. "I'm sorry, David – if you'll come back to reception with me, we'll get you signed out and on your way."

They walked back to the reception area, and Paul nodded to David again as he returned to his office.

Rose glanced at David. "Shame about your appointment – I was looking forward to lunch, even if we did have to share it with Paul."

He grinned. "Tell you a secret? If you can get away, you *are* my appointment."

She swiped playfully at him. "You!"

He pretended to look chastened. "I do have a busy afternoon, though, so will McDonalds do?"

Rose nodded enthusiastically. "As long as the offer includes a chocolate milkshake. I'll meet you there in ten minutes?"

David nodded. He walked over to the reception desk to sign out. "See you again soon, Beth."

She smiled. "Certainly, Mr Stuart."

***

When Rose reached the McDonalds, David was waiting for her. He put his arms around her, and their lips met for a brief kiss.

"What would you like?" he asked. "Apart from your milkshake, of course."

Rose glanced at the menu. "I can never resist a Big Mac – I think there's something in the sauce. And large fries, please."

David ordered their meal, and they found a seat by the window. Rose picked up her Big Mac in both hands and took a bite. "Mmm."

"I'm afraid I really do have a busy week," said David. "But the weekend's all ours."

Rose grinned. "We can work on the car."

David nodded. "But let's keep the evening free – I'll cook again."

He grinned. "And this time we'll have the fire all to ourselves after dinner."

Rose smiled softly. "Can't wait."

When they'd finished their meal, David took their trays to dispose of the debris, then came back to the table. "OK, my love, I'd better get back. Walk you to your car?"

At the car, David put his arms tenderly around Rose. "Till Saturday, then."

She nodded. "Bye, darling." His kiss was soft on her lips, then he was gone.

Rose kept her promise to text Lily every day, and her sister replied, always eager for any updates on Rose's relationship with David. Rose divided her time between the office – where things seemed to be busier than ever – and her online friends, dropping hints that maybe meeting a handsome prince wasn't such an impossibility after all.

On Friday morning, Beth came into the office with a package. "This arrived for you, Rose."

Rose pulled aside the wrapping to see dark blue fabric. She shook out the folds and held the garment up, revealing a neat pair of overalls matching the ones David had worn the previous weekend.

"He really knows how to dress you glamorously," said Beth, her expression quizzical.

"It's really sweet," said Rose. She explained about David's car restoration project. "These'll be much nicer than the old decorating clothes I was going to wear."

Beth retrieved a folded note from the wrapping paper. "What's this?"

Rose unfolded the sheet and read. 'Look in the right-hand pocket.'

She slipped her hand into the pocket, feeling something flat and square. She slid it out, and Beth smiled when she saw a velvet-covered box with a clasp. "That's more like it."

Rose opened the box. "Oh!"

Inside rested a necklace, stones sparkling in the light. Rose carefully lifted it from the case, draping it over her fingers. "It's lovely."

Inside the lid of the case was another note. 'Bring something to change into, that'll go with this?'

"Wow," said Beth. "I take it all back – he does know what he's doing."

Rose put the necklace back in its box and slipped it into her bag. When she arrived home at the end of the afternoon, she went upstairs and looked through her wardrobe, finding a dark blue dress that matched the shade of the stones. She opened a drawer, and slid the necklace to the back for safekeeping.

She heard her mother calling from downstairs that dinner was ready. "Coming, Mum."

The family sat down to eat, and the conversation turned to everyone's plans for the weekend. "I'm out again all day tomorrow at my boyfriend's," said Rose.

"Do you get on with his parents?" asked her mother.

"They live abroad," explained Rose.

"So you're there with him by yourself?" queried Charles.

"Lily was with us last week," she reminded him.

"Well, I'm not exactly happy about it," Charles said darkly.

Rose didn't reply to his comment, and the conversation moved on to other things. At the end of the meal she excused herself and went upstairs, sitting on her bed.

On impulse, she decided to try on her dress. She quickly changed, then retrieved her necklace from the drawer, managing to fasten the clasp on the first attempt. She put in her earrings, and ran a brush through her hair.

She looked at the effect in the mirror, feeling a little like Cinderella before the ball. Then an idea occurred to her. She picked up her phone and activated the camera, pointing it at the mirror and pressing the shutter.

"Picture, share, contacts, Lily," she murmured, touching the screen. "Send."

The phone vibrated to let her know that the message had been sent. As she carefully removed the necklace and put it back in its box, a quiet chime from her phone announced a reply.

"Wow wow wow!" she read. "Showing your pic to everyone in the dorm, they think you're way hot." The message ended with a smiley face and more exclamation marks.

Rose grinned. "Thanks for the confidence booster," she texted back. "I'll tell you tomorrow what David says."

She changed for bed, and put out the light, pulling the covers over her.

***

The next morning after breakfast, Rose carefully packed a small bag with her dress, the case containing her necklace, and a few other essentials. She pulled on the overalls, wondering how David had guessed her size so exactly.

As she went down the stairs, Paul was coming out of the kitchen. He glanced at her. "Very chic. But I didn't know 'Chinese utilitarian' was this year's hot trend." He grinned to reassure her he was only teasing.

Rose returned his smile. "I'll explain everything eventually."

She leaned over to kiss him on the cheek. "Have a good day."

As she pulled up the drive to David's house, he emerged from the garage and waved. Rose got out of the car, and David wrapped his arms around her tightly. "I've missed you."

"Me too. Thanks so much for the necklace. Oh, and the overalls – how did you know the size?"

He smiled mischievously. "I'd like to say that I have an eye for figures. But it's simpler than that – I texted Lily."

Rose chuckled. "Wait till I see her. But she does have one up on you – she knows what my outfit for tonight looks like."

David nodded. "Can't wait."

He glanced towards the house. "Would you like coffee? I got some pastries too."

"Mm, please."

They sat at the table by the lake to drink their coffee, and Rose ate her cinnamon whirl with relish, using her finger to pick up the last flakes of pastry from her plate.

"So what's on the cards today?" she asked.

"Big day today," David replied. "I've finished rebuilding the engine, so it's time to mount it back in the car. But it's definitely a two-person job."

"OK," said Rose hesitantly. "As long as you're sure I won't mess anything up."

David looked up. "There's no-one I'd trust more than you to help me with this."

Rose smiled. "Thanks, David."

They walked over to the garage, and David explained their task. "See, the engine's suspended from this frame, and all the mountings are prepared. We need to roll the frame over on its wheels so the engine's in the right place, then lower it."

"So which part do I do?" asked Rose.

"Once we have it in position, I'll guide the engine while you use these controls to lower it."

He smiled at her. "Ready?"

"OK."

They put their hands against the frame, and it began to move slowly towards the car. David double-checked that the engine would clear the bonnet, and shortly the engine was suspended above the mountings.

"Right," he said, steadying the engine with his hands. "Let it down slowly."

Rose hesitantly touched the controls, and the electric motor whirred. She released the button. "How's that?"

"Keep going."

Little by little the engine sank towards its intended resting place. Rose stopped for a moment to push her hair out of her eyes, and David looked up. "You OK?"

She nodded. "Fine."

"OK, nearly there," said David, not taking his eyes off the task. There was a quiet creak from the suspension as it took the additional weight, and the chains holding the engine clinked a little as they slackened. "That's it."

Rose let out the breath she'd been holding. "Phew."

She looked into the bonnet. "This might sound silly, but I feel like the car's got its heart back."

David turned to her, his face betraying his emotions. "That's exactly how I'd put it."

They stood still for a moment, then David smiled. "Come on – lots more to do. Pass me that tray of mounting bolts?"

Rose watched as he secured the engine on its mountings, then started to connect up cables. "What's that one?" she pointed.

"That's the clutch cable, and here's the accelerator."

"How fast will the car go?" asked Rose.

"With this engine, about a hundred miles an hour."

"Wow. Never mind a headscarf, I think I'll need goggles."

David straightened. "There. I still need to connect up the gearbox, and then the drive shaft, but we can do that after lunch."

Rose grinned. "What are you going to surprise me with today?"

"Come and sit down, and I'll show you."

They walked back to the table by the lake, and Rose sat down. David walked over to the house, reappearing with a tray.

"A nice chilled white wine," he said. "I'll stick to half a glass seeing as I'm working on the engine again after lunch. And the pièce de résistance, lobster salad. I cut fresh lemons for us to squeeze over it."

"Mm," said Rose, "I've not had lobster salad before."

They started to eat, and Rose looked around. "This is perfect," she said. "Sunshine, the water, amazing food."

David beamed. "I'm glad you're happy."

When they'd finished eating, they walked back to the garage. "What do you want me to do now?" asked Rose.

"Well, if you don't mind tight spaces, I could do with some help underneath the car."

Rose grinned. "Why else would I need the overalls?"

David pulled himself under the car. "OK, you slide under from the other side," came his muffled voice.

Rose lay down, and carefully inched herself under the car until she was looking up at the bottom of the engine. She turned her head, seeing David's face upside down next to her.

On impulse she leaned across and kissed him. "Ever since I saw Spiderman, I've always wondered what that would feel like."

David grinned. "Happy to solve that mystery for you."

They worked steadily on the engine all afternoon, Rose carefully following David's instructions. Finally he gave a bolt one last turn. "There. That's ready to run now."

"Does that mean we could drive it?"

David shook his head. "I still have to do the rest of the electrical connections, the lights and so on. But I can run the engine for a while – that'll be a good check that everything's connected properly."

He turned to Rose. "It should be safe, but just in case, you'd better stand outside."

She walked a little distance away. "Will this do?"

David nodded. He checked that the car was out of gear and the handbrake on, then reached over to press the electric starter. The engine turned over, then caught smoothly. David gently pulled the accelerator cable, and the engine revved, then settled down to a purr.

"Gosh," said Rose, "it's quieter than I expected."

David nodded. "These were all hand-built, and they literally machined the parts to balance to a hair's-breadth."

Rose was silent for a moment, thinking of the long-dead craftsmen who'd put so much of themselves into the beautiful car before her.

David glanced across. "OK?"

She nodded, and he pressed the stop switch, letting the engine idle to a halt.

David closed the door of the garage. "That's been a good day. Thanks, Rose."

He reached across to gently wipe a smudge of grease from her cheek. "I'm guessing you'd like a shower before dinner?"

Rose grinned. "I will need somewhere to effect my transformation."

She retrieved the bag from her car, and walked with David to the house. He led her up the stairs. "This is Poppy's room – there's an en-suite, take as long as you like. I'll get dinner started."

Rose went into the room, glancing round to see what it might tell her about David's younger sister. The colours were subdued, and on the walls hung framed prints – mostly Monet, but there was a portrait of a girl in a yellow dress that Rose didn't recognise.

She resisted the temptation to look in the wardrobes, and walked through into the en-suite. She quickly undressed, folding her overalls into a neat pile, then stepped into the shower. As she stood under the hot water, she relaxed, any stiffness from the afternoon's cramped positions seeming to wash away.

She got out of the shower, starting to dry herself on a large fluffy towel from a stack by the bath. Then she returned to the bedroom, unpacking her bag. She quickly dressed, brushing her hair, and put on the necklace and her earrings as she'd done the previous day.

Finally she dabbed on scent, remembering her shopping trip with Lily. "OK, here goes," she murmured to herself, taking one last look in the mirror then walking toward the stairs.

David was waiting to meet her, and she glanced at him in surprise. He caught her look. "Well, I wasn't going to keep my overalls on for dinner either," he teased.

He wore dark trousers and an open-necked shirt in a shade of blue which Rose was certain would complement her dress. "You look great," she said.

"So do you," he replied, holding out his hand to take hers as she reached the bottom of the stairs. To her surprise he raised her hand to his lips briefly. "Shall we?"

He led her to the dining room, and held her chair for her. He took his own seat opposite, and lifted the lid of a serving dish. "Steak in peppercorn sauce, Niçoise potatoes, vegetables in this one. And a nice Chablis."

Rose smiled. "OK, now you're officially spoiling me."

He poured wine for her. "Of course."

As they ate, Rose said, "David, I need to talk to you about something."

He put down his fork. "OK."

"Charles isn't too happy about us. He doesn't like not knowing who you are, and he certainly didn't like it when he found out I'd be here with you by myself tonight."

David nodded, reaching out to touch her hand. "I understand why you wanted to keep them in the dark to begin with."

He paused. "Rose, I love you. That's absolutely certain."

Rose's heart thrilled at his words, and she put her other hand on his.

"If you want to tell your family it's me you're going out with, that's fine. I can handle any games Charles wants to play, and I'm not going to let them drive a wedge between us."

He looked into her eyes. "And you have my word that I'll never, ever do anything that would harm you, or compromise you in any way."

Rose nodded. "I know."

She smiled, blinking back tears. "Let's not waste your fantastic cooking."

David grinned. "Leave some room for dessert, though."

Finally Rose put down her fork. "That was lovely."

David took her plate. "OK, now for the tricky bit. I'll need to be in the kitchen for a few minutes, then when I come back, you'll have to have your spoon ready."

Rose glanced at him mystified. "What kind of dessert is this?"

"You'll see."

He went out to the kitchen, and she heard the over door open and close, then the tick of a clockwork timer. The timer pinged, and David returned, still wearing oven gloves. He set a dish down in front of Rose. "Go ahead."

Rose obeyed, taking a spoonful of the dark brown contents. "Oh, my goodness. What is it?"

David grinned. "It's an Austrian speciality. Salzburger knockerl – sugar soufflé, but this one's made with dark chocolate."

Rose took another spoonful. "Gosh, it's starting to sink already."

David nodded. "I really wasn't sure I could pull it off. Over there, the waiters literally run with it when it comes out of the oven."

Rose finished the bowl. "What about you?"

"There's more mixture. It's like pancakes, I'll make you as many as you want."

She grinned. "I could go for another one."

He disappeared back to the kitchen, and this time when the timer pinged he returned with a bowl in each glove, and they raced each other to finish the soufflé before it sank.

"More?" he asked.

Rose shook her head. "You go ahead if you like."

"I'm OK, actually. It's pretty rich."

He took her dish. "Coffee? I lit the fire in the lounge while you were upstairs."

"Definitely," Rose smiled.

She went through into the lounge, sitting on the rug in front of the fire. David came through with coffee cups, and joined her on the rug, putting his arm around her shoulders as they looked into the flames.

He looked at the firelight catching highlights in Rose's dark hair. "This has been perfect, Rose, thank you so much."

"Not over yet," she smiled, turning to slide her arms around his waist and pull him to her. Their lips met, and she melted against him as their kiss deepened.

After long moments David broke the kiss, moving back a little to look into her eyes. He began to quote: "Tyger, tyger, burning bright, in the forests of the night, What immortal hand or eye, could frame thy fearful symmetry?"

As he neared the end of the poem, tears were flowing freely down Rose's face. He spoke more softly, "Did he who made the Lamb make thee?" and finally she buried her head in his shoulder. He wrapped his arms around her, stroking her hair.

Finally she looked up. "That's the most beautiful thing that anyone has ever said to me."

She hesitated. "David?"

"Hmm?"

"Do you believe it? I mean, that there's someone who made the lamb, made the tiger? I know you said church last week made you think."

David nodded. "It's hard to explain – I've always known there was something else, beyond. To be honest, church never really did much for me, but reading that story last week, Jacob having visions, believing he was travelling for a purpose, then the timing of him meeting Rachel at the well – I was absolutely certain that I understood."

He paused. "When he cried because she was the one for him – it made me shiver all over."

Another tear slipped down Rose's face, and he wiped it away gently. "And you're the one for me."

Rose smiled through her tears. "You know, Lily knew straight away."

David nodded. "I can believe it."

He looked at the fire, now falling into embers. "Sorry, Rose, I think it's time we called it a day. Will you be OK driving home?"

She nodded. "I'm fine."

He stood, helping her to her feet. "Did you leave your stuff in Poppy's room? I'll get it for you."

When he came down, Rose had wiped her face. "Everyone will probably be in bed, but I don't want them thinking you were mean to me, made me cry."

They walked out to Rose's car. "See you for church tomorrow?" he asked.

She nodded. "Wild horses couldn't keep me away."

***

The first thing Rose did when she woke the next morning was to text Lily telling her what an amazing evening she'd had. The reply came back a few minutes later, and Rose grinned at Lily's response. "Told u so. Give him a kiss from me."

Rose went down to breakfast, unable to conceal her smile. Charles looked up from his plate. "You were in pretty late last night."

He scowled. "Rose, I need to know something about this boyfriend of yours before things go any further. Who is he, where did you meet him?"

Rose took a deep breath. "You already know him. My boyfriend is David – David Stuart."

"What?" burst out Charles. "David? He's nearly ten years older than you."

He put down his fork. "Now you listen, young woman. It would be much better for us all if you forgot about him right now."

Rose looked at him steadily. "It's too late for that."

He stopped dead. "Oh God, you're pregnant, aren't you."

Rose's eyes flashed fire, then burned with a dark intensity. "It's too late because I love him. And no, I'm not pregnant. He's not like that."

Charles spread out his hands helplessly. "I'm sorry, Rose."

She turned, looking over her shoulder. "I'm going out now. We can talk at lunch."

She got ready, and by the time she left the house, she was calmer. David was waiting for her at the church gate, and she greeted him with a kiss that was unmistakably more than sisterly.

He raised his eyebrows. "Not that I'm complaining, but what prompted that?"

"Charles and I had words. He knows it's you, and I've told him in no uncertain terms that I love you and that it has absolutely nothing to do with him."

David put his hands on her shoulders. "Are you OK?"

Rose nodded. "In a way I feel better now that he knows the truth, even though he's bound not to let it go."

She looked up the path. "Let's go in."

They walked into the church hand in hand, taking the same seats as the previous week. The vicar's sermon this time was on Ruth, and Rose felt David's arm slip round her shoulders as they listened to the story of Ruth's late night visit to the threshing floor.

Rose leaned over to whisper into David's ear. "I don't think Charles would have approved of Naomi's tactics."

When the service ended, they stayed for coffee, then Rose said reluctantly, "I'd better get back. At least Mum will be there to keep Charles from frothing at the mouth."

David chuckled at the thought of Charles as a mad dog. "I don't have any meetings with Paul this week – probably a good job. I'll call you later to check you're OK, and we can decide when to meet up?"

Rose nodded. "Good idea."

They parted with a kiss at the church gate, and Rose walked steadily up the hill. When she got home, her mother was waiting in the hall. "I talked to Charles. He understands that it's up to you who you see. Try and look at it from his point of view, he feels very protective of you now your father isn't around."

Rose nodded. "He really doesn't need to worry with David. After all, they already do business together, he must trust him."

"Come on," said her mother, "let's have lunch."

Conversation over lunch was subdued but polite, and when Rose had finished, she excused herself to go up to her room. She pulled one of her poetry books from the shelf, searching through the pages till she found the poem David had quoted to her.

Again she felt her eyes filling with tears, and she quickly turned over the page. This time she laughed out loud at the first line of the poem. "O Rose, thou art sick!"

"Love-sick," she grinned to herself, starting to tidy her room. "And I hope it's incurable."

***

She didn't get a chance to see David again till Wednesday evening, and their time over dinner at a small Italian restaurant seemed all too short.

"I can't wait till Saturday," Rose said, sipping at her wine.

David nodded. "I'm determined to get the car out of the garage this week, even if we only take it to the bottom of the drive and back."

As he walked her back to her car, Rose asked, "David? When's your birthday?"

"Next month – the eighteenth."

She grinned. "Perfect – I have just enough time to look for something special."

"Don't go overboard," David smiled.

"I won't," Rose promised. "But I think you'll be pleased."

Saturday came, and true to his word David started the car and gently eased it out of the garage, reaching over to open the passenger door so that Rose could take her place.

She smiled as he carefully guided the car down to the end of the drive, then turned around. "I feel like I ought to be waving to a crowd."

David nodded. "I think we'll draw a few glances when we finally get the car on the road. It'll definitely be ready for when Lily and Poppy come back."

Rose leaned over to kiss him. "This is going to be such a great summer."

One week went by, and then another. Rose spent her Saturdays with David, and met him at least once every week for a quiet dinner, or if things were really busy, lunch at McDonalds.

At the beginning of the last week of term, Charles arrived back from the office with a pile of brochures. "We've talked about it often enough, so I thought I'd finally book us that skiing holiday. I thought we could go the first week Lily's back."

Rose hesitated. "Sorry, Charles. It's David's birthday that week, and I promised to be here to meet Poppy when she gets back from school."

Charles started to say something, then subsided. "OK. I suppose I should realise you're going to start wanting to make your own plans."

Rose smiled. "But take Lily – I know she'd love to go. Poppy will still be here when she comes back."

When she arrived at David's that Saturday, he looked at her and grinned. "Go on – I know when you have something to tell me."

"Well," Rose began, "Charles is taking the family skiing at the end of next week, but I've told him I can't go – I explained about Poppy, and about your birthday. So we have the whole week to ourselves."

David hugged her, lifting her off the ground. "That's great news."

He hesitated. "Rose?"

"Hmm?"

"It would make sense for you to come over here and stay, wouldn't it? There'd be no point in you driving all the way here and back every day. We have plenty of spare rooms, or Poppy might even want you to share with her."

Rose grinned. "You'll not get any argument from me."

The next week seemed to go more slowly than ever, but finally Friday evening came, and Rose helped Charles put the family's luggage in the car.

"Remember, drop Lily off at David's on your way back from the airport next week," she reminded him.

He nodded. "Have a good week."

"You too." Rose walked round to the passenger seat. "Take care, Lily. Remember, stick to the beginners' slopes."

Lily nodded. "I won't do anything silly, Rose. I'm looking forward to the rest of the summer too much to want to spend it with some part of me in plaster."

She glanced at Charles, still arranging the luggage in the boot. "Give David a kiss for me, and tell Poppy I can't wait to meet her."

"I will," promised Rose. She kissed her sister on the cheek. "Bye, everybody."

Charles got into the car. "Bye, Rose."

Rose watched till they were out of sight, then went back inside, closing the door. She went upstairs, and began to fold clothes and put them in a small suitcase. On impulse, she packed her blue overalls, and made sure she put in the box with her necklace, and her earrings.

She opened her drawer, and took out the small package she'd already wrapped for David's birthday, and a larger parcel with a gift for Poppy. She put the two packages into her suitcase, then zipped up the lid.

Her mobile rang, and she retrieved it from her bag. "Hi, David. Yes, I'm all packed. I'll definitely be there by ten. Love you."

Rose put the phone down, and got changed for bed. The house seemed unnaturally quiet, and she had to force herself not to go round again checking that all the doors and windows were locked.

She got into bed, putting the light out and closing her eyes, and soon fell asleep.

Sometime in the middle of the night she woke with a start, her heart pounding, images from her dream still vivid in her mind. She reached for her phone, then hesitated. Finally she picked it up and dialled.

"Rose, is that you?" David's voice answered sleepily. "What's wrong?"

"I'm sorry, I know it's late," she began. "I had such an awful dream."

His voice was reassuring. "Tell me."

"You were knocking at the door, asking to come in, but for some reason I was reluctant – I didn't know where my dressing gown was, the floor was cold – how stupid is that? – and by the time I got out of bed, you'd gone. I went outside into the street in my slippers, and suddenly someone was attacking me, hitting me, and I couldn't see you anywhere."

There was pain in David's voice as he replied. "I'm so sorry, my love. That sounds awful. I wish I could hold you till you feel better. Do you want me to come over?"

For a moment Rose was tempted to say yes, but she shook her head. "I'll be fine. I'll get up and make myself some hot milk, read for a while."

She grinned. "I'll look at our poem."

David spoke softly. "OK, darling. Remember, I love you. Goodnight, bright eyes."

Rose held the phone in her hand for long moments after he'd hung up, hearing again his final words, his special name for her. Eventually she made herself a drink, and sipped it, looking at her own favourite line.

"What the hand dare seize the fire," she murmured quietly. She vowed to herself that she would put up no resistance when David's hand finally grasped the fire of her heart...

***

The next morning in the sunlight her dreams seemed insubstantial, and Rose hummed to herself as she showered and dressed, then drove to David's house with her suitcase on the seat beside her.

He was waiting for her as usual. "No overalls today," he smiled.

Rose nodded. "They're in the case for when we need them."

David took her case, carrying it up the stairs. "I'll put it in the first guest room, the one with the en-suite, until we know what Poppy wants to do."

They went downstairs to the kitchen, and David said, "I hope you remembered that I promised you breakfast?"

Rose nodded. "So what do we have?"

"Bacon, sausages, tomatoes, mushrooms. Eggs any way you want them. Toast, muffins."

Rose thought for a moment. "I've always wanted to try Eggs Benedict."

David grinned. "Coming right up."

Finally Rose pushed back her chair. "David, that was wonderful. I couldn't eat another thing."

He glanced at his watch. "I'll pour us another coffee and we can go and sit outside. Poppy should be here any minute."

They were sitting at the table by the water's edge when they heard the sound of a car pulling up at the bottom of the drive. "That'll be her — she takes a taxi from the station," explained David.

Rose got up from her seat, suddenly less confident than she had been about meeting another member of David's family.

"You'll be fine," reassured David, seeing the uncertainty on her face. "Poppy has the biggest heart of anyone I know. She gets on with everybody."

He took her hand, and they walked together to the top of the drive. A few moments later Poppy appeared round the bend in the drive, her auburn hair shining in the sun. When she caught sight of David and Rose, she dropped her bag and ran towards them, doing her best to wrap her arms around both of them at the same time.

She stepped back, seeming suddenly shy after her enthusiastic greeting. "Hi, Rose."

"Hi, Poppy. I've been so looking forward to meeting you," said Rose.

Poppy nodded. "David said. He talks about you a lot."

"Shall we go inside?" said David. "You probably want a snack, right, Pops?"

"Please – I couldn't really get much on the train."

David picked up his sister's bag, and they walked towards the house. When they reached the kitchen, Poppy sat down at the table while David filled the kettle.

"There's something I need to get from upstairs," said Rose.

"OK."

She went up the stairs, retrieving the larger of the two packages from her case and returning to the kitchen. "I got something for you, Poppy."

Poppy put down her toast. "Oh, wow, thank you, Rose."

She tore the paper from the parcel and grinned. "I love all this bubble bath stuff, and there's some perfume."

She got up from the table and hugged Rose. "Thanks."

"Right," said David, "what's next?"

"Can I see the car?" begged Poppy. "I bet you've done so much to it since last holiday."

David nodded. "And Rose helped me – she and Lily did the inlay on the dashboard, then Rose worked with me on all the mechanical stuff."

"When's Lily coming?" asked Poppy.

"Next Saturday," replied Rose. "My brother's dropping her off on the way back from their skiing trip."

Poppy grinned. "I tried skiing once. I wasn't very good."

She tugged at David's hand. "Come on."

When they reached the garage, David said, "Now, close your eyes, Pops."

She complied, and he slid aside the door. "You can look now."

"Oh!" she said, and Rose was reminded of Lily's reaction when she first saw David's restoration project.

Poppy walked into the garage. "It's finished!" she said, grinning.

David nodded. "But we waited for you – we haven't taken it out, except to the end of the drive to make sure it was working."

"Can we go out in it later?" pleaded Poppy.

"Definitely," said David.

They walked back to the house, and Poppy said, "Rose?"

"Hmm?"

"Do you want to share my room with me while you're here?"

"I'd really like that, as long as you're OK."

Poppy nodded. "I share a room at school. It'll be fun!"

She reached out and took Rose's hand. "Let's go up, I'll find you somewhere for your things."

The two went upstairs, and Rose retrieved her case from the guest room. "Look, Poppy, here's the birthday present I got for David."

"What is it?" asked Poppy.

It was Rose's turn to feel shy. "I got him a ring, I had it engraved with part of our favourite poem."

"I bet he'll love it," Poppy smiled. She glanced at Rose. "Can I see the poem?"

Rose reached into her case again, pulling out the small volume of Blake, and opened it at the familiar page.

Poppy read carefully, then turned to Rose again, her eyes shining. "Are you the tiger?"

Rose nodded. "If he calls me 'bright eyes', now you'll know why."

Poppy thought for a moment. "That's a song, isn't it? I thought it was sad."

"Oh!" said Rose. "Of course – Watership Down. Gosh, you're right, Poppy, that is a sad one."

"We watched it last year in English, we'd been reading the book."

"Do you like reading?" asked Rose.

"Definitely," nodded Poppy. "I want to be an English teacher."

Rose found herself blinking back tears. "That's a good idea, Poppy – maybe I can help."

David tapped on the door. "Are you two OK?"

Poppy grinned. "Sure."

David came in, and Rose quickly pushed the small package under the clothes in her case. "Poppy was just telling me how much she likes reading."

David nodded. "I have a present for Poppy too."

He brought his hand out from behind his back, and Poppy squealed. "Oh! One of those electronic book things."

David grinned. "And I set it up so you can download anything you want."

She jumped up and hugged him. "That's amazing. I hope you like the present I got you for your birthday."

David smiled. "That's not till Wednesday – don't give it away, Pops."

She grinned. "Not even a hint?"

"Well…" said David. "Maybe a little one."

"OK, here goes."

She took a deep breath, and began to recite. "I saw four creatures, wondrous beings, travelling together. Their tracks were dark, their path deep and black. They coursed swiftly: faster than birds they flew through the air, dove under a wave. He strove without rest, the battling Prince, pointing the way across plated gold to the four creatures."

She stopped. "Phew – I managed the whole thing. We memorised that in English, I got class prize."

Rose glanced at David, who was looking perplexed. "I think I know, Poppy, but I don't think David has come across those riddles before."

David shook his head. "I'll just have to wait until Wednesday."

He glanced at the clock on Poppy's bedside table. "Anyway, I think it's lunchtime – and I have a surprise. You'll need to give me a hand."

They went downstairs to the kitchen, and Rose glanced at the table, now occupied by a large hamper. "I think I'm getting an idea."

David grinned. "Here, you take that side. Poppy, can you bring that blanket?"

They picked up the hamper, and Poppy followed them outside with the blanket. They set the hamper down on the gravel, then David went into the garage. After a moment Rose heard the sound of the engine starting, then settling down to its smooth purr.

"Coming out," called David, and the bright yellow roadster pulled smoothly onto the gravel beside them.

David opened the boot, and Rose helped him get the hamper in, while Poppy put the blanket on top.

"Now if you two promise to be good, you can both squeeze into the front," David grinned.

Poppy nodded. "We promise."

David got back into the car, and Poppy climbed in from the other side, sliding over to give Rose room. Rose pulled the door closed, and smiled at David. "Think we're ready."

He put the car back in gear, and they moved off down the drive. Rose closed her eyes, tilting her head up to face the sun. "This is amazing."

As they turned onto the main road, David accelerated, and Poppy squealed with delight, holding on to Rose's arm. "Wheee!"

David eased off on the accelerator. "Wow, she really does have some oomph. But I think we'd better take it steady the rest of the way."

They made their way along the valley, then David turned off onto an unmarked B-road which climbed gently. Finally he pulled onto a grassy track, driving slowly to the end and stopping the engine.

"Here we are," he said.

Rose opened her door and stepped down, and Poppy slid out to stand beside her. "What a gorgeous spot," Rose said.

David grinned. "Thought you'd like it."

He opened the boot, and Poppy took the blanket, spreading it out a little way into the grassy field.

David and Rose brought the hamper, and David opened the lid. "I think I brought everything."

Rose unpacked the hamper, passing plates and cutlery to Poppy, then plastic containers. "Mm, olives."

When their lunch was set out on the blanket, they sat down. "I brought lemonade for us," said David, "and there's ice in that coolbox."

"Chicken leg?" Rose offered Poppy.

"Mm, please."

They took their time over lunch, and finally Rose lay back, her hands behind her head. "That was lovely, David."

He leaned on one elbow beside her, while Poppy picked daisies and made them into chains.

Rose must have drifted off, and she opened her eyes to find David still looking at her. "You look so peaceful when you're asleep," he said, smiling.

He sat up. "Probably time we were getting back, it's starting to get cooler."

They packed everything up, and Poppy draped a daisy chain over Rose's hair. "Thanks, darling," smiled Rose.

They bumped their way carefully back along the track and down the narrow road, then David again gave the car her head along the straight. He glanced across at the girls, their hair streaming backwards in the wind. "This is what makes all those hours in the garage worth it."

They arrived back at the house, and Poppy helped Rose carry the empty hamper back to the kitchen while David carefully garaged the car.

He came in to find them washing up. "Oh, well done – I was going to do that later, but it'll be good to have it out of the way."

He put the kettle on. "Coffee?"

"Mm, please," said Rose.

"Can I have hot chocolate?" asked Poppy.

"Of course, darling."

David warmed milk in a pan, adding cocoa powder and dark sugar, then whisked it, pouring the frothy liquid into a mug. Poppy finished drying the last plate, and picked up her drink.

"Mm," she said, "nobody makes it quite like you."

David poured coffee for himself and Rose, and they went through into the living room.

"Do you two want to watch a film or something?" David asked.

Poppy thought for a moment. "I'd like to put some books onto my present, if that's OK."

"Are you going to light a fire, David?" Rose asked.

He nodded. "I know it's not that cold, but I really love just sitting with you and watching the flames."

"Then let's just put some music on," Rose decided.

Poppy went upstairs to fetch her present while David lit the fire. When she returned, she sprawled on the rug and began pressing buttons. "They have some really cool stuff."

David walked over to the CD player. "What do you feel like, Rose?"

She thought for a moment. "Something restful."

"Not the 1812 Overture, then," he grinned.

He slid a disc into the player, and the room filled with the gentle sound of a single violin, then another, then the deeper notes of a cello.

"Oh," said Rose, "I love Pachelbel's Canon."

David joined Rose on the sofa, and she stretched out, resting her head in his lap. He stroked her hair gently, and closed his eyes as the notes of the music intertwined.

The selection moved on through Mozart, Beethoven, Debussy, Chopin. David opened his eyes and glanced across at Poppy, who was absorbed in whatever book she'd selected.

Finally the music faded into silence, and David said, "OK, Pops, think it's bedtime."

She nodded, yawning. "I'll go and get ready, then come down to say goodnight."

Rose sat up, suppressing a yawn herself. "Gosh, must be all that fresh air. Don't worry, Poppy, I won't be far behind you."

Poppy skipped up the stairs, and David smiled. "She is good, isn't she."

Rose nodded. "I know we're going to get on."

Poppy returned in a long nightshirt with Sleeping Beauty on the front. "Night, then. And thanks for a lovely day."

She kissed David on the cheek, then hugged Rose tightly and kissed her too.

"I'll try not to wake you when I come up," Rose promised.

They watched her go back up, then David said, "I almost can't believe this is real – you being here, Poppy being home."

Rose smiled. "Maybe this will convince you."

She put her arms around him and kissed him, no longer distracted by the thought of a drive home, or whether anyone at home would notice what time the front door opened...

David gently broke their kiss. "Darling," he said. "Better go to bed, before that fire in your eyes sets us both alight."

Rose nodded. "You're right." She almost spoke again, but changed her mind. "Goodnight, my love."

She climbed the stairs, and changed for bed in the starlight. Poppy was already sleeping, her breathing slow and regular, and Rose slipped in beside her. Poppy stirred briefly, smiling in her sleep, then settled again.

Rose closed her eyes, images from the day's events bright in her mind at first, then growing indistinct as she drifted into a dreamless sleep.

***

Rose woke the next morning with a feeling of utter contentment, only increased by the promise of what the coming day might hold.

She turned over, opening her eyes to discover an empty space on Poppy's side of the bed. The murmur of voices drifted up from the kitchen, accompanied by a delicious smell, and Rose guessed that Poppy was helping David prepare something special for breakfast.

She pulled back the covers and got out of bed, walking over to the open window. From the woodland by the lake she heard the calling of doves, and further away the sound of a cuckoo.

David looked up as she walked into the kitchen. "Morning, darling."

She kissed him on the cheek, then walked over to where Poppy was stirring something in a plastic jug. "Hi, Pops. What're you making?"

Poppy grinned at Rose's use of her pet name. "More waffle mixture. David ate all the first batch."

"You had half of one," protested David good-naturedly.

"I love waffles," said Rose. "Show me how to do them?"

"Easy," grinned Poppy. "Just open the machine, pour in the mixture, and close the lid. It pings when they're done."

She demonstrated, and after a minute or so there was a quiet ping, and Poppy opened the machine to reveal a perfectly cooked waffle.

"Shall we share this one?" she suggested.

"Mm, please," said Rose. "It smells fabulous."

"Wait till you put the maple syrup on," said Poppy, gingerly lifting the waffle onto a plate and putting it on the table. "You do like maple syrup, right?"

Rose smiled. "Definitely. I don't usually go for sweet stuff, but maple syrup has that smoky flavour."

She picked up the jug. "Say when."

Poppy grinned as the syrup pooled around the edge of the plate. "When."

They sat down, and Rose winked at Poppy as she cut off the corner of the waffle and took a bite. "Shall we give David the next one, or make him wait again?"

David got up, smiling. "Why don't I make the next one for you two? I've had plenty."

By the time the girls had finished the first waffle, David had another one ready. "More syrup?"

"Mmm, please," said Rose.

Finally David coaxed the last spoonful of mixture out of the jug. "Can you manage another?"

"No, you have it," said Poppy.

She glanced up at David. "Are we going to church this morning?"

"Sure."

Poppy got up from the table. "You OK if I go in the shower first, Rose?"

"That's fine," Rose smiled. "I'll be up in a minute."

David put the last waffle on his plate and sat down opposite Rose. "Want a bit?"

She nodded, and he held out a piece on his fork for her to take.

"How far away is the church?" she asked, as David got up to rinse his plate.

"Just in the village," David replied. "It's only a short drive."

They looked at each other. "Are you thinking what I'm thinking?" said Rose.

David grinned. "It's too good an opportunity to miss."

Poppy clattered down the stairs, her hair still damp. She looked from Rose to David, catching their shared amusement. "OK, what have you two cooked up?"

148

"How would you like to make a bit of a splash when we arrive at church?" David enquired, trying to make his question sound offhand.

Poppy looked puzzled for a moment, then a broad smile spread across her face. "Could we?"

"Why not," said David. "Rose, how about you go and get ready, and Poppy can help me get the car out."

When Rose came back down, the yellow roadster was outside the front door, David explaining the controls to Poppy. "OK, Pops, do you want to go in the back?"

She moved to the back seat, and Rose got in beside David. He started the engine, and they set off down the drive.

As they entered the village, the church bells began to ring, and David grinned. "Perfect timing."

Poppy leaned forward, resting her hands on the back of Rose's seat. "There's Alice," she said, waving.

David drew into the car park and set the handbrake, stopping the engine. "OK, here we are."

He opened Rose's door, taking her hand as she stepped down. Poppy jumped from the car and ran over to her friend, and the two of them walked up the path, arms around each other's waists.

David and Rose followed, still hand in hand, and the vicar greeted them at the door. "Good to see you, David. And your co-pilot?"

David grinned. "Rose, meet Arthur Wood, our vicar. He's been at the church since we moved here."

Rose shook the vicar's hand. "Great to meet you."

They walked into the coolness of the church, a hint of incense lingering in the air.

"I'm afraid the pews are a little hard," smiled David.

Poppy waved to them, and they slipped into the end of the pew she'd chosen. The organ started to play, and Rose watched fascinated as a small group of white-surpliced choristers processed up the aisle to their places.

The organist finished his piece, then sounded a soft note. A single chorister picked up the note, then the others joined in with their parts, and Rose was irresistibly reminded of the Pachelbel that they'd listened to the previous evening.

The last note faded away, and the choir took their seats. The vicar made his way to the front, and began the service with the traditional words. "The Lord is here."

"His Spirit is with us," came the reply from the congregation.

"Please sit or kneel as we pray," requested the vicar.

Rose sat, bowing her head, as the choir sang again. The vicar led the familiar prayer: "Almighty God, to whom all hearts are open, all desires known…"

Just for a moment, Rose had a strange sense of feeling both reassured and at the same time exposed. Her heart open, her desires known? She felt for David's hand, and he squeezed her fingers reassuringly.

The prayers continued, and Rose glanced at Poppy, who was kneeling, her hands folded, an expression of utter peace and tranquility on her face.

At the end of the prayers, the vicar announced a hymn, and they stood to sing. Poppy leaned over to share Rose's hymn book, and Rose was unsurprised to discover that Poppy too had a clear, tuneful singing voice.

The Bible reading was from the old version, but Rose immediately recognised the words: "Thou preparest a table before me in the presence of mine enemies: thou anointest my head with oil; my cup runneth over."

She leaned over to whisper to David. "I certainly feel as though my cup is running over, the last few weeks."

The vicar's sermon was short, encouraging his hearers simply to be grateful for everything good that they had. He finished with a blessing, and the choir sang a final anthem as they processed back down the aisle.

Rose smiled at David. "That was really lovely. I'm glad we came."

Poppy seemed uncharacteristically quiet, and Rose touched her shoulder. "You OK?"

Poppy nodded. "Everything's going to be fine."

Before Rose could ask her what she meant, Poppy had slipped out to join Alice, and the two whispered animatedly as they slipped out of the church into the sunshine.

"Shall we go?" asked David.

Rose nodded. "Had you thought about lunch?"

"The meat's already in the oven," he grinned. "And roast potatoes, and parsnips. Just the Yorkshire puddings to make, and we're set."

Oblivious to anyone around them, Rose leaned over to kiss him. "You're going to have to tell me sooner or later, you know."

"Tell you what?" David looked puzzled.

"What's not perfect about you," she teased.

"Hardly," David snorted.

They walked out of the church, shaking hands with the vicar at the door, and found Poppy and Alice playing on the railings by the path.

"Sorry, Alice," said David. "We're going to have to take Poppy away from you."

"But you can come round in the week," said Poppy. "I'll text you."

They made their way back to the car, and David opened the door on the driver's side. But instead of getting in, he glanced at Rose. "Want to drive us home?"

Rose caught her lip between her teeth. "If you're sure?"

"Of course – just take it steady."

Rose got in behind the wheel, and David slid into the passenger seat while Poppy took her place in the back.

"Handbrake's on," said David, "so just make sure you're not in gear and press the starter."

The engine roared into life, and Rose pressed down on the clutch, engaging the gears. She looked around, then with an expression of intense concentration let the clutch up and released the handbrake.

The car moved forward, and David said, "Brilliant! Let's get round this corner, and you can change up."

As they made their way out of the village, Rose's confidence grew, and she pressed down on the accelerator, feeling the breeze picking up her hair as they travelled down the straight.

They approached the gates of the drive, and Rose slowed, changing down through the gears and being careful not to cross her hands over the steering wheel as she turned.

As they drew level with the front door, Rose braked gently to a stop, and set the handbrake, stopping the engine.

"Well done," said David. "You can take us out next time we go for a picnic."

Poppy looked wistful. "It'll be ages before I get to drive it."

David grinned. "Actually, Pops, I have a surprise for you. I was going to tell you later, but while you're home I've booked you some time at one of those places where you can drive off-road. And I promise, the moment you're seventeen you'll have lessons, and I'll take you out in my car to practice."

Rose took a deep breath. "And I'll take you too, Pops – my car's a bit smaller, it'll be easier for you with some of the manoeuvres."

She glanced across at David. The expression on his face combined surprise, hope and unmistakeable joy.

Poppy grinned, putting her arms round both of them. "You two are the best."

David got out of the car and walked round to help Rose down. "Right, let's get those Yorkshires going, shall we."

Poppy sat at the kitchen table with her book, while Rose watched David mixing milk, flour, an egg. He carefully poured batter into the depressions of a baking tin, and slid the tin into the oven. "Right, twenty minutes."

"I'll make us some coffee," offered Rose.

David sat down next to Poppy, looking at what she was reading, while Rose poured coffee. "Cream, Poppy?"

Poppy nodded. "Thanks, Rose."

They sipped their coffee for a while, then David got up. "OK, gravy next."

He opened the oven, taking out the dish with the meat, and used a fork to transfer the joint to a plate. He lit a gas ring, and set the dish on it, then mixed cornflour with a little milk and poured it into the meat juices.

The gravy thickened, and David poured it carefully into a jug, then started to slice the meat thinly. "You'll like the end bits, won't you, Rose."

"Mm, please."

"Right, think we're ready to go."

David took the plates he'd set to warm, and lifted slices of meat onto each one. He took the oven gloves and pulled out the trays, dividing up the roast potatoes and parsnips between the plates. Finally he used his fingers to pick up the Yorkshire puddings and distribute them, blowing on his fingers to cool them afterwards.

He put plates in front of Rose and Poppy, then brought his own plate to the table. "Would you say grace for us, Poppy?"

She smiled, and bowed her head. "Bless, O Lord, this food to our use, and us to your loving service. Amen."

Rose and David echoed the Amen, and David passed Rose the gravy. "Take plenty."

She poured gravy carefully into her Yorkshire puddings, then a little over her potatoes, and passed the jug on to Poppy.

Poppy poured a little over her meat. "There, plenty left for you, David."

They started to eat. "Wow," said Rose. "This beef is fantastic."

"There's a farmer a little way down the road, he raises his own cattle," explained David.

"So what shall we do this afternoon?" asked Rose.

"It's such a lovely day, we could just sit on the grass by the lake," suggested David.

"Cool," said Poppy. "I'll bring my book."

When lunch was over, Rose and Poppy washed up while David gathered a few things for their afternoon outdoors.

"I've put some ice in the coolbox, and we've got bottles of fruit juice. I'll take the blanket out – is there anything else we need?"

"Don't think so," said Rose. "Oh, I suppose some sun cream would be useful – Pops, do you want a hat?"

Poppy nodded. "I've got one with a wide brim, I'll put that on."

They finished putting away the dishes, and Poppy skipped up the stairs, returning with her hat.

Rose nudged David as Poppy walked ahead of them to the spot by the lake where the blanket was spread out. "She looks like something out of an Impressionist painting, doesn't she."

He grinned. "Tell her – she loves their pictures. You've seen the posters in her room."

Poppy stopped, taking off her shoes. She sat down by the edge of the lake and dangled her legs in the water. "This feels lovely – come on, Rose, give it a try."

Rose joined her, slipping off her shoes. "Mm, you're right. Look, there are a couple of goldfish – hope they don't take a fancy to our toes."

After a while she got up, and walked over to the blanket where David was sitting. "Did you find the sun cream?"

He nodded. "Here."

Rose poured a little of the lotion into her palms and went back over to Poppy. "Let me just do your shoulders, Pops."

"Brr," said Poppy. "That's cold."

Rose quickly applied some lotion to her own arms, then returned to David. "Want some?"

He shook his head. "Fortunately, I don't burn."

Rose sat down next to him, looking out over the lake to the woodland beyond. "I can't imagine anything more perfect."

She lay back, leaning her head on one arm and closing her eyes. David joined her, and she turned, putting her other arm round his waist. The combination of their Sunday lunch and the warm sun finally overcame her, and she dozed off.

When she opened her eyes, David was smiling at her. "You OK?" he asked softly.

She nodded. "Think I'm thirsty, though."

David fished a bottle out of the coolbox and passed it to her. Rose drank deeply, then handed the bottle back. "Poppy," she called, "do you want something to drink?"

Poppy walked over, the droplets of water on her legs glistening in the sun. "Please. What flavours are there?"

Rose glanced into the coolbox. "Orange and pomegranate – that's my favourite – or apple and mango."

"Mm, apple and mango please."

Rose passed her a bottle, and Poppy tilted her head back to drink. "Wups!" she said. "There goes my hat."

She retrieved her hat, and joined Rose and David on the blanket, picking a piece of pond weed from her ankle.

David glanced at his watch. "I'm afraid I'm going to have to do some work this afternoon – I'm meeting the board tomorrow. It won't take long, though. How about I come out and get you when I'm finished, and we have tea? I bought some cake."

At the mention of cake Poppy's eyes lit up. "Yes please."

She turned to Rose. "Shall I go and get my Scrabble set? We can have a game while David's busy."

"Great idea," said Rose. "Lily and I used to play all the time before she went away to school."

Poppy walked with David to the house, returning with a well-worn box. "You pick first," she offered, holding out the bag of letters.

Rose got the first go, and carefully laid out six letters. "A, l, b, e, d, o – the brightness of a heavenly object."

Poppy grinned. "I can see I've got my work cut out here…"

When David returned, Rose glanced up. "We're on our third game – this is the decider."

He nodded. "I'm not allowed to help, right?"

Poppy shook her head. "I think I've got one."

She looked from her tiles to the board and back again. "Here goes."

She concentrated as she laid out her tiles. "H, e, n, then this 'n' here, then a."

Rose nodded. "Henna, and it's on a triple word score – well done, Poppy, your game, and you win the match."

"Yay!" grinned Poppy.

David smiled. "Definitely well done, Pops. Let's go in, shall we? I've made the tea, and the cake's on the table."

Poppy put the Scrabble away, slipping the score sheets into the box. "I'd love to play again sometime, Rose."

They stood, and David picked up the blanket and the coolbox. "Don't forget your shoes."

When they'd finished their tea, David said, "I could really do with an early night – it's going to be a busy week."

Rose smiled. "That's fine. Poppy and I have a few things to talk about, isn't that right, Pops?"

Poppy nodded, getting up from her chair to hug her brother and kiss him on the cheek. "G'night."

"I'll look in on my way to bed," promised Rose. "If you're asleep I won't disturb you."

When David had gone upstairs, Poppy glanced at Rose, grinning. "Do you have an idea how we can surprise David for his birthday?"

Rose nodded. "See, what we do is…"

When she finished outlining her plan, Poppy said, "Great – I bet he'll never guess in a million years."

She held back a yawn. "Gosh, I'm tired all of a sudden."

Rose nodded. "Let's go up, then."

They got ready for bed, and Rose said, "I'll just pop in and say goodnight to David."

She walked along the landing, her bare feet silent on the carpet, and pushed open David's door. She stood by his bed in the faint light from the window, and listened to his slow, regular breathing.

Somehow he must have sensed her presence, and he opened his eyes. "Hello, darling."

Rose smiled. "I didn't mean to wake you."

"It's fine, I'll drop off again as soon as you're gone."

She leaned over to kiss him, her hair brushing his cheek. "Goodnight, darling."

"Sleep tight, my love."

***

While David was at work, Rose and Poppy occupied themselves sitting in the sun, playing Scrabble, reading. Poppy showed Rose the summer house, and the tree in the woods where David had built her a tree house.

"Alice and I used to sit up there and pretend we were wood fairies, and when David came we'd put spells on him and he'd pretend he was lost and couldn't get out of the wood – like Bottom in that play we read."

Rose smiled. "You said you'd text Alice, didn't you – how about you invite her to lunch tomorrow?"

"Great idea," said Poppy.

When David came home, they were in the kitchen. "We made dinner," said Poppy proudly. "Look, beef stew."

David grinned. "Well done."

They spent the evening in front of the fire, Poppy lying on the rug with her book, Rose's head pillowed on David's shoulder as they talked, watching the firelight.

Reluctantly David sat up, stretching. "Another early night for me, I'm afraid."

"You're sure you won't stay a little longer?" asked Rose. "We were going to toast some marshmallows, weren't we, Pops?"

David shook his head. "Maybe one night later in the week."

Rose made herself and Poppy hot chocolate to go with their marshmallows, and they both sat on the rug, their cups on the edge of the hearth.

When they went up to bed, Rose again looked in on David. This time he didn't wake, and she whispered her 'Good night', closing the door quietly behind her as she left.

Alice came the next day in response to Poppy's invitation, and they played a game of hide and seek around the garden in the morning. Lunch was fish fingers and chips – "My favourite," grinned Alice – and afterwards Poppy asked, "Would you like to go and look at the car?"

Alice's eyes lit up. "Please."

Rose helped Poppy slide the door aside, and Alice walked up to the car.

"Could I sit in it?" she asked hesitantly.

"Sure," said Poppy. She opened the driver's door. "Go ahead."

Alice carefully climbed up, resting her hands tentatively on the steering wheel. "Wow."

"It'd be nice to go out," said Rose, "but I'd rather David was here – I don't know the car well enough to feel completely safe."

Alice nodded. "That's OK. Can I come one weekend?"

"Of course," said Poppy. "We have the whole summer."

Alice's father picked her up at tea time, and as they drove away towards the village, Rose saw David's car approaching from the other direction.

"You just missed Alice," she said as she wrapped her arms round him in welcome. "She loves the car, she'd like to come out with us one weekend."

"Of course," David said. "Now, let's go inside. I have a surprise for you."

They went in, sitting down at the kitchen table. "What's up?" said Poppy, coming down the stairs.

"I got Rose a present," grinned David, pulling a small box from his pocket.

Just for a moment Poppy's mouth dropped open a little, then she caught herself. "Cool."

David passed Rose the box. "I hope you like it."

She opened the lid, and carefully took out a small, bright object, laying it in the palm of her hand and draping the fine chain across her fingers. "Gosh, it's lovely."

"Open it," said David, smiling.

She pressed the tiny catch, and the locket opened. Rose looked at the inscription inside, and as she smiled softly, Poppy saw a tear slip from the corner of her eye.

Rose looked for a moment longer, then held out her hand to Poppy. "Look."

Poppy carefully took the locket, reading the delicately-engraved words. "When the stars threw down their spears, And watered heaven with their tears, Did he smile his work to see? Did he who made the Lamb make thee?"

She looked up, her eyes shining. "That's beautiful. Here, let me put it on you."

Rose held still while Poppy fastened the chain at the back of her neck, and David smiled. "Perfect."

That evening when David had gone up to bed, Poppy grinned at Rose. "When I saw that box, I thought –"

Rose nodded. "Me too, just for a second. But I know David, he'd lead up to it a little more."

Poppy smiled ruefully. "Probably he won't do it when I'm there."

Rose was silent for a while. "You really think he'll ask me, though."

Poppy nodded. "You told me, remember – when he first gave you the poem, he said you were the one for him."

When Rose went in to David's room to say goodnight, she kept the locket on, and as she bent over to kiss him, it swung gently on its chain, reflecting a gleam of moonlight into his eyes.

***

The next morning, Poppy's alarm clock went off early, and she turned over to silence it. "Ready, Rose?"

They went quietly down to the kitchen and started to put their plan into action. Poppy put the frying pan on the top of the stove with a clatter, and stood still, holding her breath. "I don't think he heard us."

A few minutes later, they carefully made their way back up the stairs, Rose carrying a tray, Poppy following behind with the cafetiere.

Rose carefully eased David's door open. "Good morning, darling. Happy birthday."

He stirred, opening his eyes. "Wow – what's all this?"

"Bacon sandwiches, fruit, orange juice…" said Rose, putting the tray down on the bed.

"And coffee," chipped in Poppy, pouring.

David sat up. "Thanks, you two – this is wonderful."

He bit into a sandwich. "Mm, crispy, just the way I like it."

The girls sat down on the bed while he ate, and he put an arm around Rose's waist. "This is going to be the best birthday ever."

Poppy suppressed a giggle, then caught Rose's eye. "Sorry," she mouthed silently, and Rose grinned in return.

"Do you want your presents now, or later?" asked Rose.

David considered. "I want to say now, but can we leave it till later? I don't want to rush it."

"That's fine," grinned Poppy. "Only, don't be late from work."

"I won't," he promised.

Poppy carefully carried the tray downstairs, while Rose swung her legs onto the bed and leaned back on David's pillow, his arm still around her.

"I wish I could have got the day off," he said, "but there's just so much going on at the moment – it doesn't feel like the holidays."

Rose nodded. "I understand. With Charles and Paul away, I'm amazed I haven't had a call from the office with some problem or other to solve."

David stirred reluctantly. "Well, I'd better get going. But I'll definitely be home on time."

They watched his car disappear down the drive, then Poppy said, "We have plenty of time to get everything ready, don't we?"

Rose nodded. "I know what we could do, though – if we do all the housework, change the beds, do the washing, then everything's ready for when Lily gets here."

Poppy grinned. "Saturday's not far away now – I can't wait to meet her."

They spent the morning on the housework, until finally Rose switched off the vacuum cleaner. "Phew – that took longer than I thought."

Poppy nodded, pushing her hair out of her eyes. "I think we deserve a break. I know – instead of cooking, let's walk down to the fish and chip shop."

"Great idea," agreed Rose.

They walked down the drive, turning towards the village, and quickly reached the small stone building which served as the fish and chip shop.

"What do you fancy, Pops?" asked Rose.

"Actually I really like their chicken nuggets," said Poppy.

"OK," said Rose. "Two lots of six nuggets and chips," she told the girl behind the counter.

They walked back to the house, and Poppy found the salt and vinegar in the kitchen cupboard. "Ketchup?" she asked.

"Please," nodded Rose.

When they'd finished eating, Rose made coffee and they sat outside on the table by the lake.

"So where shall we start?" asked Poppy.

"Well, we can blow up the balloons, and tie them up," said Rose. "Then there are the streamers."

Poppy nodded. "It's a good job the shop in the village had all this stuff."

They set to work decorating the house, then Rose said, "Right, it's probably time we made the cake."

As the baking progressed, Poppy glanced around the kitchen. "Gosh, we seem to be making a bit of a mess. We'll have to clear up again before we can cook dinner."

When the cake was in the oven, they sat for a while drinking tea. "Right," said Rose, "I'd better start cooking."

Poppy nodded. "I have something I need to do, though – it's a surprise for both of you."

Rose began peeling, chopping, frying. The kitchen timer pinged, and she took the cake out of the oven, setting it on a wire tray to cool. In its place she slid a large casserole dish into the oven, turning the temperature up.

Poppy came back into the kitchen. "That's my special surprise ready."

She glanced at the cake. "Is it cool enough to ice yet?"

"Think so," said Rose. "How about you put the filling on this half."

Poppy carefully spread the chocolate filling on the cake, then set the other half on top. Rose stirred the icing, and covered the top of the cake with a thick layer.

"It doesn't quite look like the ones in the shop," she said.

"So what," said Poppy. "We did it – that's what David will care about."

She glanced at the clock. "OK, cake's done, dinner's in the oven. Why don't you go up and shower first, then I'll get ready."

Rose went upstairs, making sure the dress she'd chosen was laid out carefully before she went in the shower. When she came down, carrying the small package containing David's present, Poppy smiled. "You look amazing."

"I'm just sorry I can't wear the necklace and the pendant at the same time, seeing as they're both presents from David," said Rose.

Poppy nodded. "Right, I'll go and get ready now."

They were sitting at the kitchen table when they heard the sound of David's car in the drive. "OK," said Rose, "let's get to our places."

They walked to the front door, and as David turned the key and came in, they chorused, "Happy birthday!"

David grinned. "I might have known you two would cook something up between you. You both look fantastic."

He kissed Rose, then gave Poppy a bear hug. "Oof," she protested, smiling.

"Dinner's ready," said Rose, "come on in."

David followed them into the kitchen and sat down. Rose got the dishes out of the oven and piled rice onto plates, then a generous serving of the casserole. She glanced at Poppy, smiling.

"Thank you, Jesus, for this food, Amen," said Poppy.

"Amen," said David. "And thank you for the hands that made it."

He picked up his fork and took a bite. "Mm, this is great."

Rose poured wine for each of them. "To David – many happy returns."

When they'd finished eating, Poppy took the plates to the sink. "I hope you left some room," she said, returning with the cake.

"You baked as well?" said David. "Wow."

Poppy cut him a slice of cake. "You deserve it."

David grinned, and took a forkful of cake. "Perfect."

"Now you have to come with us," said Poppy when he put his fork down. "Close your eyes."

David obeyed, and Rose took his hand to lead him through into the living room. "OK, you can look now."

"Fantastic," David said, looking at the streamers and the balloons.

"Your presents are on the table," said Poppy.

David sat down on the sofa and pretended to look indecisive. "Which one first?"

"Open mine," said Poppy. "That's OK, isn't it, Rose?"

"Of course."

David picked up the small, slim package and carefully peeled away the tape, then unwrapped the paper. He opened the box inside, and Poppy grinned. "Do you remember my clue?"

"Four creatures, their tracks dark, their paths deep and black," said David. "Of course, fingers holding a pen."

He took out the fountain pen from its box. "Gosh, this is a pretty special one."

"The nib's solid gold," said Poppy. "Dad had to help me get it."

David put the pen down carefully and hugged his sister. "Thanks, Pops, really. I'll carry it with me, but I'll only use it for signing special things."

He picked up his second gift, glancing at Rose. "I honestly have no idea what this could be."

He removed the paper to reveal a small velvet-coloured box. Rose watched, holding her breath, as he opened the lid. The ring inside was gold, plain on the outer surface, and just for a moment Rose saw in her mind's eye David holding his hand out to her, her fingers slipping a gold band onto his ring finger.

She pulled herself back to the present as David eased the ring from its box and turned it over in his fingers.

"What the hand dare seize the fire," he read quietly. He lifted his head to smile at Rose. "I think I have an idea what that means."

He slid the ring onto his right hand, holding it out for Rose to see. "It fits perfectly," he said.

Poppy took his hand. "It suits you."

She stood up. "Now for my special surprise."

She walked over to the small table in the corner, and Rose noticed that her laptop was set up. Poppy opened the lid, and pressed a couple of keys.

For a moment the computer made a quiet ringing noise, almost like an old-fashioned telephone, then a voice came from the computer. "Hello, darling. Is he there?"

The screen lit to show a couple side by side, what looked like a hurricane lamp hanging from a beam behind them. Inset into the picture was a small window showing Poppy's face.

"Hi, Mum," said Poppy. "Yes, David's here."

David stepped forward, Poppy moving aside to let him face the camera. "Mum, Dad, this is a lovely surprise."

"Happy birthday, son," said his father. "Is everything going OK?"

David nodded. "Wonderful. I've got a lot to tell you."

Poppy stuck her head back into the camera's view. "There's someone else here to talk to you."

She grinned at Rose. "Come on."

Rose took a deep breath, and stepped forward to stand beside David. Poppy leaned toward the microphone. "This is Rose."

"Hello, dear," said David's mother. "Of course David has told us about you, it's wonderful to finally meet you."

"Thank you," said Rose shyly.

She paused, and in the background she could hear a strange chirping sound, not exactly like a bird. "You're in India, is that right?"

David's father nodded. "Near the Himalayas – on a clear day, you can see them from the fields behind the house."

"Wow," said Rose. She glanced at David. "It'd be lovely to visit."

"You'd be very welcome," said his father. "Come in January, the weather's perfect. We always go out for lots of picnics."

David nodded. "We'll do our best. I think Lily – that's Rose's sister, I'm sure I mentioned her – would love to come too."

He looked at the clock in the corner of the screen. "Gosh, it's pretty late over there – thanks for waiting up."

"No problem," assured his father. "Now, Poppy, you're OK, aren't you?"

Poppy nodded. "I'm having a great summer, Rose being around and all. We've been playing Scrabble, sometimes I beat her."

Her mother smiled. "Well done. Anyway, it is late, we ought to call it a day. Call us again soon. And congratulations again, David."

"Night, Mum, Dad," he said.

Poppy closed the connection, and grinned at Rose. "That was OK, wasn't it?"

Rose nodded. "Thanks so much, Poppy – I had no idea how I was going to introduce myself to them, I so wanted them to at least have an idea who I am."

David squeezed Poppy's shoulder. "I'm glad I've got such a sensible sister."

He smiled. "Now, why don't I make us all some hot chocolate before we go to bed."

When he returned from the kitchen, Poppy was explaining to Rose how to use the laptop. "As long as you know someone's ID, if they're online you can call them. If they don't have a webcam, it's just like a telephone."

She closed the computer, and the light on the edge pulsed slowly "See, it tells you when it's asleep."

When they'd finished their drinks, Poppy said, "I'll say goodnight, then."

She kissed David, then Rose. "See you in the morning."

As she disappeared up the stairs, David looked at Rose. "Thanks so much for my present – I'm so glad I got you the locket, they really go together, don't they."

Rose smiled, then her face became serious. "Hold me, darling?"

David put his arms around her. "Are you OK?"

She nodded. "It's been a wonderful day – I think I'm just a little overwhelmed."

David stroked her hair. "And you'll be tired – you did get up early to make breakfast."

He looked into her eyes. "You have a couple of days before Lily gets here, you can relax. Poppy won't mind if you need a bit of time by yourself, she has her books. You can go into the summer house, take the CD player from the kitchen."

Rose nodded, a tear running down her cheek. "Thanks for being so thoughtful."

David kissed the track of her tears. "Come on, let's get you to bed."

They walked up the stairs hand in hand, stopping at the door of Poppy's room. Again David took Rose in his arms, kissing her softly. "Goodnight, my love."

***

The next day, Rose took up David's suggestion, and after she and Poppy had had breakfast, they went into the living room to pick a few CD's of classical music from the shelf in the living room.

"If you haven't reappeared by lunchtime, I'll bring you a sandwich," said Poppy.

"Thanks, Pops."

Rose walked across the grass and pushed open the door of the summer house, breathing in the pleasant scent of sun-warmed wood. She glanced around, seeing an old-fashioned rocking chair in one corner, and pulled the chair towards the open door so that she could sit facing out onto the lake.

Her fingers played with the locket at her throat, and her thoughts drifted back to her conversation with Poppy the day before David's birthday. She was sure that if David did propose to her, he'd do it the old-fashioned way, on one knee.

Rose decided to let her imagination have free rein just for a while, and tried to picture her ideal honeymoon. She remembered Lily's description of a tropical beach, a chalet looking out over the surf, but her mind wouldn't settle on the image. Instead she found herself imagining the scene she'd glimpsed briefly on Poppy's computer screen the previous night; the evening air still warm from the heat of the day, but now scented with flowers, and filled with unfamiliar sounds.

She wondered again what kind of creature was responsible for the chirping she'd heard in the background of their conversation with David's parents. She imagined fireflies, and – where had she seen this? – wisps of soft down floating on the evening breeze.

Elephants – of course there'd be elephants, perhaps painted, carrying howdahs, with a turbaned mahout in front, making their way in single file through the jungle...

"Rose?" she heard as if from far away. She opened her eyes. "Oh, hi, Pops. It can't be lunchtime already?"

"Not quite. But I made you a cup of coffee, and I've brought you sandwiches for when you want them – look, I boiled some eggs, then sliced them."

She put the tray down. "Are you OK on your own for a bit longer?" asked Rose.

Poppy nodded. "The book reader thing that David got me is the best present ever – there are so many things I want to read."

"Great," smiled Rose. "But if you do want some company, just come and get me."

Poppy walked back to the house with a glance over her shoulder and a smile, and Rose turned back to the view across the lake. This time she imagined a road winding up through dusty villages to a wooden lodge in the foothills, overlooking tea plantations and with the mountains as a backdrop. David guiding a old-fashioned car through the gates, opening the door for her, offering her his hand...

She shook her head, smiling, and sipped her coffee, then picked up one of Poppy's sandwiches and took a bite. She saved the crusts for the ducks, walking over to the water's edge to scatter the bread for them, then returned to her seat. She watched the ducks eating – the ducklings now much larger – then paddling back to their roost in the reeds at the far side of the lake.

She heard the sound of an engine, and wondered if David had returned early. But when she glanced towards the drive, she saw the distinctive red of a post van, and she heard Poppy speaking to the driver, then the van turning and going back down the drive.

Poppy walked across the grass towards her. "Were the sandwiches OK?"

"They were great, thanks, Pops. Do you want to do something now?"

Poppy nodded. "Could we go into town? I'd like to get something for Lily."

"Of course. Let me get my bag."

Rose went upstairs, returning with her bag. She fished out her car keys and unlocked the doors. "Hop in."

They set off, and Rose glanced across at Poppy. "It seems really strange – apart from church, and walking to the village for our lunch, this is the first time I've been out since I got here."

When they reached the multi-storey car park, Rose locked the car, then grinned at Poppy. "Where do you want to go?"

"I thought we could look in the department store. You'll help me, won't you, Rose – you know what Lily likes."

"Of course, darling."

They walked to the precinct, and Poppy glanced into the big display windows of the department store. "They have some great stuff. Where shall we start?"

Rose thought for a moment. "How about the jewellery counter? It doesn't have to be something expensive, maybe just some bangles, or a bracelet."

Poppy nodded. "Like a friendship bracelet or something."

They took the escalator to the next floor, and walked over to the brightly-lit glass cases.

"This stuff is beautiful," said Poppy, looking at a tray of pendants set with stones in shades of blue.

"Maybe I can drop a hint in David's ear," grinned Rose. "When's your birthday?"

"October – ages yet. Oh, look, Rose, what about these?"

Poppy pointed to a tall case with silver bracelets. "See, there's one there with a little enamel dove."

Rose looked. "You know what, Pops, I think Lily would really like that."

She caught the assistant's eye. "Can we take a look at this one, please?"

The girl opened the cabinet and took out the bracelet, draping it over Poppy's hand. "We have these with different charms, if you'd like to see them."

Poppy shook her head. "No, the dove's perfect."

She took out her purse and walked over to the counter with the assistant, returning with a small carrier bag. "Thanks, Rose, that was a really good choice."

Rose grinned. "I have another idea. When Lily and I come in here, we always go up to the restaurant – their milkshakes are amazing. Come on, I'll treat you."

They went up to the top floor, and found a table by one of the potted palms. The waitress approached them, smiling. "What can I get you?"

Rose glanced at Poppy. "What's your favourite milkshake?"

"Vanilla, please," said Poppy.

Rose smiled. "That's Lily's too. I'll have chocolate, please."

When their milkshakes arrived, Poppy sucked on her straw. "Mm, these are pretty good."

Rose nodded. "Anything else you want to get while we're here?"

Poppy thought. "David did say he'd toast marshmallows with us one evening, didn't he. And I bet Lily likes them?"

Rose chuckled. "My sister has a sweet tooth – you'll see."

"So we'd better get some more," decided Poppy.

They finished their milkshakes, and made their way out of the store back to the precinct.

"There," pointed Rose. "I bet they'll have sweets and stuff."

They went in, and Rose picked up a basket. "Over there," she pointed.

Poppy put three bags of marshmallows into the basket. "Look, Rose, they have those hot chocolate things, you know, on a stick – you put them into the milk and they dissolve."

"Mm," said Rose. "They sound fantastic – let's get a few."

She thought for a second. "We'd better get some more coffee, and syrup. Oh, and some fresh cream."

They took their basket to the checkout and Rose paid, then they walked back to the car with their bags. As Rose drove, Poppy took her gift for Lily from its box and looked at it. "Do you think she'll like it?"

Rose nodded. "Definitely."

They reached the house, and Poppy helped Rose find places for everything. "We can do the proper shopping tomorrow with David."

Rose glanced at the clock. "He'll be back soon. What shall we do for dinner?"

"There are some lamb chops in the freezer," suggested Poppy. "And I know there's mint sauce – we have both sorts, the vinegary one and the sweet kind."

When David opened the door, Rose went to greet him with a kiss. "Good day?"

He nodded. "Pretty good, really – I think I'm on top of things at the office. How about you?"

Rose smiled. "Definitely. I had a quiet morning by the lake – Poppy made me sandwiches – then we drove into town, got a few things."

They went through to the kitchen, and David gave Poppy a hug. "Careful," she grinned, "or you'll get flour on your suit."

"What are you making, Pops?"

"I thought I'd do something a bit special with these lamb chops – see, I've put flour on, and then egg."

She dropped the coated chops into a frying pan, and they started to sizzle.

"I'm impressed," nodded David.

"Drink?" offered Rose.

"Please."

She opened the fridge, taking out a bottle of white wine. "That should be just nicely chilled."

David sipped his wine. "You know you're spoiling me, right?"

Rose grinned. "You deserve it – you work hard."

She glanced at Poppy. "But there's a condition."

David pretended to look concerned. "What?"

"We bought marshmallows," said Poppy, "and this time you have to stay and toast them with us."

"I think I can manage that," he chuckled.

When they'd finished dinner, David lit the fire while Rose made hot chocolate and brought it in.

Poppy opened a bag of marshmallows and put one on a stick for each of them, then dropped a couple into her hot chocolate. She glanced at Rose mischievously. "Is that cheating?"

Rose grinned. "No – actually I was just about to suggest it. Lily always does that."

They sipped their hot chocolate, then toasted marshmallows, blowing on them to cool them a little afterwards.

After a few minutes, David moved to the sofa. "Getting a little warm there."

Rose leaned back against his legs, and he stroked her hair gently. "Anything else you need?"

She shook her head. "This is perfect."

When the fire started to die down, David said reluctantly, "Well, one more day to go, then we can really relax."

Rose squeezed his hand. "Can't wait. Although when Poppy and Lily get together, things might go a little bit crazy."

Poppy grinned. "Don't worry – we can go and hang out in the tree house if you two want a bit of peace."

Rose reached out to ruffle her hair. "I was only teasing, Pops. You two do whatever you like – David and I will help, or give you some space, whichever."

She leaned forward to let David stand up, and he offered his hands to help her to her feet. As she stood, he wrapped his arms around her. "See you upstairs in a minute."

Poppy took the poker and stirred the embers, sending a shower of sparks up the chimney. "What do you want to do tomorrow, Rose?"

"We can make a shopping list, and you can wrap Lily's present," Rose said. "And we can make sure the tree house is OK – you can find some old blankets and stuff so that you and Lily have something to sit on."

They went up the stairs and got ready for bed, then Rose looked in on David.

"He's fast asleep," she said as she walked back into Poppy's room. "We'll have to make sure he gets time to wind down at the weekend."

Poppy nodded. "Maybe you can drive me and Lily to the early service on Sunday, let David have a lie-in. Then we can make him a late breakfast in bed."

"Twice in a week," chuckled Rose. "He really will think we're spoiling him."

***

The weather the next day was duller, and Poppy looked out of the window apprehensively. "I hope it doesn't rain this weekend – I was so looking forward to us all going out in the car."

"Don't worry," reassured Rose. "The forecast on Saturday is fine."

At about four o'clock David called Rose's mobile. "I'm done for the day – shall I meet you at the supermarket?"

"Sure," said Rose. "I'll bring the list."

When they got to the supermarket, Poppy pushed the trolley while Rose ticked items off the list.

"Don't forget the ice cream," said Poppy as they walked through the freezer section. "Can we have a tub of that one with the chocolate dinosaurs in?"

"Of course, Pops," grinned David, opening the door of the cabinet.

At the checkout, Poppy and Rose packed the bags while David unloaded the trolley. "That should keep us going for a while," he said, putting his wallet away.

Rose followed David's car back to the house, and they put everything away. "What did we get for dinner?" asked Poppy.

"Pizza," grinned David. "Rose has given me a taste for the spicy one, and I got ham and pineapple for you."

"Yummy," said Poppy. "I like the pineapple, it's juicy."

When they'd eaten, David said, "I picked up a surprise for us when we were shopping."

He walked over to the kitchen counter. "I thought you two would enjoy this."

Poppy glanced at the DVD case. "Oh, I've heard of this one. Doesn't she keep losing her memory?"

David nodded. "So he has to find a way of telling her every day that he's her boyfriend, she has no idea who he is when she wakes up."

They went through to the living room, and David put the DVD in the player. He sat down on the sofa, and Poppy sat beside him, snuggling into his shoulder.

"Hmm," said Rose, pretending to consider. "Where am I going to sit?"

"By me," said Poppy firmly, patting the cushion next to her.

David grinned. "That's OK, Pops."

The film started, and Rose glanced across at David. "It must be awful having something like that happen to you."

He nodded. "I sometimes wonder if there's a way we could get involved, help people who aren't as fortunate as we are."

The film drew to its conclusion, and Poppy gasped as the camera zoomed out in the final scene, showing Antarctic icebergs, then a boat, a little girl in her father's arms. Rose heard a quiet sniffle, and put her arm round Poppy's shoulders.

"It's happy really, Pops," she whispered.

"I know. I wish she could remember, though."

Rose nodded. "Come on, darling. Let's get you to bed – big day tomorrow."

Poppy nodded. She sniffed again, and David handed her a handkerchief. "Blow."

She blew her nose, then smiled. "I'm OK."

Rose leaned across to kiss David. "I'll go up with Poppy – I'll come in to you in the morning, but not too early."

He nodded. "That'll be great."

Rose walked up the stairs with Poppy, and they got ready for bed. As they got under the covers, Poppy turned, and Rose hugged her again. "Sweet dreams, Pops. You know you can wake me up if anything disturbs you."

Poppy nodded. "Thanks, Rose."

***

When Rose looked in on David the next morning, he was sitting up in bed. "Is Poppy OK?"

"She's fine – I think she was a little tired. She's back to her normal self this morning, full of plans for her and Lily."

The three of them had breakfast together, then David washed up while Rose and Poppy got ready. "What time does the flight land?" he asked when Rose came back down the stairs.

"About eleven, Charles said. So they'll be here before twelve."

Poppy came into the kitchen, and Rose said, "Pops?"

"Hmm?"

"Had you thought where we're all going to sleep? Your bed's big, but I think it'd still be a bit of a squash."

Poppy grinned triumphantly. "I've already got the answer. We can get the tent out, put it up on the lawn. If it rains too hard, we can always dive into the summer house."

"Great idea," said David. "I'll go and look for the tent."

Rose glanced at Poppy, her eyes twinkling. "Have you read Love's Labour's Lost yet?"

Poppy looked puzzled. Then she put her hand over her mouth. "Oh! Of course – the princess and her three noble ladies, camping out because the prince has made a vow."

She frowned. "But there are only three of us – you have to be the princess."

Rose grinned. "You can always ask Alice to come for a sleepover."

Poppy nodded. "Maybe later in the week – I want to really get to know Lily first."

She glanced in the direction of the garage. "So David has to be the prince – what about the other three?"

Rose looked thoughtful. "Your prince will come eventually, Pops."

She smiled wryly. "That probably means Charles and Paul have to be Don Armado and Costard."

David came back in. "OK, found the tent, I've laid everything out on the grass. Can you give me a hand?"

They soon had the tent up, and Poppy tugged on Rose's hand. "Come on inside."

"I thought we'd have jacket potatoes for lunch," said David. "I'd better go and put them in the oven."

Poppy and Rose stood in the tent, the bright sunlight muted by the canvas. "This is going to be so cool," said Poppy.

Rose nodded. "I have another idea. I saw a camping stove in the garage, I bet we could get an old frying pan and cook ourselves something one day, like real camping."

They emerged from the tent, finding David in the kitchen putting the kettle on. Rose's phone beeped, and she checked the screen.

"OK," she said. "Paul says they're just coming through the village."

They walked outside and stood at the top of the drive. A few moments later, Charles's car turned in through the gates, Lily in the front seat waving excitedly. As soon as the car stopped, she opened the door and dashed over to Rose, wrapping her arms around her sister tightly. "I've missed you."

"Me too," smiled Rose. Lily next hugged David, then looked at Poppy.

Poppy stepped forward without hesitating and gave her a hug. "Hi, Lily. Come on, I've got something to show you."

David grinned as they disappeared into the house. "I knew they'd be fine."

Charles got out of the car. "Hi, Rose," he said, kissing her on the cheek.

He turned to David, his expression neutral. "I hope everything's been OK."

David nodded. "We've had a great week, actually. I think Rose and Poppy have had a wonderful time."

Rose hesitated. "It's OK if Lily and I stay over, isn't it, Charles? Poppy thought of getting the tent out for us all to sleep in."

Charles frowned, then pursed his lips. "I suppose it'll be fine, seeing as all three of you are together."

He turned to get back into his car. "You won't forget to come over one evening and see Mum, will you."

Rose nodded. "Maybe Wednesday."

They watched him drive away, and Rose let out the breath she'd been holding. "I'm glad Charles didn't try to be difficult."

David nodded. "Right, let's see what mischief those two have got into."

When they went inside, Poppy and Lily were sitting at the kitchen table. "Look what Poppy got me," said Lily, holding out her wrist.

"It's lovely," said Rose, looking at the bracelet. Poppy winked at her.

"Who's for some lunch?" asked David. "Jacket potatoes, and I made chilli, or there's grated cheese. And butter, of course."

Rose and Poppy had chilli, while David and Lily divided the cheese between them. "So, Lily," said Rose. "Tell us all about your trip."

"Well, I did OK at skiing," Lily began. "But it was all the other stuff that made it really special – going up to the top of a glacier and throwing snowballs at Charles and Paul, riding the cable cars, looking down from the top at all those gorgeous Alpine valleys."

"Wow," said Rose. "What else did you see?"

"There's a palace – built by some mad king – he was a practical joker, and there are fountains under the paths, they go off when you're walking on them and you have to dodge."

Poppy grinned. "He sounds a bit loopy."

Lily nodded. "But the palace is amazing. There was a huge hall, all lit with candles, and they had a quartet playing some of that, what's it called, chamber music."

She carried on with stories about the hotel, the journey – "I love planes!" – and other people they'd met on the trip. David got up from the table, listening while he made coffee.

"Here you go, Lily," he said, putting a tall mug in front of her. "And there's cream, and syrup."

"We made sure we had everything," said Poppy.

Lily glanced up. "Thanks, Pops."

Rose caught David's eye, and he smiled.

"OK," said David when they'd finished their coffee, "I think we need to get the tent sorted out."

Rose helped him carry bedding down from upstairs. Poppy and Lily were arranging their side of the tent, and Poppy said, "Can we have the big duvet from my bed, Rose?"

"Of course, Pops."

When everything was in place, David came to the entrance of the tent and stood outside. "Knock knock, can I come in?"

Lily looked at Rose. "What does the princess say?"

Rose pretended to look unsure, then grinned. "Of course – come on in, David."

He glanced around. "Very cosy – you've done a great job."

Rose nodded. "The girls were very thoughtful, they let me go near the entrance so I can come in after I've said goodnight to you."

David smiled. "Thanks, girls. Well, it's not bedtime yet, so who fancies a walk before dinner?"

They walked down the drive, Poppy and Lily in front, David following hand in hand with Rose.

"Which way?" asked Poppy when they got to the gates.

"Why don't we walk up to the farm," suggested David. "We can look at the pigs."

"Yay!" said Lily. "I like pigs."

They reached the farmyard, and David nodded to the farmer who was stacking bales in the far corner. They walked over to the sty, and Lily looked over the wall, leaning on her elbows. "Look, Pops, she has piglets."

The sow grunted gently as the piglets pushed at her, and Lily giggled. "That doesn't look very comfortable."

"It's the same for people," said Poppy. "We had a lesson about it at school."

For a moment Rose felt an odd sensation, as she thought back to her imaginings of a few days before. She knew in her mind that starting a family was the next step after a wedding and a honeymoon, but Poppy's words somehow made it seem more real.

"Are you OK?" asked David. "You've gone quiet."

Rose nodded, smiling. "I'm fine."

They looked at the pigs for a few more minutes, then set off back towards the house. When they reached the top of the drive, Lily said, "Can Poppy and I go in the tent again for a bit? We'll help clear up after dinner."

"Of course," said David. He turned to Rose. "Give me a hand in the kitchen?"

As they prepared dinner together, Rose said, "They'll be OK by themselves next week while you and I are out at work, won't they?"

David nodded. "They both have their mobile phones, and Poppy knows what things she shouldn't do while I'm not here. Don't worry."

Rose smiled. "I won't."

The girls came in, and David grinned. "Perfect timing."

"What are we having?" asked Lily.

"Spaghetti bolognese," said Rose. "And we got ice cream with chocolate dinosaurs in it for afters – Poppy chose it specially."

Lily grinned at Poppy. "Great."

David served, and they began to eat. Rose rolled her eyes as Lily sucked a strand of spaghetti into her mouth noisily. "I don't know, I can't take you anywhere," she teased.

They took their ice cream into the living room, and David lit a fire. "Marshmallows tomorrow?" he asked.

Poppy nodded vigorously. "And hot chocolate."

"We thought we'd let you lie in tomorrow, David," said Rose. "I'll take the girls to church first thing."

David nodded. "It would be nice to have a lazy morning."

Poppy finished her ice cream and stood up. "Come on, Lily, we promised to sort the kitchen out."

They went out, the murmur of their voices mixing with the sound of the washing up. Rose snuggled closer to David on the sofa. "This is the best part of the weekend – we've had a nice day, we can sit in front of the fire, we don't have to work tomorrow."

David nodded, tightening his arm around her shoulders. "Only one way it could be any better," he said, then stopped, as though he'd said more than he intended to.

"I know," said Rose softly. "But we have plenty of time."

Poppy looked round the door. "Everything's sorted," she said. "Lily and I are going to change, then go out to the tent."

She reappeared with Lily a few minutes later, and David got up to hug her, then kissed Lily on the cheek. "Goodnight, you two. Rose won't be long."

When they were gone, he sat down again, and Rose pillowed her head in his lap while he stroked her hair. The glow of the fire gradually died down, and Rose's eyelids drooped, then closed, her breathing slowing.

David smiled to himself, and changed position a little, moving slowly so as not to wake her.

The fire was out, its ashes still warm, when Rose opened her eyes again. "Mm," she said indistinctly. "What time is it?"

David looked across at the clock. "About one."

Rose sat up, blinking. "The girls must have been asleep for hours."

She turned to look at him. "Did you sleep? It can't have been all that comfortable."

David smiled. "Doesn't matter. There's nowhere –" he emphasised the word – "I would rather be than with you, waking or sleeping."

Suddenly Rose was in his arms, trembling. "Hold me?"

David wrapped his arms around her, kissing her hair. When she lifted her head, her face was wet with tears. "I love you."

"And I love you," David replied, his eyes not leaving hers.

She smiled. "I'd better get changed."

When Rose came back down in her nightshirt, David put his arms around her again. "Sweet dreams."

She nodded. "You too."

He watched her slip across the lawn, bright like an angel against the dark hedge, and close the tent flap behind her.

***

The next day David was awoken by the sound of the car door closing, and the murmur of the girls' voices as they came back in to the house.

Rose came up the stairs. "Morning, sleepyhead."

David grinned. "Seems to me you were the sleepy one last night. How was church?"

"Great – it's the communion service at eight o'clock on Sundays."

David got out of bed, and Rose chuckled. "Not seen you in shorts before."

They went downstairs, and Poppy said, "Bacon's nearly ready – I made enough for all of us, breakfast was a long time ago."

"Can we use the waffle maker as well?" asked Lily.

"Of course," grinned David. "And there's honey in the cupboard as well as maple syrup."

Breakfast – second breakfast for the girls – was a leisurely affair, bacon and eggs, then waffles as often as the machine could produce them. David made a second cafetiere of coffee, and Poppy grinned. "We'll have to get some more cream."

The girls went upstairs to change, and Rose said, "We won't need to make lunch, really – there's lots of cake and stuff for tea later. What would you like to do?"

David smiled. "Actually, I have another surprise for you. I'm amazed Poppy hasn't mentioned it, we used to do it all the time."

"I'm intrigued," said Rose. "Will I need to wear anything special?"

David shook his head. "Poppy can find you a hat."

The girls returned, and David said, "OK, let's go."

Rose was mystified as they turned right out of the front door instead of left, walking past the summer house and down to the far end of the garden.

David unbolted a gate, and Rose followed Poppy and Lily through. "Oh," she said, "I didn't know the river was so close."

David nodded. "You're OK with water, aren't you?"

"Definitely. I used to love the paddle boats in the park."

"Then this'll suit you perfectly."

They rounded a bend in the river, and Rose stopped. "Oh!"

Tied up to a small landing stage were half a dozen long, low shapes, moving up and down in the slight swell as a brightly-painted barge went past.

"I've always wanted to try this," said Rose.

David grinned. "There's a bit of a knack to it – why don't I take us along the river a bit, out of the traffic, and you can have a go."

He took a long pole from a rack on the wall, and lowered it into the water, holding the punt steady. "Hop in, girls. Let Rose sit at the end where she'll be facing me."

Lily and Poppy took the two nearest seats, and Rose carefully made her way to the far end. David stepped on to the boat, and pushed them gently away from the bank, then dug the pole into the river bed, propelling them along.

"What do you think?" he asked Rose.

"It's marvellous," she grinned.

They travelled upstream for a while, then as they passed a grassy meadow David said, "Let's stop here for a bit."

He maneuvered the punt into the bank, and used the pole to secure it. Poppy scrambled onto the bank, and held out her hand to Lily. "Race you to the other side of the field!"

David watched them go, then grinned at Rose. "Is there room for me on that seat?"

She slid across, and he joined her, leaning back against the wood. "This is the life."

Rose nodded. "I'll try not to fall asleep on you this time."

They sat for a while, the water gently rocking the boat. "Look!" David pointed.

Rose glanced up, shading her eyes from the sun. She could just see a small dot rising high into the blue, then the unmistakeable song of a skylark filled the air.

Poppy and Lily returned, breathless. "We saw a kestrel," Lily said. "I think it caught a mouse."

They got back into the punt, and David glanced at Rose. "Want a turn?"

"You'd better help," she said. She stepped up onto the end, and David picked up the pole, standing behind her. "Put your hands here," he said, "and push gently."

The punt moved out into the stream again, and Rose shifted her feet to keep her balance. "Oh, I see how it works."

David nodded. "You're doing fine."

They continued upstream for a little way, then David said, "There's a lock in a bit – there are rollers we could take the punt across, but it's a bit tricky."

"That's OK," said Rose. "Maybe next time. This has been a lovely trip."

David took her place, turning the punt downstream and letting the current do most of the work. When they got back to the moorings, he tied the punt up carefully and replaced the pole in its rack.

They walked back to the house, and David said, "Why don't you three stay in the garden? I'll bring you some tea."

When he returned, the girls were sprawled on the grass in a circle, giggling over Poppy's book. "What's so funny?"

"We were pretending Rose was the princess in the play," said Poppy. "It's a bit hard to understand at first, but the princess and her ladies are really clever – I think they get the better of the men."

David rolled his eyes, pretending to sigh heavily. "I don't stand a chance, do I?"

"And Alice is coming for a sleepover on Thursday," said Poppy. "Then you'll have to cope with all four of us."

"Anyway," said David, putting down the tray he was carrying, "I brought you tea, and there's some chocolate cake."

Rose smiled and put her hand gently on his arm. "We were only teasing. Thanks for our trip, and for doing this."

They made room for him to sit down, and Rose leaned against him as she sipped her tea. "How about we have a game of Scrabble when we've finished our cake?"

Poppy grinned. "OK. Lily and I will see if we can beat you two."

Her words proved prophetic, and Rose shook her head. "You two are way too smart."

She turned to Lily. "When do you get your exam results?"

"Next week – I have to go in to school to fetch them."

David nodded. "If you've done OK, we can go out and celebrate."

Lily hugged him. "You're on."

They sat in the garden talking until the sun dropped behind the trees. David took a deep breath. "Well, work tomorrow for both of us, Rose."

She nodded. "And in bed on time tonight, not like yesterday."

"I thought I didn't hear you come in," grinned Lily.

The girls went to get ready for bed, while Rose and David washed the tea things.

Rose sighed. "I'm going to miss this when Lily and I are back home the week after next."

David moved behind her as she stood at the sink, putting his arms round her waist. "Me too."

She turned in his arms, kissing him hard on the mouth. "But we'll make the most of the time we have."

They heard footsteps, and David glanced up. "Hi, you two."

Rose slipped out of his arms to hug Lily, then Poppy. "I really will come soon – we didn't finish our talk about the princess this afternoon, did we?"

David kissed both girls on the cheek. "Sleep tight."

When they'd gone, he turned back to Rose. "I suppose we'll take both cars tomorrow?"

She nodded. "I'll probably finish earlier than you, and I can pop in and see Mum, then come back here and help the girls make dinner."

She wrapped her arms around him. "Night, then."

"Sweet dreams, my love."

***

Rose's day went much as she'd anticipated, working through some of the correspondence that had arrived at the office while the family had been on holiday. She bought sandwiches from the staff restaurant, and sat in reception with Beth while she ate, telling her about her week with David.

"I'm really happy for you," said Beth. "I don't think Charles is so pleased, though."

"I don't get it," said Rose. "He can see I'm really happy, and Lily gets on with Poppy like a house on fire — you know she's never had that many friends of her own age."

She shook her head. "And after he blurted out that he thought I was pregnant, I've made it crystal clear that David and I aren't…"

She blushed, and Beth nodded.

"Anyway," said Rose, getting up. "I'd better carry on with these letters – if there's one thing Charles is sure about, it's that he wants his correspondence organised."

Rose worked till four, then drove the short distance home. "Hello, stranger," said Paul as she opened the door.

"Hi, Paul," Rose said, kissing him on the cheek. "I wondered why I hadn't seen you at the office."

He nodded. "Mum needed a couple of things doing around the house after we got back."

Rose's mother came out of the kitchen. "Hello, dear."

"Hi, Mum. You OK?"

She nodded. "I really enjoyed our holiday – it was great to have Lily all week. Is she having fun with – Poppy, isn't it?"

Rose smiled. "They get on brilliantly."

She thought for a moment. "Poppy can come over with Lily on Wednesday, can't she – David won't mind having an evening by himself."

Her mother nodded slowly. "You know that David's very welcome here, don't you."

"I know, Mum, but I don't want to rub Charles's nose in it."

Her mother smiled. "You're very wise, Rose. Do you want a cup of tea?"

They sat at the kitchen table and talked as they drank their tea, then Rose glanced at her watch. "Sorry, Mum. I have to go back and help Poppy and Lily make dinner."

"That's all right, dear. It's nice that you get a chance to see how you want to do things when you have your own place, and it's easier with them to help you."

Rose got up to hug her mother. "Thanks, Mum. I really appreciate the way you're seeing this."

She drove back to David's, and looked around for the girls. There was a scrap of paper on the kitchen table in Lily's writing: "In tree house."

Rose walked into the woods. "Are you two OK?" she called.

Poppy stuck her head out of the tree house. "Fine."

"Thanks for leaving the note," said Rose, "that was really thoughtful. Are you ready to come down now?"

The girls clambered down the ladder, brushing at smears of bark on their jeans. "What are we making for dinner?"

Rose thought for a moment. "David really liked that stew we made last week, Poppy. Why don't you and Lily have a go at that?"

When David came in, he looked tired. Rose kissed him, and said, "Are you OK?"

"I'm fine. Just a lot going on at work."

Rose looked at him, concerned. "Dinner will only be a few minutes, the girls are doing brilliantly. Come in and sit down for a bit."

David sat on the sofa, closing his eyes with a sigh. "How was your day, darling?"

"Pretty good. I caught up on all the correspondence, had lunch with Beth, then popped round to see Mum. She wondered if Poppy could come over when Lily and I go round on Wednesday."

David nodded. "No problem. I need to get the household accounts up to date, anyway."

He smiled wryly. "More figures, as if I don't see enough at the office."

"Maybe I could take a look, if you show me how it all works?"

David opened his eyes. "Would you?"

Rose nodded. "You know I do all the spreadsheets for Charles, right?"

David laughed. "You've really cheered me up. I had no idea he didn't do them himself."

Lily came in from the kitchen. "Hi, David. Dinner's ready."

They went through, and David hugged the girls. "Thanks for making dinner."

"You haven't tried it yet," grinned Poppy.

"It smells delicious," said David firmly.

When they'd finished eating, Rose said, "I don't think any of us feels up to anything too taxing tonight. Shall we do what we did the other day, just put some music on?"

"OK," said Poppy. "Can Lily and I choose today?"

"Of course, darling."

They went into the lounge, and the girls looked through the CD's, whispering to one another. "Here," said Poppy triumphantly. "I knew we had it."

She slid the disc into the player, and Rose looked puzzled as the unmistakeable sound of a ship's horn came from the speakers. Then a voice started to sing wordlessly, a haunting melody, and Rose nodded in recognition.

She turned to David, her eyes bright, her lower lip caught in her teeth. "Do you know it?"

He shook his head. "Don't think so."

Rose grinned. "You will when it gets to the theme."

She shifted position, resting her head on his shoulder, and closed her eyes. A couple of instrumental tracks followed, then again a chorus of voices began their haunting, wordless melody.

David's arms tightened around Rose. "Now I know."

Poppy shifted a little closer. "This is Rose's theme."

Understanding flooded David's face. "I'd forgotten that was the name of the character."

He held Rose more tenderly, even desperately, and as the words reached 'Love can touch us one time, and last for a lifetime, and never let go till we're gone', David made no attempt to hold back the tears streaming down his face.

As the track faded out, Rose lifted her head. "I've made your shirt all soggy," she said, managing a smile.

He kissed her eyelids. "Don't worry."

Lily looked sad, a little lost. "We didn't mean to upset you."

Rose reached out her hand. "It's OK, angel. It's good to cry, and sometimes it's happy tears. We have each other, nobody's lost."

She took a deep breath. "That was lovely. Thanks, girls. I think it's time we called it a day, though."

The girls went to get changed, Lily still subdued, then returned for their goodnight kiss. "I won't be long," promised Rose.

She looked into David's eyes, seeing a determination she hadn't noticed before. "Will you be OK?"

He took a deep breath, then nodded. "I'll be fine. Sleep well, my love."

***

The week seemed to pass quickly, Rose dividing her time between the busy office and the all-too-short evenings with David and the girls. She and Lily made the promised visit home on Wednesday night, and Poppy shyly presented their mother with the flowers she'd picked from the garden. "Thank you, darling, they're lovely."

Saturday came, and Lily watched as David folded up the tent. "I've had a really nice time," she said.

Poppy nodded. "You can come over every weekend if you like – we can share my room."

"What about R–" Lily started to ask, then stopped herself. Rose stood a little way off, absorbed in her own thoughts.

Finally Rose and Lily got into the car. "We'll see you tomorrow at church," said Rose.

David nodded. "Drive carefully. Call me when you get home, just so I know you're both OK."

When they reached the house, Lily went upstairs and sat on her bed. "Come on, angel," said Rose, putting an arm around her shoulders. "It'll be all right, you'll see."

Lily nodded wordlessly. "Let's go downstairs," said Rose. "I brought some marshmallows and a couple of those hot chocolate sticks."

Lily brightened a little. "OK."

As they lay in bed that night, Lily said, "Rose?"

"What is it, angel?"

"Are you going to marry David?"

Rose didn't answer for a moment. "He has to ask me first. I know he loves me, I think he's being really thoughtful."

"I don't understand," said Lily.

"Well, angel, I'm still young, really, and we haven't known each other all that long. And he doesn't want to make things any more difficult than they already are with Charles."

Lily muttered something under her breath.

"Sorry, angel, didn't hear you?"

"I said I hate Charles."

Rose turned towards her. "Darling, don't say that. I know he's difficult sometimes, but he's worked hard for us, given us a lot. Especially after Dad wasn't here any more."

Lily sighed. "You're right. But he should just see what we see, how good David is."

"I can't argue with that," smiled Rose. "Now, let's get some sleep. And we'll see David and Poppy in the morning, remember."

***

When they got to church, David and Poppy were waiting for them at the gate, and David gave Rose her usual kiss. "Shall we go in?"

They sat in their usual pew, and Rose put her heart into the hymns, hearing David's warm baritone next to her.

The reading was one Rose wasn't familiar with, about a young woman whose father made a very unfortunate promise and ended up having to allow his daughter to be put to death. The young woman – she wasn't even named – asked permission to go and roam the hills with her friends for two months, because she would never marry.

Rose felt shaking next to her, and realised that Lily was crying. She put an arm round her sister's shoulder. "Do you want to go out?"

Lily nodded, and as soon as the next hymn started, Rose stood, taking Lily out into the sunshine. "Are you OK?"

"It was so sad," choked Lily.

"I know, angel. But it was a long time ago." Rose held Lily, stroking her hair.

David and Poppy joined them, and Poppy hugged Lily, giving her a hanky. "Thanks," she smiled, wiping her tears away.

"I think I should take Lily home," said Rose.

David nodded. "I'll call you later."

Lily and Rose walked back to the house, and Rose made sure Lily got up to their room without her brothers seeing. She couldn't face explaining what had made her sister so upset.

"Do you want some lunch?" Rose asked.

Lily shook her head. "Tell Mum I don't feel very well. Could you bring me a sandwich later?"

"Is Lily OK?" asked Paul, when she didn't appear at the table.

"She's got a stomach ache," said Rose, pushing away her guilt at the untruth.

She took Lily up a sandwich, finding her sister sitting up in bed looking brighter. Lily ate her sandwich hungrily. "I feel better now."

Rose stroked her hair. "I'm sorry – we had such a lovely time last week, but it's all been a bit much for you, hasn't it?"

Lily nodded. "But Poppy's right – I can go over there at weekends, and then in September I'll be back at school."

The next day, Rose went to the office as usual, while Lily helped their mother arrange their holiday photos in an album. When Rose got home, Charles and Paul were both there for dinner, and they went into Charles's office when the meal was over. Rose saw Paul bring up some figures on the computer screen, then Charles closed the door, cutting off her view.

At first Rose thought nothing of it, but the more she thought about it, the more it bothered her. What could they possibly be doing with the numbers that they didn't want her to see?

She sat at her laptop, looking at her online forum, until she heard the door open again. She got up silently, and stood by the doorway, out of sight.

Charles came out of the office first, continuing his conversation with Paul. "I don't see how he can find out – we'll put it to him as though it's in his favour, and when the accounts are published for the quarter, it'll be too late – we can just say we didn't know things were going that well, we landed some new contracts towards the end of the period."

Paul joined him in the hall. "I really don't agree with it."

"Are you going to tell him?" demanded Charles.

"Well, no."

"Then it's settled," Charles snapped.

They went through to the kitchen, and Rose sat back down at her computer, bewildered. Who were they talking about, and what were they going to do? Obviously it was completely wrong, something fundamentally dishonest, and she felt a flash of disgust that Paul had caved in so easily.

The next day when she arrived at the office, Beth glanced up. "Oh, hi, Rose. I have a surprise for you – David's going to be here for a meeting, Paul gave him a call first thing."

Rose's pleasure at Beth's words suddenly gave way to a sick feeling. What if it was David they'd been talking about?

She forced a smile. "Thanks, Beth."

She was checking invoices when Paul came into the office. "Hi, Rose. Can you sit in on a meeting with me and David?"

Rose smiled. "Of course."

When she got to the conference room, David looked up. "Hi, Rose." He made no move to kiss her, but she could see that the smile on his lips was meant only for her.

"Thanks for coming, David," began Paul. "We've been reviewing the terms of the investment you've made with us, and we have a suggestion."

He looked up, but Rose could tell he was having trouble meeting David's eyes. "You've probably noticed our share price has been a bit flat in the last few weeks."

David nodded. "Of course, I keep an eye on it."

"It's nothing to worry about long-term," assured Paul. "But on current performance, it occurred to us that it'll undervalue your quarterly dividend. We wondered if you'd agree to a variance to the contract, to change the dividend to an average basis over the quarter."

He pushed a piece of paper across the table. "Obviously we're not quite at the end of the period yet, but this shows the difference based on the two."

David looked at the figures. "It seems plain enough. Do you have the papers drawn up?"

Paul passed across a folder. "Of course, you don't have to sign immediately – the terms of the contract are that you have seven days to review any proposed variance."

He got up and turned to look out of the window, as though to reinforce the impression that there was no urgency.

David reached into his jacket, taking out his pen. Rose recognised the present Poppy had given him for his birthday, and something inside her gave way.

She glanced under the table, and very carefully aimed the toe of her shoe at David's ankle, giving him a sharp kick.

She silently blessed David's patience. He looked up at her, and caught her eye, his face puzzled.

Rose glanced at the contract, and shook her head slightly. David frowned, and Rose shook her head more vehemently.

"Ah, Paul," said David, standing up. "I think I'll take you up on your suggestion, and sleep on this, if you don't mind."

Paul turned back to face them, and only Rose's prior knowledge allowed her to catch the flash of panic in his eyes. "Of course, that's fine."

"I'll get going, then," said David, picking up the documents.

"Great to see you," said Paul. "Rose, you'll see David out, of course."

When they reached reception, David signed out, smiling at Beth. "Can I buy you lunch?" he said to Rose, his voice casual. "I'll drive."

She followed his lead. "Oh, I think that's allowed." She winked at Beth as she passed, and Beth smiled.

When they got out to the car, David drove away, and as soon as they were out of sight of the offices, he pulled over. "Darling – what's going on?"

Rose breathed a sigh of relief, and took his hand.

"You're trembling," he said, his voice betraying his concern.

Rose took a deep breath. "Paul is lying to you."

"What?"

"There's something going on with the business — I think they're about to announce some really good results, and they think the share price will go up. They don't want you to benefit."

David's face showed a bewildering array of emotions. "Is Charles behind this?"

Rose nodded dumbly.

David shook his head. "I never thought he'd go this far."

"What are we going to do?" asked Rose.

"The end of the quarter's only a few days away. They'll have to publish the figures as soon as the accountants have finished, and at that point whatever happens to the share price fixes the rate of the dividend. If I stall, don't sign, there's absolutely nothing they can do."

Rose nodded. "Then that's what we'll do."

David put his hand on hers. "Rose, I am desperately sorry you've been put in this position."

She shook her head. "You're not responsible for this."

She forced a smile. "Now, you offered me lunch?"

***

Rose heard nothing for the rest of the week about Charles's deception, though Paul looked increasingly harried. On Friday, as she was arriving at the office, she recognised the car driven by their accountant, and concluded that the figures must have been finalised.

Her assumption was proved correct when Paul came out of his office after lunch. "Beth, could you fax this please? The auditors first, then the FT and the local press."

Rose watched as the papers slid into the fax machine, then pulled out her phone and dialled. "David? Thought you'd want to know, the numbers are public now. I'll meet you at the house in an hour and let you have them."

She ended the call, and walked up to the reception desk. "Could you run me a copy of the figures off, Beth?"

"Of course."

Rose took the papers, still warm from the photocopier, and folded them, pushing them into her jacket pocket. She drove home, stopping only long enough to pick up Lily and let her mother know they wouldn't be in for tea, then went on to David's.

David kissed her, then ruffled Lily's hair. "Poppy's been so excited – go out to the garden, she's waiting for you."

Lily skipped off, and Rose followed David into the kitchen. "Here are the numbers."

David carefully scanned down each sheet. "These are fantastic. Your brothers have obviously done an amazing job."

"Except for one thing," said Rose, pointedly.

David opened his briefcase and took out his laptop. "Let's see how the share price is doing."

He switched the computer on, and started the stocks application. When the line for Middleton Sons appeared, Rose gasped. "Oh, my goodness."

David tapped at the calculator pad. "Trading hasn't finished for the day yet, but even at this price..."

He turned the display so that Rose could see it. "That's the quarterly dividend payment."

Again Rose's eyebrows shot up at the figure displayed. She thought for a moment. "Would that amount make a big difference to the final quarterly profit?"

David grinned. "Never let me forget how smart you are. No, not really. It's a big number, but compared to the bottom line in the quarterly numbers, it's not really a lot."

"So they wouldn't lose substantially by letting you have the full dividend?" Rose asked.

"Not really. It'd take their bonuses down a bit, but..."

Rose shook her head. "So they're either just greedy, or —"

She looked at David. "Or it's somehow become personal."

He closed the laptop, all thought of figures and dividends forgotten. "I'm sorry, Rose."

She nodded. "Well, I'm not the first person to have to make a choice."

"Oh, Rose, no, not unless it's completely unavoidable," said David, his voice anguished.

"The next move is up to them," said Rose. "If they admit their mistake and pay the dividend, maybe we can let this go."

She took a deep breath. "Anyway, it's the weekend. I won't let this spoil our time together."

Poppy and Lily tumbled into the kitchen, out of breath. "Can we help cook?" asked Lily.

David grinned. "Of course. How about we make a pie? I have some pastry in the fridge, and there are tins of pie filling so we don't have to do it all from scratch."

After a few minutes' work, the pie was in the oven, and the girls were nibbling on leftover pieces of raw pastry.

"I'm not totally sure that's good for you," smiled Rose, "but never mind."

While they waited for the pie to cook, Lily showed Poppy the album she'd brought with the family's holiday photos. "See, here's me on top of the glacier. And this is the ice caves – they're fantastic, but absolutely freezing."

The timer on the oven pinged, and David took out the pie. "Looks perfect, girls."

He served out slices of pie, then fetched salad and pickles from the fridge. "Tuck in."

When they'd finished eating, David said, "Now, how about a game of Scrabble? I'm still hoping Rose and I can get our own back on you two after last week."

This time David and Rose managed to win two out of the three games, and David grinned. "Seems we can salvage some of our credibility."

Rose took a deep breath. "Well, I'd better be getting back. I'll come over in the morning after breakfast."

Lily glanced across at her. "I wish you could stay, like before."

"Me too," said Rose. "But last week was different – this is like a sleepover for you, but I can't really do that. Not every weekend, anyway."

Lily nodded. "OK."

Rose hugged her, then kissed Poppy on the cheek. "Walk to the car with me, David?"

When they reached the car, David put his arms around her. "Thanks, Rose. I know it's frustrating, but we should do the right thing."

He kissed her softly, then said, "We'll get through this, darling, I'm certain."

Rose nodded. "You'll make sure the girls go to bed, won't you."

He grinned. "Of course. But I can't stop them talking till all hours."

Rose smiled. "Well, they can sleep in tomorrow if they like."

She kissed David again. "Night, my love."

***

When Rose arrived the next morning, she found a very sleepy-looking Lily and Poppy sitting at the kitchen table yawning over their cereal. "Try not to fall asleep in your cornflakes," she teased.

David came in, wiping his hands on a cloth. "Morning, darling. The car's all sorted, so once these two are ready, we can set off."

Lily looked up. "Where are we going?"

David grinned. "There's an air show today — I thought you'd like to see some of the old planes."

"Wow," said Poppy. "That'll be great."

"So eat up," encouraged Rose, "then you two can have a quick shower and we'll get going."

When the girls were ready, they set off, David taking a route that Rose was unfamiliar with. Finally they saw a sign pointing off the road, and David turned, driving over the grass to a gate manned by a steward in a yellow jacket.

The steward stepped forward. "Good morning, sir. I think you've taken a wrong turn — the entrance for competitors is a little further on."

David gave him a puzzled smile. "We're just here for the air show?"

"Ah, sorry — seeing your car, I thought you'd entered the vintage rally." He cast an admiring eye over the bodywork. "You've certainly made a fantastic job of it, if you don't mind me saying so."

Poppy leaned forward from the back seat. "Can we see if we can enter, David? Please?"

"Don't get your hopes up," cautioned her brother. "Probably we would have needed to fill in all sorts of forms. But OK, we'll give it a go."

He backed the car up, and they carried on along the road to the next gate. Another steward, this time with a clipboard, walked over to them.

"Hi," he said. "I don't see your number plate on the list?"

David grinned. "We didn't know about the rally, but the girls begged me to see if we could get in."

The steward looked at Poppy and Lily in the back, giving him their best hopeful expressions, and smiled. "That shouldn't be a problem. I just need to check – the car is based on an original vehicle, and you've done the restoration work yourself, it's not been done commercially?"

David nodded. "Absolutely."

"Rose and I did the inlay on the dashboard, look," piped up Lily.

"Then there's no problem – I'll put you on the list, and the very best of luck."

He opened the gate and they drove in, seeing a row of vintage vehicles in the field just ahead. David drew level with the end one, and a man in an old-fashioned suit with goggles pushed up onto his forehead nodded to him. "That's a beauty you've got there."

David winked at Rose. "Sorry, darling, I think he's talking about the car." There was giggling from the back seat, then Poppy said, "Come on, Lily, let's see what else is here."

"Don't go too far," said Rose, smiling.

David opened her door and offered his hand as she got down. "If I'd known, we could have dressed the part too," he said.

"Never mind – we can think about it next time."

They walked down the row of vehicles, admiring the immaculate restoration work and the attention to detail their owners had obviously paid.

A voice came over the tannoy. "Good morning, ladies and gentlemen, and welcome to our show today. We're very fortunate to have a fly-past of some very special planes today, and the first group will be over in just a minute or two, so please keep an eye upwards and enjoy them."

As the announcement ended, Rose heard a burst of music, and she glanced across to see a brass band tuning up. From somewhere in the distance, a low drone grew louder, and the band leader lifted his baton, the band striking up.

"Oh!" said Rose. "That's the Dambusters, isn't it."

She looked up, shading her eyes, and watched as a group of planes approached in perfect formation, their silhouettes unmistakeable, the roundels on their wings bright.

"Fantastic," said David, his voice full of emotion.

"Are you OK?" asked Rose, touching his arm.

"I should have said, Dad was in the Air Force before he retired," David replied. "So this has always meant a lot to me."

Rose rested her head on his shoulder and they continued to watch. As the planes passed overhead, something streamed from the back of the lead aircraft, drifting gently down to the ground.

"What's that?" wondered Rose aloud. She spotted the girls coming towards them, clutching something in their hands.

"Look, poppies," Lily said, holding out her palm to show the crimson petals.

David nodded. "For remembrance. That's partly why your name, Pops."

Now it was Poppy's turn to hold back tears as the aircraft drew slowly out of sight.

The tannoy crackled back into life. "We hope you enjoyed the fly-past. Next there's something quite different. One of our exhibitors has very kindly agreed to offer a lucky few visitors the chance to be a passenger in their vintage biplane. I'm afraid this is for over-eighteens only, but for the kids we have the flight simulator near the refreshment tent."

David glanced at Rose, his eyes twinkling. "Want to give it a try?"

She took a deep breath. "Yes, please – I think."

They walked toward the airstrip, and Lily pointed. "Look, there."

"It's awfully small," said Rose.

The pilot, marked out by his flying suit and goggles, walked over to them. "Any takers?"

Rose stepped forward nervously. "Please."

"Great. Captain Jim Richards at your service, ma'am."

He stuck out his hand for Rose to shake. "Didn't you arrive in the yellow Rolls?"

She nodded, glancing at David.

"Well, then, we share a decade — my kite was built in the nineteen-thirties too."

"What is it?" Rose asked, glancing at the fragile-looking aircraft.

"Best biplane ever built," he grinned. "The de Havilland Tiger Moth at your service."

He handed her a flying helmet and goggles. "You'll need these — and there's an intercom built in, just plug this into the dash when you're in."

Rose pulled on the helmet, and David chuckled. "Wish I'd brought the camera."

Poppy fished in her bag. "My phone takes pretty good pictures." She held it up, and Rose blinked at the flash. "Got it. I'll take some more as you climb in."

Captain Richards took Rose's elbow. "Up these metal steps — take your time."

Soon she was safely strapped in to the rear seat, and Jim Richards took his place in front.

"If you'd like to stand back a little," he called down to David and the girls.

The engine spluttered, then caught, and the propeller began to turn. He opened the throttle, and the plane began to roll forward.

Rose remembered to plug in her intercom, and Jim's voice came through the headphones. "You OK?"

"Fine," she said, her voice less than convincing.

The plane moved faster, the wind rushing past Rose, and her hands gripped the sides of the cockpit involuntarily as the wheels lifted from the tarmac and the plane rocked.

The ground dropped away beneath them, and Jim climbed steadily, then levelled out the controls. "Look, you can see the motorway."

Rose leaned over gingerly, seeing the sun glinting off moving dots on the narrow ribbon. "Wow."

Jim banked the plane, circling round over the airfield, and Rose could just make out a yellow fleck between the landing strip and the road.

"Want a go?" Jim asked.

"What?" said Rose, confused.

"In front of you – the controls. Just rest your hands on them to start with."

Rose placed her palms on the yoke, feeling the vibration of the control surfaces. "OK."

"Now pull back just a little."

As she eased the yoke backwards, she felt the plane climb, the note of the engine changing. She pushed the yoke forward again, and the plane levelled.

"Well done," came Jim's voice. "I'd love to show you a few aerobatics, but I think we'd better get back, see if anyone else would like a jaunt."

He turned the plane, and they started to descend. "You know what the pilot's motto is?" he asked.

"Noo," said Rose slowly.

"Always let the number of landings equal the number of takeoffs."

The plane seemed to fall like a lift, and Rose swallowed, hoping her stomach could cope. Finally the front wheels touched down, and Jim Richards glanced over the side of the plane, slowing the propeller and letting the tail drop as they slowed to a stop.

He climbed out, and brought the metal steps. Rose eased out of the cockpit and climbed down, the ground somehow seeming less than steady.

She saw David and the girls approaching. "Well done," he said, hugging her.

He turned to Captain Richards. "Thank you so much – do come by and take a look at the car later if you have time."

They walked back towards the refreshment tent. "Anybody hungry yet?" asked David.

Rose nodded. "Good job we didn't have lunch before I went up, though."

David glanced around. "Look, there's a snack van. Burgers, or hot dogs?"

"I'd like a hot dog," said Lily. "Me too," chipped in Poppy.

"Rose?"

"A burger for me, please. With a slice of cheese?"

David went to the van to buy their food, then they made their way back to the car. Rose spread out the picnic blanket, and they sat down to eat.

"Can we go and look round again?" asked Lily when they'd finished. "Maybe we can get a turn in the flight simulator."

The two girls went off hand in hand, chattering animatedly, and David stretched out on the blanket. "This was a good idea."

Rose nodded. "Oh, look, here comes that chap who was on the gate this morning."

David sat up again. "Hi, can we help?"

"I just thought I'd let you know that the judging committee will be along in a minute. You don't have to do anything special, just stand by the car and answer any questions they have."

David got to his feet, helping Rose up. "Thanks."

A small group of blazer-clad officials were making their way along the row of vehicles, pausing occasionally to talk with their owners. When they reached the Rolls, the leader glanced at the list, then up at David. "I'm Andrew Johnson, the chairman of the committee. You're a newcomer, aren't you, Mr Stuart?"

David nodded. "Bit of an accident that we entered, to be honest – we just came for a day out."

The chairman nodded. "Well, we're very impressed with your car. Please, if you're not rushing off elsewhere we'd really like you to stay for the judging – we'll be announcing the prizes at four o'clock."

"Of course," said David. "That's very thoughtful of you."

They moved on, and Rose grinned at David. "Do you think that means we'll win something?"

He thought for a moment. "Not sure. I wouldn't want the established competitors to feel as though we'd barged in."

He glanced at his watch. "That gives us about an hour – do you want to walk round, see what else there is?"

They strolled around the site slowly, looking at the various displays and the aircraft on the ground. As they reached the far end, the tannoy came to life again. "Ladies and gentlemen, it's time for our next fly-past. We're privileged to have another piece of history, accompanied by some planes that are very much up-to-date."

David leaned back on the fence, and Rose rested against him, looking upwards. This time the note of the engines was very different, and Rose gasped as a huge delta-winged aircraft thundered low over their heads, followed by two smaller, futuristic-looking planes.

As they disappeared from view, David wrapped his arms round Rose's waist. "I'm glad we don't need the Vulcans any more."

She folded her arms over his. "Why, what were they?"

"Those were our nuclear first-strike aircraft, back at the height of the Cold War," explained David.

Rose felt a brief chill despite the warm sun. "And the smaller ones?"

"F22's – American stealth fighters."

Rose nodded. She turned in David's arms, tilting her face up for him to kiss her. "Shall we get back to the car? It's nearly four."

When they reached the car, Poppy and Lily were waiting for them.

"Did you have fun?" asked Rose.

Lily nodded. "I nearly managed to land at Paris, but I crashed."

"You shouldn't have picked a jumbo jet, silly," said Poppy. "I actually got the Cessna down without it blowing up."

David grinned. "Obviously you take after Dad."

"Here come the judges," pointed Rose.

A small crowd gathered round the committee, and Andrew Johnson stepped forward.

"I have to say in introduction that the standard this year has been exceptionally high," he began. "We're particularly pleased to see the American marques so well represented – Mr Wood, I'm delighted to say that we've awarded first prize in that class to your Chrysler."

There was scattered applause as he affixed the rosette to the curved bonnet.

"As for the British entries, I have to say we found ourselves with a dilemma. As most of you will know, Bill Symcox has been showing his three-litre Crossley – now absolutely unique – for many years, and even though he's made a stunning job of the restoration, somehow he's always been pipped to first prize by another entrant.

"Bill tells me it's his last year showing – he and his wife are moving to Australia to live with their daughter. So after much deliberation, the committee have decided to honour Bill with a special lifetime achievement award."

The applause was louder this time, and a white-haired man stepped forward to shake Andrew Johnson's hand, taking the rosette.

"So," the chairman continued, "that left us free to award first prize in the British category to our dark horse entrant – David Stuart and his yellow Rolls-Royce roadster."

David stood rooted to the spot, and Rose poked him gently. "Go on."

He stepped forward, turning to face the small group of car owners. He cleared his throat. "I don't know what to say. The car was a personal project, I never even thought about showing it. But thank you so much for letting us take part."

He beckoned to Rose and the girls. "I can't leave my co-pilot out, and the girls really helped too."

They joined him, and he put his hands on the girls' shoulders while Rose slid her arm round his waist.

"Congratulations," said the chairman, handing David the rosette.

Bill Symcox was the first to start the applause, and he shook David's hand. "I hope you'll bring her back next year."

David looked confused, and the older man chuckled. "The car – they're always 'she', you know."

David grinned. "I'll give it some serious thought. And I hope Australia really suits you."

Bill nodded, and turned back to the small group of admirers gathered round his car.

David glanced at Rose. "Wow, what an amazing day. I don't suppose anything else unusual could happen, eh?"

Rose smiled. "Guess not."

She ruffled the girls' hair. "Come on, you two. I think it's time we got back."

Poppy and Lily climbed into the back seat, Lily clutching the rosette, and David helped Rose up, closing her door.

He slid behind the wheel and started the engine, then pulled slowly forward, conscious of the eyes on them. The car bumped over the grass, and David glanced left and right before pulling back onto the tarmac and accelerating.

As they neared the village, David glanced into the back seat. "Those two are out for the count," he grinned.

"I'm flagging myself, to be honest," said Rose.

David chuckled. "Tell you what, how about I drop you at your place, then take the girls home and put them straight to bed after tea?"

Rose nodded. "What about my car?"

"Easy – I'll meet you at church, then drive you back."

They passed the gates of the house, then carried on into town. David pulled up outside Rose's, and opened her door, helping her down.

Rose glanced at the front window, then kissed him hard on the lips. "So what if Charles is watching?" she said, tossing her head.

David looked back as he pulled away, and Rose waved, then opened the front door. "I'm home."

"Hello, darling," her mother said, coming down the stairs. "You're back early."

Rose grinned. "We wore the girls out, I think David's going to give them some tea, then send them straight to bed. I'm pretty wiped myself."

"Would you like a sandwich, dear?"

"That'd be lovely, Mum. Are Charles and Paul about?"

Her mother shook her head. "Some Chamber of Commerce dinner."

They went into the kitchen, and Rose sat down at the table while her mother busied herself at the worktop.

"I met David's parents last week, sort of," she said. "Poppy's laptop has a camera and we talked."

Her mother nodded. "I'm glad – they're such a long way away."

She put Rose's sandwich on the table. "Your favourite ham, and plenty of that wholegrain mustard."

When Rose had finished eating, she said, "Thanks, Mum. Think I'll go up to bed now."

"Are you meeting David for church?"

Rose nodded. "Then we're at his for lunch – is that OK?"

"Of course, dear."

Rose climbed the stairs, and changed for bed. She sat for a while leafing through her volume of Blake, feeling her eyelids starting to droop.

She put her book down, and pulled the covers over her, reaching for the light switch. "The tygers of wrath are wiser than the horses of instruction," she murmured to herself, as her eyes closed.

***

When Rose woke the next morning, she stretched luxuriously, feeling refreshed. She showered, then went downstairs to the kitchen.

"Morning, dear," her mother said. "What would you like for breakfast?"

"I'll just get some cereal, thanks, Mum."

After breakfast, Rose decided to walk down to the church early, and she was sitting on a bench in the churchyard when David's car pulled into the car park. Lily and Poppy got out, and David followed them up the path.

Rose walked to meet them. "You two feeling a bit more with it?"

"You bet," grinned Lily, and she and Poppy headed for the church, holding hands.

David hugged Rose. "You OK?"

"Definitely. Mum and I had a good chat."

She glanced at the church clock. "Come on, the service will be starting in a minute."

After church David drove them back to the house. "Gareth offered me a special treat when I went round to get the meat – a joint of venison. I remembered you said you liked it, so that's lunch today."

Rose smiled. "Fantastic."

They sat down to lunch, and this time Lily said grace. "Thank you for the food we eat, thank you for the world so sweet, thank you for the birds that sing, thank you God for everything. Amen."

She opened her eyes. "Oo, cranberry sauce," she grinned, reaching for the dish.

Dessert was chocolate ice cream, then David said, "OK, girls, I think it's mine and Rose's turn to wash up – why don't you go and make the most of the sunshine?"

"We can go to the tree house," grinned Poppy. "I printed out some of the pictures from yesterday, we're going to put them up in there."

They put their dishes in the sink and went up the stairs, clattering down a moment later with a sheaf of photos. "We think this is the best one," said Poppy, putting a picture on the table, then following Lily out of the door.

David picked up the photo. "She's really caught the moment," he said, holding it out for Rose to see.

"Hmm, I do have a bit of an Amelia Earhart thing going on there, don't I," she grinned.

She took the photo. "Can I borrow your pen?"

David stepped out into the hall, fetching his fountain pen from his jacket pocket. Rose unscrewed the top, and wrote carefully, replacing the top and blowing on the ink to dry it. "There."

David took the picture, reading the flowing inscription. "For David, with all my love, Rose. 'On what wings dare he aspire?'"

"Blake again," he smiled, propping the photo carefully on a shelf in front of a row of cookbooks, then turning to kiss Rose.

He rolled his sleeves up. "Right. I'll wash and you dry?"

They worked steadily, the pile of washing-up quickly diminishing.

"Oh, here's another spoon, sorry," said Rose, dropping it into the sink with a splash.

She giggled. "Oops – you have bubbles on you..."

"So do you," said David, scooping up a handful of foam and blowing into his palm, sending a spray of bubbles in Rose's direction.

"Oho!" said Rose. "So that's how it is, is it?"

She dipped her hand in the sink and flicked a shower of droplets over David, then squealed and ducked as he scooped up a whole handful of water and sent it towards her, splashing her blouse.

She reached for a glass, moving to fill it from the sink, and David wrapped his arms around her to stop her. She struggled for a second, then suddenly stilled, looking up into his face, breathing rapidly. "You win."

He bent down and kissed her on the lips, gently at first. Her eyes widened, then she put her hand behind his head, pulling him closer.

David moved back, loosening his grip. "Sorry, Rose."

She shook her head. "I'm fine. But that was fun, wasn't it." She quickly reached for the glass, and dumped the contents over his head. "Got you!"

He held out his hands, palms up in surrender. "You win."

Just then the girls came back in. "It's going dark, and Poppy's torch battery has run out," said Lily.

She looked at them. "What have you two been up to?"

"Nothing," said Rose, innocently.

Poppy smiled. "Right."

She glanced at the shelf where the photo stood. "Oh, I love the inscription, Rose."

"Shall I make us a drink?" asked David.

"Mm, please," said Rose. "We still have some of those hot chocolate sticks, don't we?"

They sat sipping their hot chocolate, then Rose said reluctantly, "We should be getting back, Lily."

"OK," Lily said. "Can you give me a lift over on Wednesday? Poppy's invited Alice for tea."

"Sure, angel."

David and Poppy walked with them to the car, and David said, "I'll call you tomorrow, Rose – maybe another evening I can drop Poppy at yours and just the two of us can go out for pizza or something."

He kissed Rose, then hugged Lily, and stepped back. "Take care."

***

The next morning, Rose went into the office, busying herself with invoices as usual. She heard footsteps in the corridor, and Charles and Paul came in.

"Oh, hi, Rose," said Paul. Charles just nodded curtly.

The two went into Paul's office, and Charles pushed the door closed behind them, not stopping to make sure that the catch engaged. The door opened a crack, and Rose wrestled with her conscience for a moment before walking quietly over and standing outside.

"David didn't sign," she heard Paul's voice. "I think you've lost this one, Charles – I've already made out the draft for the dividend."

"Don't be stupid," Charles replied. "I'm not going to let this go. Call him in for another meeting, I'll deal with him this time. I'll tell him we'll return his original investment with interest at base rate. If he won't accept, we'll see him in court – I'm sure our legal team can find a loophole in the contract somewhere."

"I–" began Paul, but Charles must have made some gesture, cutting him off.

Charles's heavy steps came toward the door, and Rose hastily retreated, sitting down at her desk just as he emerged.

Rose's thoughts whirled as she considered options. She reached for her phone, then stopped as an idea occurred to her.

She worked steadily for the rest of the day, stopping only to grab a sandwich from the restaurant. As the hands of the clock passed six, Beth came in. "Still here?"

"Just a couple of things to finish off."

Beth smiled. "OK – the security guard's here, anyway."

Rose watched her go, then walked into Paul's office, searching on his desk for the document she was certain would be there.

She picked up the draft, and sat down slowly in Paul's chair as she read the figure, nearly twice David's estimate.

She hesitated briefly, then switched on Paul's computer, logging in and starting the invoicing program.

"Lewis's, Lewis's," she muttered, searching through the payee list. "There."

She keyed in the figure, double-checking it, then clicked the icon to run the process.

A window opened requesting the authorisation key, and Rose got up from the desk, walking over to the safe. She turned the dials, opening the heavy door, and took out a plastic wallet, returning to the desk.

She tapped the code into the small electronic device, then carefully transferred the sequence of digits from the display to the computer.

There was a click, and she heard the familiar tones of the modem dialling the bank, then the hiss of the negotiation. The modem fell silent, and a progress bar moved quickly across the screen.

The printer in the corner whirred, and Rose retrieved the single sheet, checking the confirmation code.

She took a deep breath, then picked up the draft again, tearing it into tiny pieces and dropping them in the confidential waste bin.

Carefully she closed down the computer, then shut the safe and spun the dials.

She folded the printout, slipping it inside her jacket, and left Paul's office, switching the light off and closing the door.

As she passed the security guard, she nodded. "All done – have a peaceful night, Sam."

When she got home, she leaned into the kitchen. "Hi, Mum. Sorry I'm so late – something came up at the office."

"That's all right, dear. I saved you some soup, and there's home-made bread."

Rose pushed down the surge of emotion she felt. "Thanks, Mum, you're the best."

She forced herself to eat, then went upstairs, finding Lily in their bedroom reading, already in her pyjamas. Lily looked up. "Rose? Are you OK? You look as white as a sheet."

Rose nodded. "I'm fine – just a long day. Do you mind if I just go to sleep?"

"No problem."

Rose got changed, and pulled the covers over her, wishing she could talk to Lily, wrestling with whether she should call David. But for no reason she could explain, she resolved to let David hear Charles's proposal from her brother's own mouth.

Lily closed her book. "OK, I'm ready to sleep now too."

She put out the light, and slid in beside Rose. She snuggled up close to Rose's back, and Rose drew comfort from the contact. "Night, Lily. Love you."

"Love you too," came the sleepy answer.

***

When Rose arrived at the office the next morning, Beth greeted her with her usual warm smile.

"Charles asked me to set up an urgent meeting with David," she said, "so perhaps he'll take you for lunch."

Rose nodded. "I had an idea Charles had something to discuss with him."

She walked over to one of the sofas and sat down, trying not to betray her nerves. Beth picked up the phone, speaking for a short while, then ended the call.

Charles walked in. "Have you set that meeting up, Beth?"

"Mr Stuart will be here at ten," Rose heard Beth's reply.

Charles turned. "What are you doing there, Rose? Never mind. I need you in my meeting with David when he gets here."

Rose watched the clock, and as the time approached ten David came through the door. He signed in, then turned, seeing Rose.

"Hi, darling," he said, kissing her. "Charles seemed in a hurry to see me."

She returned his kiss. "Let's go in, shall we."

Charles was waiting for them in the conference room. "Ah, David. Take a seat."

He glanced at his sister, then back to David. "This is going to be a difficult meeting, but I thought Rose ought to be here."

"Go ahead," said David.

Charles crossed his arms. "I'm sure by now you have an idea of the value of the quarterly dividend. I need to tell you that I have no intention of paying that figure. Just because Paul and I managed to secure some very valuable contracts, we don't see why you should benefit to that extent from something you did nothing to achieve."

Rose was tempted to break in, all the arguments bubbling up in her brain – how would you have secured those contracts without the production capacity David's money paid for, you wrote the terms of the contract yourself, Paul was prepared to stick to the agreement. But she held her tongue.

David raised his eyebrows. "I see. So what do you propose?"

"We made you a reasonable offer – a dividend based on the average value – but you weren't smart enough to take it."

Rose wondered why the edge of the table didn't crack under her grip, as her brother continued.

"So here's the deal. We return your original investment – I'm prepared to add base rate interest. Take it or leave it, or we see you in court. I'm sure that contract could be broken if we get our legal team on it."

Rose was absolutely certain that she'd never seen anger in David's eyes, but it burned there now.

She held her breath as David sat straighter in his chair. "I won't argue. Make out a draft. I want it before I leave, and a written guarantee that you'll meet the production schedules we've already agreed, until we can find another supplier who can meet our specifications. It's a pity, because the work you've done for us is exceptional."

"And this stays between us," said Charles, trying to regain the initiative.

"Certainly," said David. "Though it'll be difficult to explain why Lewis's won't give you any more business, given your reputation for quality and a competitive price."

Rose wanted to scream at her brother – Don't you see what you're doing, if you would work with David instead of against him you could achieve so much more.

Charles nodded curtly. He started to get up. "I'll write out the draft."

Finally Rose spoke. "That won't be necessary."

David turned to look at her, and her heart sang as she saw not the slightest hint of a question in his face, only complete trust, and acceptance that she must have something important to say.

Charles sat down again, his face showing utter confusion. "What do you mean, Rose?"

"What you owe David —" she emphasised the word — "is already in Lewis's bank account. I transferred it last night."

She looked directly at Charles, her eyes flashing. "Don't worry, I tore up the draft, so there'll be no mistakes."

His mouth worked. "You… you…"

"You didn't think I'd go against you? You assumed I'd blindly stick with the family, even when what you've done is so appalling?"

"I don't believe you," Charles ground out.

Rose pulled the printout from her pocket. "Here."

He scanned the sheet rapidly, then reached for the conference room phone. "I can still have that transaction reversed."

Rose put her hand on the phone, holding the receiver in its cradle. "David may have promised to keep this between the two of you, but I haven't. If you make that call, I'll make sure everyone knows what you did. What do you think will happen to your share price then? And your new contracts?"

Charles's eyes bulged, and for a moment Rose thought he was about to have some kind of seizure. But he got up from the table. "Very well. But you have to live with the consequences."

He left the conference room, slamming the door behind him.

Faster than Rose had ever seen him move, David was beside her, his arms encircling her. For long moments he didn't speak, and Rose closed her eyes, leaning back, somehow drawing strength from his touch, her racing heart slowing.

Finally David spoke. "Rose, you didn't have to do that for me. It's only money, and they're your family."

She shook her head. "I couldn't let Charles do that. It was wrong. And he thought he could do what he wanted to you. I'd never have been able to live with myself if I'd said nothing."

She squeezed his hands, then got up from her chair. "I need to go home."

David nodded. "Call me – whatever time, I'll be there."

Rose got in her car and drove home. She opened the front door, and stopped dead. Lily was struggling down the stairs with a suitcase, her cheeks wet with tears. "Oh, Rose," she sobbed, throwing herself into her sister's arms.

Rose stroked her hair. "Lily, darling, what are you doing?"

Lily could hardly get the words out. "P-P-Paul rang Mum from the office. She took the phone into her bedroom, but I saw the look on her face as she went up the stairs and I picked up the other phone down here. Paul told Mum –"

She choked again, and something snapped inside Rose. "Come on, angel," she said, putting her hand gently under Lily's chin and lifting her head.

She took the suitcase in one hand, her other arm round Lily's shoulders, and guided her sister to the car. She pushed the case into the back seat, made sure Lily's seatbelt was fastened, and got behind the wheel, starting the engine and pulling away.

When they reached the gates at the bottom of David's drive, Rose glanced at Lily. "Everything's going to be OK."

She turned into the drive, stopping the car just short of the front door, and helped Lily out. Ignoring the suitcase, they walked to the door, and Rose fished out the key David had given her.

She opened the door, and Poppy came out of the living room, followed by David. Poppy looked at Lily's face and gasped. "What's happened?"

Lily shook her head wordlessly, and Poppy stepped forward to do the only thing she could think of, enfolding Lily in her arms.

David looked at Rose. "Have you—"

She nodded, walking into his outstretched arms. "Oh, David."

"Come and sit down, I'll make us some hot chocolate."

They went into the kitchen, Lily clinging to Poppy's hand. David quickly heated milk, putting steaming mugs in front of them.

Rose sipped at the froth on top of her mug. "That's better."

Her phone rang and she fished it out of her bag, walking out into the hall. She heard Paul's voice at the other end of the line. "Rose? Are you at David's, is Lily with you?"

"Yes."

She heard him sigh with relief. "We didn't know what had happened."

Charles cut in, obviously having taken the phone from Paul. "You get straight back here, you hear me? And what's Lily doing over there?"

Rose tried to keep her anger under control. "Lily overheard Paul telling Mum what had happened. When I got home, she was beside herself."

Her voice was dangerously calm. "Whatever it is you've got against David, I can live with, but I'm not going to let you hurt Lily."

Charles hesitated. "Rose, I – listen, we could pay you a proper salary. Hell, I'll make you a partner, profit share in the company, the whole thing. But give this up?"

For a moment Rose stood, stunned into silence. Then she replied, her voice even lower than before, every syllable like a shard of glass. "Charles. I told you. I love David. When you have the slightest idea what that means, perhaps we can talk."

She switched off the phone and went back into the kitchen, taking her place.

David reached out and put his hand on hers, not speaking. She met his gaze. "It's finished."

Lily spoke for the first time since they'd left the house. "We're not going home?"

Rose shook her head. She turned to David. "Where are we sleeping?"

For a moment his eyes widened, then he nodded. "Lily, you'll go with Pops, won't you?"

"Come on," said Poppy, getting up and drawing Lily gently to her feet. The two went upstairs, disappearing into Poppy's room and closing the door.

David turned to Rose. "I'll go in the guest room, and you can have my bed."

He grinned. "I wouldn't inflict the guest room wallpaper on anyone."

Rose nodded. "David?"

"Mm?"

"Thanks for all this – I don't want you to think I'm taking you for granted."

He shook his head. "Rose, I love you. That means whatever it takes. I know in the scheme of things it hasn't been that long, but I can't imagine life without you now."

He got up from his chair. "Don't move."

"Where would I go?" Rose said, her voice matter-of-fact.

David went out into the hall, returning a few moments later. "This isn't how I imagined it would be," he said, "but..."

He took his hand from the pocket of his jacket, holding it out palm upwards. "Rose, will you marry me?"

In his palm lay a ring, a circle of tiny diamonds glittering in the light, in their centre a sapphire the colour of a mountain lake under a perfect blue sky.

Rose glanced at the ring, then lifted her eyes to meet David's, for the first time seeing in them something less than total confidence, knowing that he was truly giving her the freedom to choose.

She took a deep breath. "Yes, David." As she spoke, she saw his assurance return, and knew without the shadow of a doubt that she was his.

As he slipped the ring onto her finger, she heard a rustle from up the stairs, and a whispered "Yay!"

"Come on, you two," David chuckled. "How long have you been listening?"

Lily looked over the banisters, Poppy beside her. "We heard you come out into the hall."

The girls came down the stairs, standing in the doorway. "I got my wish," grinned Poppy. "I said I wanted to be there when you asked her."

David went over to the wooden wine rack in the corner of the kitchen. "I think this deserves something special."

He took a bottle from the rack, unwrapping the foil from the top then starting to loosen the wire holding the cork. "Pops, could you get us some glasses? The tall ones on the shelf."

The cork shot from the bottle, ending up in the hall, and David poured for them, letting the bubbles settle then topping up the glasses.

Lily took a sip, then sneezed twice in quick succession. "That always happens to me," she grinned.

David looked at the clock. "Is anyone hungry?"

Rose glanced at Lily. "I don't feel like eating, but I think we need to."

"I'll do us beans on toast," said David. "And I think we have some of those little sausages too."

He lit the grill, then started opening tins. A few minutes later, he brought plates to the table. "Tuck in."

Lily took a mouthful. "This is good."

When they'd cleared the lunch things away, David said, "Rose, I think I should go back into the office, just for a couple of hours. At the very least I need to explain about the bank transfer."

He glanced at her. "Will you be OK?"

"We'll look after her," said Poppy. "Won't we, Lily?"

Lily nodded. "We can go up in the tree house and show you all the pictures we put up."

David grinned. "I think you're in safe hands."

He got up from the table. "I'll see you in a while... my love."

Rose submitted to being pulled towards the tree house by both hands. "The ladder isn't as hard as it looks," assured Poppy.

"OK," said Rose, setting her foot gingerly on the first rung. Finally she stepped into the tree house. "Wow, you've really made it nice up here."

"We brought some squash, and a big bottle of water," Poppy said. "Shall I make us some?"

"That'd be lovely," said Rose. She took the paper cup Poppy held out. "You want to know a secret?"

The girls glanced at each other, grinning. "Yes please."

"I'm not all that keen on champagne – I prefer squash, or that fruit juice we had the other day."

She looked out of the opening that served as a window. "Now, when David comes back, we can play that game you told me about, where we pretend we turn him into something when he comes looking for us."

"A donkey!" Lily said, giggling.

"Or a tiger," suggested Poppy. "He couldn't climb up and eat us, could he?"

Rose smiled. "I thought I was the tiger."

"A lion, then," said Poppy firmly.

Rose was glad of the distraction as they continued their make-believe, and she was surprised how quickly the time had gone when they heard David calling. "You three still up there?"

"Now," whispered Poppy.

Lily leaned carefully on the window ledge and opened her hand. A shower of glittering flecks drifted down, catching the late afternoon sun.

"Now you're a lion," she said dramatically.

David looked up, smiling. "Grr!" he said. "I'm coming to eat you!"

Lily and Poppy pantomimed dismay as David climbed the ladder, growling, then squealed with delight as he cornered them, pretending to gobble them up.

"I'm still hungry," he said in a low voice, rich with laughter.

Rose backed against the wall, her burning eyes meeting his. He trapped her, his hands either side of her shoulders, and as he kissed her, she slid her arms around his waist. "I think you've eaten me all up," she murmured.

David released her, glancing at the girls. "That was a fantastic game – bet you didn't know lions could climb, though."

He grinned. "Now, talking of eating – I brought fried chicken back with me, it's keeping warm in the oven."

"Yay!" chorused the girls, scrambling down the ladder.

Rose looked apprehensively after them. "I'm not sure it's as easy going down as it was coming up."

"I'll go first," volunteered David. "That way I'll break your fall if you do slip."

They reached the ground without mishap, and walked back to the house. Poppy and Lily had already found plates, and David took their food out of the oven.

"Chips too," grinned Lily. "Is there any ketchup?"

They ate with their fingers, licking off the crumbs from the coating. "Thanks, David," said Rose. "We didn't really think about cooking."

"We'll wash up," said Poppy.

"Thanks, Pops," said David. "And then I think it's bedtime for you two – you can read for a while, if you like."

"OK."

The girls made short work of clearing up, then went upstairs. "Can I have my suitcase?" Lily called.

"I'll get it," replied David. Rose handed him the key to her car, and he fetched Lily's case, taking it up to their room.

When he came down, Rose was waiting for him on the sofa. She smiled as he sat down beside her. "Wasn't it a little early to send the girls up to bed?"

David nodded. "But I wanted us to have a chance to talk. Unless you're not feeling up to it? I know a lot's happened today."

"No, I'm fine," said Rose. "You're right, we need to think things through."

"Would you like a drink?" asked David.

Rose nodded. "Have you got any liqueurs? I really like the coffee one."

David grinned. "Your wish is my command."

He opened the drinks cabinet, taking out a dark bottle. "Just the thing."

Rose took a sip from her glass. "So where shall we start?"

"I'm thinking about Lily," said David. "She did really well in her exams, didn't she?"

"Definitely – that revision we did together at half-term really paid off."

"I know the principal at Poppy's school quite well," David mused. "Do you think it would make things easier for Lily if she could move?"

Rose thought for a moment. "I don't think she's made any really close friends where she is. That sounds like a really good idea. Let's ask her tomorrow what she thinks, and if she likes the sound of it, you can talk to the school."

"OK."

David paused. "The next thing I thought we could talk about was, well, the wedding."

Rose looked at the ring sparkling on her finger. "I'm still getting used to the idea."

She leaned over to kiss him. "I know you'd probably have preferred things to be different, but I'm so glad you asked me today."

He smiled. "Me too. I assumed you'd want Poppy and Lily to be bridesmaids, so…"

Rose nodded. "I thought we could ask Alice, too."

"So maybe it would work out best if we had the wedding before they all went back to school?" David suggested.

Rose blinked. "That's really not far away," she said, counting on her fingers.

She looked up. "But you're right – why wait?"

The smile on David's face reminded her of a little boy finding out he'd been promised a treat. "Fantastic."

He looked thoughtful. "So we'd better tell Reverend Wood before Sunday to start reading the banns."

"It sounds so simple when you put it that way," chuckled Rose.

"The big decisions are the easiest," David said confidently.

Rose's mind filled with a million things to do, to arrange, but she pushed them down. "Settled, then. What's next?"

David paused. "I was saving this one. When I went into the office this afternoon, the MD was waiting for me. He'd already heard from the Finance Director about the dividend on our investment in Middleton's, and he called me into his office."

"Was there a problem?" asked Rose apprehensively.

David shook his head. "Not at all. He was so pleased with the outcome that he offered me a partnership in the business. That's very unusual – generally you have to have been with the firm at least ten years."

He grinned. "And he gave me a sizeable bonus too. We'll definitely be flying first class for our honeymoon."

Rose raised her eyebrows. "Have you already decided where we're going?"

"I thought about keeping it a surprise," David replied, "but with all the practical arrangements – visas, inoculations, the pills you'll have to take – it wouldn't really be possible."

He paused. "Would you be OK if we went to India – we can see my parents, but we'd definitely have most of the time to ourselves."

Rose wrapped her arms around him. "That would be brilliant!"

She hesitated. "Do we have to decide about the partnership straight away?"

David shook his head. "We have plenty of time to make a decision."

"I'm just not sure about the commitment," said Rose. "Let's leave it till we get back?"

"Of course," David nodded.

Rose suppressed a yawn. "Sorry – I think things are catching up with me."

David smiled. "I think we've sorted the really important things."

He got up from the sofa. "I just need a couple of things from my room, then it's all yours."

They went up the stairs into David's bedroom, and Rose looked around. "I'm not sure what I imagined, but…"

On one wall was a large pinboard, with family photos side by side with hand-drawn sketches. Rose walked up to the board, looking more closely.

"The sketches are Poppy's," said David. "She's always been quite good."

"This one's me," said Rose, a note of surprise in her voice.

David nodded. "She did it for my birthday – she was just a little shy about me showing it to you."

He opened a drawer, taking out a small pile of clothes. "Right, I think that's everything I need."

Rose hesitated. "David – I didn't have time to pack anything when I came. I can use Lily's toothbrush, but… Can I borrow something to wear for bed?"

David stopped. "Sorry, Rose, I didn't even think. Of course – let me take a look."

He flicked through hangers in his wardrobe. "Here, this should do."

Rose took the long t-shirt he held out. "Perfect."

She put the t-shirt on the bed. "Goodnight, then, my love."

David wrapped his arms around her. "If there's anything you need, I'm only along the hall."

He bent to kiss her. "Sleep well."

He slipped out, closing the door behind him, and Rose was alone. She quickly undressed, pulling David's t-shirt over her head, and went across the hall to the bathroom. She cleaned her teeth, and looked in the mirror, somehow finding it hard to believe that she looked the same after so much had happened.

She returned to the bedroom, getting into bed and reaching over to turn out the light.

As she laid her head down, she caught a hint of David's aftershave from the pillow. She pulled the covers over her, and curled up, the cotton of his t-shirt soft against her skin. Her last thought as she drifted off was that there was only one way now she could be any closer to him…

***

When David came in the next morning he was already in his suit, his briefcase in his hand. "Morning, darling. I'm off to work now, but call me if you need anything, or if you want to talk. I heard the girls moving around, but they're not down yet."

He walked over to the bed, bending down to kiss her. "See you later, Sleeping Beauty."

Rose listened to the sound of David's car fading as he turned at the bottom of the drive, then stretched luxuriously, looking round the room again in the morning light.

She heard footsteps in the hall, and there was a tap at the door. "Rose?"

"Come in, Pops, it's OK."

Poppy opened the door and came in. "Lily's just making coffee. Did you sleep all right?"

Rose nodded. "Thanks, Pops."

She paused. "How's Lily?"

"I think she's OK," Poppy said.

She glanced at Rose. "We talked till quite late."

"That's fine," Rose reassured. "I'm really grateful you're here to help her."

She pulled back the covers and swung her legs out of bed. "Coffee sounds good."

"Is that David's t-shirt?" grinned Poppy.

Rose nodded. "I feel like a bit of a refugee."

She thought for a moment. "It's not going to be easy, but I need to take a trip back to Mum's, get some of my stuff."

"Do you want me to come?" asked Poppy.

Rose shook her head. "I'd rather you stayed with Lily."

She stood up. "Anyway, that can wait till after breakfast."

They went down to the kitchen, and Lily hugged her sister. "Look, I made espresso, just the way you like it."

Rose sipped the dark liquid. "Thanks, Lily, it's perfect."

Poppy fetched bowls and cereal. "Here's that one you like, Lily."

Lily poured on milk, listening to the crackling from the bowl then starting to eat. "Mm, great."

"So, you two, David and I were talking last night–" began Rose.

"We think it's so cool," interrupted Lily. Poppy nodded, grinning.

"– and we have some things to tell you."

Rose looked at Lily. "We wondered if you'd like it if you could join Poppy at school next term."

She held up her hand. "*If* it's possible – David would have to talk to the principal."

The two girls turned to look at each other. "I'd have to catch up," said Lily. "You'll have been doing different lessons."

"I'll help you," promised Poppy.

"And we talked about the wedding," Rose continued. "You two are bridesmaids, of course, and I thought you might like to ask Alice."

She saved the biggest surprise till last. "We're arranging it so we can get married before you go back to school."

"Wow," said Poppy. "That's soon. And you have to get a dress, and everything."

"Well," grinned Rose, "you two can help me with that – there's a bridal shop in town."

"You wait," said Lily. "We'll find you the most romantic dress *ever*."

Rose put down her spoon, and took a deep breath. "Right. I'd better get dressed and go over to Mum's, get some stuff."

Lily's expression became troubled. "You'll tell her I'm OK, right?"

"Of course, darling. And I'm sure we can go over there and see her very soon."

Rose held back from mentioning her brothers, pushing away the problem of how – if? – she could achieve some kind of reconciliation.

She left the girls finishing their breakfast, and went upstairs, pulling on her clothes.

"I'll be back before lunch," she reassured Lily as she went out of the door.

When she reached the house, she was relieved to see no sign of Charles's car. She opened the front door, and her mother came out of the kitchen. "Oh, thank goodness," she said. "Are you both all right?"

"We're fine, Mum."

Rose hesitated, then lifted her hand so that her mother could see her ring. "David and I are getting married."

Her mother nodded. "I know I didn't say very much before, but I trust David. I'm not surprised it was the first thing he did."

She hugged Rose. "Congratulations, darling. And you're staying over there till then?"

Rose nodded. "I think it's better for Lily – she gets on so well with Poppy. And with David."

She paused. "We suggested to Lily that she join Poppy at her school next term."

"I don't see a problem with that," her mother nodded.

She looked thoughtfully at Rose. "Have you set a date for the wedding?"

"Before the girls go back to school – so I suppose it'll be the last weekend in August."

Her mother smiled. "I'd better start looking for a dress – and a hat."

Rose nodded. "Well, I need to pack up some stuff."

She went up the stairs and pulled her suitcase from the top of the wardrobe, laying it on the bed. She opened drawers, and transferred clothes into the case, then folded dresses and lay them on top.

She looked round the room, deciding that everything else could wait. She closed the case, and carried it downstairs to the hall.

"Don't forget your laptop, darling," her mother called.

Rose went into the lounge, picking up her laptop bag and slinging the strap over her shoulder. "OK, Mum, I think I've got what I need."

She hugged her mother. "I'll probably see you at the weekend – I'll call first."

When she reached David's, the girls came out of the house at the sound of the car. "Can we help you unpack?" asked Poppy. "I put some more of David's stuff in the spare room, so there's space for your things."

"Poor David," said Rose, "he'll feel like a guest in his own house."

She carried her case up the stairs, and opened it on the bed. "Wow," said Poppy, "you have some lovely dresses."

She carefully unfolded them, hanging them in the wardrobe next to David's other suits.

When everything was put away, they went back downstairs. "Are you hungry yet?" asked Rose.

Lily nodded. "Can we have fish fingers?"

"I like to make mine into sandwiches," chipped in Poppy.

"OK," grinned Rose, "if there are any."

They sat at the kitchen table to eat their lunch, Lily facing the window. Suddenly she pointed. "Look, out in the garden."

Poppy turned. "Oh! Aren't they sweet."

On the grass opposite the summer house, two fox cubs rolled playfully together, their russet fur catching the sunlight.

"I wish we could keep one and tame it," said Lily.

Rose smiled. "I think foxes are usually a little wild for that."

The cubs finished their game, and trotted out of sight into the woods. "Maybe we'll see them again," said Rose.

She put down her fork. "Now, let's clear up the kitchen, then you can come and help me make a list of everything we have to do for the wedding."

When David arrived home, they were absorbed in sheets of paper covered with Poppy's handwriting. He picked up one sheet and read. "Flowers – church, car. Flowers – button holes. Bouquet." The last word was underlined.

He smiled. "Have you decided what flowers you want, Rose?"

"I quite like the idea of honeysuckle and clematis."

David nodded. "The scent will be gorgeous."

He glanced at the clock. "Before we get started on dinner, can we talk to my parents? I sent them a text from work, so they'll have the computer on."

"OK," said Poppy. "Let me get the laptop."

They went into the living room, and Poppy brought her computer, putting it on the small table and flipping up the screen.

She tapped keys, and again Rose heard the quiet ringing sound. The screen lit, this time showing an outside scene, David and Poppy's parents sitting on plastic chairs. In the background stood a building with thatched walls, and through a doorway Rose could see a cooking fire.

"What are those?" asked Lily, pointing at something straight and vertical running from top to bottom of the picture.

"Hello, darling," said David's mother. "Those are tree trunks – some of them are betel nuts, and some are coconuts."

She smiled. "It's nice to see you, Lily. Have you come over for the evening?"

David stepped closer to the camera. "Sorry, Mum, there are a couple of things we need to tell you. I thought it'd be easier if we were all here."

His father cut in. "David, what's wrong?"

David shook his head. "We're OK, Dad, don't worry."

He smiled. "First things first – Rose and I are getting married."

"Oh, that's wonderful," said his mother. She turned her head slightly. "Welcome to the family, Rose. And Lily, you too – I'm sure Poppy always secretly wished she had a sister."

"It's not all good news," said David. He outlined the events of the previous day. "So Rose and Lily are over here now."

His father nodded. "Have you decided on a date?"

"Four weeks," David replied. "Three Sundays to have the banns read, then the Saturday after that."

"I think we'll struggle to get back, sorry, darling," said his mother. "You'll have to take lots of video, and post us a disc."

David grinned. "Better than that – we'll bring it. We'll be honeymooning near you, I thought the lodge at Hathipota would be a good place to start."

Rose remembered the journey she'd imagined up into the foothills. "It sounds amazing."

David's father nodded. "Send us your flight times and we'll sort everything out – we'll meet you at the airport, get you across here."

He grinned. "Don't worry, once you're here, we'll stay out of your hair – you can choose when you see us."

"That's great, Dad, thanks so much. I'll let you know."

David glanced at his watch. "Anyway, it's getting pretty late over there – we'll let you go. See you in a few weeks!"

"Bye!" chorused Lily and Poppy.

Poppy ended the connection and closed the laptop, putting it back in its bag.

Lily looked across at Rose. "Wow, India! Wish I was going with you, it sounds awesome."

David smiled. "Tell you what, we'll all go next summer. After all, you'll be starting your A-levels when you go back to school that September."

He paused. "Talking of school, I called Poppy's principal today. He's fine with Lily starting there in September."

"Yay!" said Lily, and the two girls hugged.

"Now," said David, "how about something to eat?"

"I saw some mince in the freezer when I was getting lunch for us," said Rose. "We could make chilli, and you could do some of your special rice for us."

The girls sat at the kitchen table while Rose and David cooked. "You two look so right doing stuff together," said Lily. "Anyone would think you'd been together for years."

David piled rice onto plates and brought them to the table while Rose put the chilli into a serving bowl. "Dig in."

"Mm, it's great," said Poppy. "Just spicy enough."

"Do you two want to go and do your own thing?" asked David when they'd finished eating.

Poppy glanced at Lily. "We could take the laptop upstairs, I'll introduce you to some of my school friends – we're all on Facebook."

She grinned. "We could upload some new pictures – the ones from the air show."

They went upstairs, and David looked at Rose. "Anything special you want to do?"

"Let's go for a walk," said Rose. "I really like the garden and the woods, and we should make the most of the late evenings – when we get back from India it'll be autumn, and who knows what the weather'll be like?"

As they walked across the grass by the summer house, Rose said, "There were a couple of fox cubs playing out here earlier. I think Lily wanted to keep one as a pet."

David chucked. "They are cute, aren't they. But they do have a habit of chewing at the bottom of the wisteria, I don't really know why."

They reached the edge of the wood, walking into the shade a little and sitting down on the trunk of a fallen tree.

"When I was a boy," David said, "I used to imagine that these woods went on forever. Somewhere deep in the forest there was a stag, with magnificent antlers, and if I watched for long enough I'd catch a glimpse of him."

"Stags, lions," teased Rose gently. "what next?"

Her face softened, and she touched David's hand. "If you're the stag, I'll be your doe."

He smiled. "I'd seen you more as a lioness."

Even as he spoke, somehow Rose felt something fierce, untamed, rising up in her heart. "David, I love you."

His arm tightened round her shoulder. "I love you too."

Rose nodded. "I know there's a lot to do these next couple of weeks, but it's all worth it. I'm almost jealous that you have to be at work. Having Lily and Poppy around will really help."

David grinned. "Let's see what those two have got up to. Race you back to the house!"

Rose did her best to keep up with him, and when he stopped at the front door and turned, she ran into his arms, out of breath. He held her for long moments until she got her breath back. "Nearly caught you," she managed.

As they went into the house, the girls came down the stairs. "We got the photos posted," Poppy said. "My friends really like Lily, they can't wait till September."

Rose smiled. "That's good. Would you like a drink before bed? I think we just have four of the hot chocolate sticks left."

They went into the kitchen and David heated milk, then the girls competed with one another over whose chocolate would all be melted first.

"OK," said Rose reluctantly, finishing her drink. "Time for bed."

They followed the girls upstairs, and David kissed Rose at the door of his room. "Sleep well, my love."

***

The next day Rose and the girls continued with their preparations, Poppy crossing through items on the lists as Rose made phone calls.

"When are we going to do dresses?" asked Lily.

"Let's go into town tomorrow," said Rose. "And this evening David and I are going over to see Reverend Wood."

When David arrived home, they met him in the hall, and he kissed Rose, hugging the girls. "Something smells good."

Lily nodded. "We made a pie again, a bit like the one we did before."

They sat down to eat, and David listened carefully as Rose went through the things she and the girls had managed to do. "I think we're getting there."

He nodded. "Well, tonight we're going to the vicarage, and how about tomorrow we all go out for a meal? You deserve a treat."

Rose nodded. "That'd be nice."

Lily chipped in. "Alice asked if Poppy and I can go for a sleepover on Saturday – we can show her the pattern for the bridesmaids' dresses."

"Of course," said Rose. "That'll be all right, won't it?" she asked David.

He smiled. "Sure."

"Oh, one other thing," said Rose. "I got my appointment with the doctor for Friday afternoon, so that'll take care of all the injections."

David nodded. "Good. Fortunately mine are all up to date from the last time Poppy and I went out."

He glanced at Lily. "Sorry, Lily, you'll have to go through that before next summer."

Lily shrugged. "I don't mind needles."

David put down his knife and fork. "OK, girls, are you all right to clear up while Rose and I go and talk to the vicar?"

They left the girls nudging one another good-naturedly by the sink. "Let's walk," said David. "It'll only take a few minutes, and there's a short cut over the fields."

They went down the drive, turning onto the lane and walking a short distance. "Here's the stile," said David, climbing over and offering Rose his hand.

"What do you think the vicar will ask us?" she queried as they set off across the field.

David looked thoughtful. "I don't know, really. I was just expecting to talk to him about the banns, booking the church, maybe about the flowers."

When they reached the next stile, David again helped Rose over. "There's the vicarage," he pointed.

They stood in front of the door, Rose admiring the ivy climbing over the porch. David knocked, and the door was opened by a determined-looking woman with greying hair.

"You must be David and Rose," she said. "Come in."

They followed her along the hall, and she indicated an open doorway. "The reverend is in his study."

David preceded Rose into the room, and the vicar got up as they entered. "Please, have a seat."

"So," he said. "You're getting married."

David nodded. "I know it seems quite short notice, but there are valid reasons."

He briefly explained the events of the last few days. "So we thought it made sense to have the wedding before the girls go back to school."

The vicar nodded. "So you and your sister are staying at David's now?" he asked Rose.

"That's right. I've seen my mother and she's fine, and we've talked to David's parents."

"What about your brothers?" asked the vicar, his voice containing no hint of reproach.

Rose sighed. "I wish I could talk to Paul. I know he didn't want to hurt me, but at the end of the day he didn't stand up for what he knew was right. And Charles – I'm just not ready even to see him."

The vicar again nodded. "I understand, it's hard. Will you invite them to the wedding?"

Rose glanced at David. "Yes. I just hope Charles has the sense not to make a fuss, if he comes at all."

"Well," said the vicar, "there's nothing he can do to stop you being married. Unless there's anything you need to tell me?"

David shook his head. "Nothing."

"Then that's fine. I'll read the banns for the first time of asking on Sunday, and of course the church is yours on the last Saturday in August. If you want to start decorating it beforehand, everything will be ready from Friday afternoon – we have some very dedicated volunteers who keep the place tidy."

David smiled. "We appreciate that – and we'd like to make a contribution over and above the usual fees."

Rose nodded at his thoughtful suggestion. "And you'll have the flowers to enjoy on the Sunday," she added.

"Now," said the vicar, "something else you might like to consider. I always offer couples who are about to be married in the church, the opportunity to come over here for a couple of evenings before the wedding. It gives each of them the chance to talk about what they're hoping for from marriage, what their expectations are. If there are any surprises, things they hadn't discussed, often they can work out an answer more easily with someone to help them talk it over."

David nodded. "That sounds very wise."

He glanced at Rose. "We'll give that some serious thought – can we let you know on Sunday?"

"Of course," replied the vicar.

"Well, thanks so much for your time," said David, getting up. He held out his hand to help Rose to her feet, and she thought she caught an approving smile from the vicar.

As they walked back down the lane, Rose said, "I like the vicar. He really seems to care, and I think talking to him would be good, even though you and I have a pretty good idea what we're expecting."

She grinned. "You remember what Lily said? We look as though we've been together for years."

David nodded, slipping his arm around her shoulders. "I think we've got the best of both worlds – total certainty, but still so much to discover too."

When they got back to the house, the kitchen was spotless, everything neatly in its place, and the girls were in the living room playing draughts.

"Was it OK?" asked Poppy.

"Definitely," smiled David. "We might go over there again a couple of times – I think Reverend Wood has some wise things he can tell us."

They finished their game, then Rose played against Lily while David and Poppy brought in hot milk and slices of cake.

"We can get some more hot chocolate when we go into town tomorrow to look at dresses," said Lily.

David glanced at Rose. "Have you decided on a style?"

She smiled secretively. "Stop fishing."

He grinned. "OK – I promise."

The girls picked up the last few crumbs of cake with their fingers, and Rose said, "Right, time we went up."

The girls disappeared into their room, and David stood with Rose in the hall for a moment.

"Is there anywhere particular you want to go tomorrow night?" he asked. "Or shall I surprise you?"

He grinned. "Either way, let's make it a surprise for the girls."

She considered. "How about an Indian place? If we're going over there, I wouldn't mind trying a couple of different things to see what else I like."

"OK," said David. "I'll book somewhere while I'm at work tomorrow."

He leaned over to kiss her softly. "Night, darling."

***

After breakfast the next day, Rose and the girls set off into town. When they reached the precinct, Lily pointed. "I've always liked the look of the wedding dresses in that shop."

They went into the shop, and an attractive woman in her early forties approached them. "Hi there. I'm Sarah Tyler, please call me Sarah. I'm guessing you're looking for a dress, and maybe something for bridesmaids?"

Rose smiled. "It is a bit of a giveaway, isn't it. Actually there's another bridesmaid too, she couldn't come today."

"Well," said Sarah, "why don't we start by looking at a few photos? These are from weddings where we've done all the dresses for the bridal party, so point out anything you like and we can look for something that has a similar style."

They sat down, and Sarah brought out an album, pointing out particular features as they leafed through the pages.

"I think you should have one like that, Rose," pointed Lily.

"Are you sure?" said Rose. "I hadn't thought about leaving my shoulders bare."

Poppy nodded. "Lily's right, it'll look nice."

Rose grinned at Sarah. "Well, my style gurus have spoken."

They carried on looking through the photos, and Poppy said, "Look, Lily. Didn't you show me a dress of yours like that?"

Lily looked more closely. "Oh, yes. I really like that one, actually – it's quite simple, but the skirt's a bit fuller. Better than loads of frills and puffs around the shoulder, eh, Pops?"

Sarah nodded. "OK. Well, let's have a look and see what we've got. You first, Rose."

They walked to the back of the shop, and Rose's eyes widened at the seemingly endless rails of dresses in white and ivory.

Sarah glanced at her expression. "Don't worry – I think there are perhaps four or five that fit what you have in mind, that I think would really suit you."

She hummed to herself as she looked at the hand-written labels on each hanger. "Ah, here."

She carefully took a dress from the hanger. "Right, girls, give us a moment or two, and then you can tell us what you think."

Rose followed Sarah into one of the changing rooms. "Those little cubicles like they have in the department stores would never do for this, would they?" she grinned.

After a few minutes Rose emerged, and Lily gasped. "Oh, Rose, that's gorgeous."

Poppy nodded. "I can't think of any way you could look more beautiful."

Rose glanced at Sarah. "Doesn't sound like I need to try anything else."

Sarah smiled. "You'll not hear any protest from me. I wish all my customers were as easy to please."

She picked up a diary from the counter. "Can you come in for a final fitting on, say, the Thursday before the wedding?"

"That's fine," said Rose. "Now, what about these two? It'd be nice to get their dresses made specially, and of course they can keep them for other occasions."

Poppy grinned. "You bet."

"So you like that style with the full skirt?" asked Sarah.

Lily nodded. "Definitely."

Sarah found a tape measure and deftly took their measurements. "That'll be no problem. If you give me a call when you know Alice's measurements, I can get the dressmaker on it straight away."

As they left the shop, Rose said, "I didn't think it would be that easy. We have some time before lunch – what else would you like to do?"

Poppy thought for a moment. "Aren't you and David supposed to get each other presents? We could help you look for something."

They walked down the precinct, and Lily pointed. "There's a jeweller's – shall we try in there?"

They went in, and Lily said, "Look, Pops, there's a bracelet like the one you got me."

Rose walked over to the other side of the shop, looking at the men's jewellery.

"Can I help you?" the assistant asked.

Rose looked thoughtful. "I'm looking for a present to give my fiancé."

For a moment the word felt strange on her tongue, and she remembered the day – it seemed like an eternity ago – when she'd watched David signing his name and wondered how her signature would look.

"How about something from this section?" suggested the assistant. He indicated a case with trays of cufflinks.

Rose looked for a few moments. "Could I look at that tray there?" she pointed.

He reached into the case and slid out the tray. "Are there any that you were particularly interested in?"

"Those ones with the blue stones – lapis lazuli, isn't it?"

The assistant nodded. "It's what's called 'cabochon' cut. Quite unusual."

He carefully removed the cufflinks from the tray, putting them in Rose's palm.

"They're gorgeous," she said. "Let me ask the girls what they think."

"Poppy, Lily," she called. "What about these?"

They came over. "Oo," said Lily, "they're really pretty."

Poppy grinned. "They are nice – and I think they'd suit David. He really likes blue."

Rose made up her mind. "In that case, we'll take them."

She handed the cufflinks back to the assistant, and he carefully boxed them. Rose handed over her card, and the assistant swiped it, handing it back.

"Thanks so much for your help," she told him. "My fiancé and I will definitely come back here first to look for our wedding rings."

They went back out to the precinct, and Rose said, "Definitely lunchtime now – shall I take you to the place in the department store?"

"Paninis!" said Lily.

Poppy grinned at her. "And milkshakes."

They charged off in the direction of the store, and Rose shook her head. "Get us a table!" she called after them.

As they were eating, Rose said, "The only other thing we need to get today is stationery – wedding invitation cards."

She smiled wryly. "I'm going to need you two to help me – addressing envelopes, sticking stamps."

"No problem," said Poppy firmly. "We can do that tomorrow."

After lunch they went further down the precinct to a large stationers. "What sort of thing do you want?" asked Poppy.

"Something quite simple," said Rose. "Look, they have a book of sample cards here."

They leafed through the book, glancing at the cards on offer. "Look," said Lily, "what about that one?"

Rose looked at the card by Lily's finger. "Mm, I quite like those. The flowers are really delicately drawn."

Lily nodded. "Definitely."

"I'll go and ask if they have them in stock," said Poppy, slipping the sample card out of its plastic sleeve.

When she returned she was smiling. "They have plenty."

They left the shop with the cards carefully wrapped in a sheet of paper. "Right," said Rose. "Let's get back home, then we can start getting ready to go out."

Lily grinned. "We can take all our dresses out of the wardrobe and see which ones go best together."

***

When David arrived home, Rose met him in the hall. "The girls are just putting the finishing touches to their makeup – you've got plenty of time to get changed."

David looked at her admiringly. "I'm glad you chose the blue dress."

"What else would I wear?" Rose grinned. "It goes with the necklace – the first present you ever bought me."

He pretended to look concerned. "I'll have to buy you another necklace – don't want you limited to just one colour."

Rose put her hand on his arm and said softly, "You already spoil me, darling."

The girls came down the stairs, and David raised his eyebrows. "You two look fabulous."

Lily wore a pale blue dress, and Poppy had plaited her hair, then pinned the plaits in an almost medieval style. But Rose's attention was taken by Poppy's outfit, loose cotton trousers with a long embroidered tunic, her hair in a single braid down her back. "Wow, Poppy, that's amazing."

Poppy smiled shyly. "I was really hoping this would fit Lily, but it doesn't quite."

She turned to Lily. "Don't worry, we can go to my favourite shop next summer and get you all sorts of stuff."

David grinned. "And Rose and I will bring you something back with us."

Lily hugged him. "Thanks!"

He glanced at his watch. "I'd better get ready, though there's no way I'm going to match you three."

When he came back down the stairs, Rose said, "Well done – you found that same shirt."

David grinned. "Can't go clashing, can I."

They got in the car, David holding Rose's door for her, and set off.

"We're not heading for town?" queried Rose.

David smiled. "I thought we'd go somewhere a bit more special."

"Still Indian though?"

"Of course – I promised."

They drove on, and after a few minutes Lily pointed. "Is that it?"

David nodded, turning in to a small car park some distance from a low building. They got out, and walked along a gravelled path towards the restaurant.

Rose looked at the greenery either side of them. "They seem to have some unusual plants."

"Well spotted," nodded David. "Pops, you're good with the names, what are these?"

Poppy considered for a moment. "Well, this one's Himalayan balsam – it grows at our favourite picnic spot by the river, remember. And this is a sort of magnolia."

She looked a little further on. "Oh! Look at this one. It's a blue poppy – they're quite difficult to grow."

They reached the restaurant, and David held the door for them, glancing back at the exotic flowers.

They were seated quickly, and the waiter stood with his pad poised to take their orders for drinks.

"I don't mind if you want to have a drink or two, David," Rose said. "I can drive us home."

He nodded. "Thanks, Rose. In that case, I'll have lager."

He grinned at her. "There's a picture of a tiger on the bottle."

"Can Poppy and I share some of that yogurt and fruit juice stuff?" asked Lily. "I've never tried it."

"Of course, darling. And I'll just have a Coke, please."

The waiter went off to fetch their drinks while they looked at the menus. "This one sounds amazing," said Lily. "With green peppers and fresh chillies."

Poppy pantomimed fanning her face. "I like the korma – it's more creamy."

David nodded. "Rose?"

"I usually have something with masala, and I do like naan bread."

"Try the peshwari one," suggested David. "It has nuts, but raisins as well, it's quite sweet."

"I'll share one of those with you, Rose," offered Lily.

Their drinks arrived, and they gave the waiter their orders. He returned with a plate of poppadoms and small bowls of dips, and Lily said, "Mm, lime pickle. Does anyone else like it?"

David glanced at Rose and Poppy. "It's all yours, Lily," he grinned.

When their food arrived, the waiter lit the small brazier on the table with a flourish. "Enjoy your meal," he wished them as he left.

Rose tried her sauce. "This is pretty special," she said.

"Want to try a bit of mine?" offered Lily.

Rose shook her head, grinning. "I might get a chilli by mistake."

She turned to David. "Is this anything like the food we'll get at your parents' place?"

"Not at all, really. But I'm sure you'll enjoy it – their cook is really good."

Rose paused. "They have someone to cook for them full-time?"

He nodded. "It works better that way – otherwise, what with getting firewood, preparing all the spices, going to the market to get meat, they'd never get anything else done. And it gives her a job, my parents are very conscious about putting their money into the local community where they can."

"I can see I have a lot to learn," said Rose thoughtfully.

When they were nearly finished, the waiter approached, and David grinned at Rose. She stopped with her fork halfway to her mouth as David spoke to the waiter in what was obviously his own language.

Poppy's face lit up. "Yes, please, if they can."

The waiter nodded and left again. "OK," said Rose, "what did I miss?"

"Sorry," chuckled David. "I should have said – Pops and I have picked up a few words, we're not really as fluent as we might look."

"David asked if we could have some of their special dessert," explained Poppy. "It's sort of rice pudding, but with spices and sultanas."

The waiter returned with bowls, putting one in front of each of them, and Rose tentatively tried a spoonful. "Mm, I like this."

Finally David went to pay the bill, and returned with a small plate containing foil-wrapped after dinner mints.

Rose looked at Lily's hopeful expression and smiled. "Of course you can have mine, Lily."

They walked back to the car, the plants in the garden now filling the air with exotic fragrance in the warmth of the late evening.

David sighed. "I can imagine myself back there," he said.

"You really love the place, don't you," asked Rose.

He nodded. "I can't wait to be there, and it'll be so amazing to explain everything to you."

Rose remembered his words of the previous day: Still so much to discover. "I'm really looking forward to it, darling."

When they got home, Rose said, "It's been a lovely evening, but I think I'm ready for bed."

David nodded. He grinned at Poppy and Lily. "Knowing you two, you probably won't get much sleep, even though it's a sleep-over."

Poppy smiled sadly. "Means I have to take off my outfit, though."

David paused. "I'll get the camera — sorry, I forgot before we went out."

He went into the living room, returning with the camera, and Poppy and Lily stood either side of Rose.

"Ready?" asked David, then pressed the button. "Oh, yes, that really captures you."

Lily looked at the display. "That's another one for your Facebook page, Pops."

She took the camera from David's hands. "Can we upload it now? We promise to go to bed straight away as soon as we've done it."

"Of course," he smiled.

Rose and David followed the girls upstairs, and David stood with her outside the door of her room.

"Thanks for a lovely evening," Rose said.

He nodded. "And we have the place to ourselves tomorrow night, maybe we can sit by the fire, put some music on."

He kissed her softly. "Sleep well, dearest."

***

The next morning, Rose wrote invitation cards while the girls addressed envelopes. Lunch was fish fingers again, then Rose glanced at her watch. "Time I left for my appointment — are you two OK to carry on for a bit?"

Poppy nodded. "We can get all these done, and put them in the post box on the way to Alice's."

Rose drove into town, finding a space in the medical centre car park. She walked up to the reception desk, and the receptionist looked up. "Miss Middleton? You're with Doctor Scott as usual. Please take a seat."

Rose sat down, leafing through the magazines on the table beside her. After a few minutes the chime sounded, and her name flashed on the display.

She walked down the corridor and tapped on the door. "Come in," she heard.

Rose pushed the door open. "Good afternoon, Rose," the doctor said. She indicated a chair. "So you're off to India?"

Rose nodded. "It's my honeymoon."

The doctor nodded. "Well, first of all you'll need malaria prophylaxis. You can get that over the counter, but some people have a reaction to the standard product – disturbed sleep and so on. If you have anything like that, come back and I'll give you a prescription for something different."

She got up and crossed the room, opening a small fridge. "We have everything you'll need in stock, fortunately."

She returned with three small boxes, removing a syringe from the first. "These will sting a little."

Rose closed her eyes briefly at each injection, then smiled. "Not so bad."

The doctor nodded. "It's possible you may have a slight reaction in a few hours - you may feel a little feverish. It's nothing to worry about – drink plenty, and don't do anything too strenuous, and you'll be fine."

She paused. "You said you're travelling for your honeymoon - are you happy with your contraceptive arrangements?"

Rose felt herself blushing. "I hadn't even thought about it."

The doctor looked mildly surprised. She reached across to her desk and picked up a small packet. "Most young women try these to begin with. Just take one a day; if you forget, then take it as soon as you remember, then take the next one as usual."

She handed Rose the box. "They take two weeks to become effective, so..."

Rose smiled shyly. "That won't be an issue."

The doctor looked at her thoughtfully. "Is there anything else you'd like to ask me?"

Rose shook her head. "Thanks," she said. "You've been very helpful."

From the surgery she walked to the chemist's and picked up the malaria tablets, then drove back to David's. As she stopped her car in the usual spot, she realised she'd already started to think of the Georgian house by the lake as home.

As she went in, the girls came down the stairs with their overnight bags. "Alice's dad is picking us up in a minute," said Poppy. She held up a neat bundle. "And we finished the invitations, so we'll post those."

Rose smiled. "Thanks, darlings. Be good, and we'll see you for tea tomorrow."

The girls stood outside, and as Rose went into the kitchen, she heard the sound of a car arriving, then pulling away down the drive again.

Rose sat down at the table, thinking to herself that this was the first time she'd been alone in the house. She realised with relief that she didn't feel uncomfortable; the clock ticked reassuringly on the wall, and outside she could hear the sound of the woodpigeons roosting on the chimney stacks as usual.

She felt thirsty, and walked over to the sink to fill a glass of water. Outside she thought she caught a glimpse of a russet shape disappearing into the bushes, and she smiled.

She hard the sound of David's car in the drive, and walked out to the hall to meet him. "How did it go today?" he asked. "I passed Poppy and Lily going the other way, they waved."

Rose smiled. "Fine. The girls finished addressing the invitations, so everyone will have those next week."

"What would you like for dinner?" asked David. "I'm afraid I haven't had time to think of anything special."

Rose shook her head. "I'm not really all that hungry. I'll make us a sandwich, if you like. Unless you want something a bit more substantial?"

"No, that's fine. I think there's some cheese in the fridge – hope you like strong cheddar?"

Rose grinned. "If anything would tempt me to eat, it's a decent bit of cheese."

She cut bread for sandwiches while David made a pot of tea, and they sat down at the table to eat.

"Think I'll leave the crusts for the ducks," Rose said, pushing her plate away.

"Are you all right?" asked David, concern in his voice. "You look a bit flushed."

Rose nodded. "The doctor did say I might feel a bit feverish after the injections."

David nodded. "Shall we go through into the living room?"

Rose stood, then held onto the back of her chair. "Actually, I think I should lie down."

David held her elbow as she walked up the stairs, then watched as she got into bed, pulling the covers over her. "I'll get you a glass of water."

When he returned, Rose's eyes were closed and there was a thin sheen of perspiration on her forehead. David quickly went back to the bathroom and ran a flannel under the tap, squeezing it out.

He sat down beside Rose and gently sponged her forehead. She stirred, and turned towards him. "That feels better."

"Try to sleep," suggested David. "If you feel any worse, tell me."

She closed her eyes again, and David rested his hand on hers. After a few minutes her breathing slowed, and she slept. Occasionally she shifted position, and David kept hold of her hand as she murmured indistinctly.

Grey light was filtering through the curtain when she awoke, turning her head to look at David. "How do you feel?" he asked.

She sat up slowly. "A lot better, actually."

She glanced at him. "Did you stay the entire time?"

286

"Of course."

Rose grinned. "So it's finally happened."

"What?" asked David, puzzled.

"We've spent the whole night together."

He chuckled. "Well, when you put it like that..."

"I hope Lily doesn't have such a bad reaction when she has her injections," said Rose thoughtfully.

David nodded. "Well, now we know, we can take it in turns to sit with her."

He stretched. "Do you feel like breakfast?"

Rose nodded. "Actually I'm starving."

"Right," said David. "Bacon sandwiches, waffles, coffee, the works."

He went downstairs, returning after a few minutes with a loaded tray. Rose moved over a little, and said, "You can sit next to me, I'm sure that's allowed, isn't it?"

David propped a pillow against the headboard and sat down. "I think this would be a great way to start our Saturday mornings," he said.

"If the girls aren't rampaging around wanting to do something," grinned Rose.

"They'll be at school most of the time," reminded David. "I really will have you all to myself."

Rose felt the same fierce longing rising in her as before, and wrapped her arms around him. "It'll be wonderful."

He hugged her, then hurriedly reached to steady the tray. "Wups."

Rose smiled. "Pass me a sandwich?"

When they'd finished breakfast, David said, "Do you feel like going out?"

Rose shook her head. "I'm still a little light-headed."

"Sure that's not my influence?" he teased. "Tell you what, I'll get out some of the family photo albums."

He went down to the living room, returning with a stack of albums. "These first ones are from when my parents got married."

Rose looked at the photos. "Poppy really does look like your Mum when she was younger, doesn't she."

David smiled. "I'm sure she'll break a few hearts."

They spent the morning flipping through the albums, David telling Rose more about his family.

"We were fortunate," he said. "Most families in the military get moved around a lot, but even though Dad was away quite a lot, he was always based near here."

"Does he still fly?"

David shook his head. "They're pretty tight on restrictions out there. But they are close to an Indian Air Force base, so Dad gets to go over there and spend time with the pilots and the technicians."

He grinned. "The base commander is a very interesting chap – one of the perks that goes with his job is a vintage car quite a lot like ours, he claims it used to belong to a Maharajah."

Rose shook her head slowly. "It sounds like the most wonderful place – where almost anything could be true."

David nodded. "Now, are you ready for some lunch yet? I could make us scrambled eggs on toast."

"Mm," said Rose. "I think I could come downstairs for that."

David went down and started cooking, and Rose joined him in the kitchen a few minutes later. "Smells good."

He nodded. "No spices, but a little fresh black pepper makes all the difference."

Rose grinned. "You seem pretty confident with cooking."

David shrugged. "I've been looking after myself and Pops pretty much since I came back from university, and Mum left all her cookbooks. I like it."

After lunch, they ventured out into the garden, and David spread a blanket on the lawn for them to sit on. "I might have a bit of a nap," he said, lying back.

Rose nodded. "You can't have slept all that well in the chair."

When the girls arrived back, David was asleep, and Rose was beside him, finding shapes in the clouds.

She sat up. "Hi, you two. Did you have a nice time?"

Poppy nodded. "Alice loves her dress, and we got her measurements –"

"She's ticklish," interrupted Lily. "She wouldn't hold still."

"OK," smiled Rose. "Are you hungry?"

"Alice's Mum took us to McDonalds," said Poppy. "But that was ages ago."

Rose grinned. "Now I know why David is so good at cooking."

At the sound of his name, David opened his eyes. "Hi, girls. How about I light the barbecue, do you think you can survive until things are ready?"

"I'll make some salad," said Rose. "We can start with that."

Lily followed her into the kitchen while Poppy helped David with the charcoal. "Are we at church tomorrow?"

Rose nodded. "We were planning to go anyway, but this Sunday's special – our banns will be read."

Lily nodded. "Alice says there's a fete in the afternoon, can we stay?"

"Of course, angel."

Rose opened the freezer and piled boxes onto a tray. "Take this outside, darling, and I'll be out in a minute with the salad."

When she got outside, the barbecue was well alight, and Poppy tugged at David's apron. "Can we start cooking yet?"

"Sorry, Pops," he grinned. "It's still too hot, everything would burn to a crisp. Have some salad first."

"OK."

The girls crunched on carrot sticks, and after a few minutes David passed his hand carefully above the grill. "I think we can start with a couple of things round the edge."

He carefully arranged burgers round the edge of the grill, and Rose cut some rolls. "I brought mustard, and ketchup, and there's some chilli sauce."

"Yummy," said Lily, taking the bottle and squeezing it over her roll.

"OK," said David, "I think a couple of these are ready. Come on, girls, bring your rolls."

"Do you want something to eat now, David?" asked Rose, after she and the girls had finished a couple of burgers each.

David nodded. "The heat's going down now, I can just leave things cooking."

He grinned. "Did you notice I saved a couple of bits of steak?"

Finally Rose sat back. "I don't think I could eat another thing."

"I almost forgot," Lily said, "We made fairy cakes at Alice's."

She went into the house, bringing back a plastic tub. "See, we put sprinkles on and everything."

Rose took a cake. "Well, maybe just one."

David returned from cleaning the grill. "Anyone fancy a game of badminton?"

"In a minute," chuckled Rose. "I thought I was full, and after the girls' cakes, I'm even fuller."

"I'll have a go," said Lily. They went to the garage, returning with racquets and a shuttlecock. David walked over to the summer house, and they started to knock the shuttle back and forth.

After a few minutes Rose got to her feet. "Are there any more racquets?"

"There," David pointed. "I thought we might want to play doubles."

Poppy shook her head. "I'm happy just watching for a bit."

David grinned. "OK, you two can play me, then."

Rose and Lily did their best to wear him out, hitting the shuttle to opposite sides, and he played along, throwing himself into seemingly impossible shots.

Rose shook her head. "You're trying too hard," she teased.

David looked sheepish. "I should have said – I was on the university badminton team. But two against one makes it fair, doesn't it?"

Just then Rose looked up. "I think I felt a spot of rain."

"We can shelter in the summer house," said Lily, and she and Poppy dashed over to the wooden building, trying to dodge the raindrops.

David and Rose caught up with them, and Rose took the old rocking chair while David leaned against the wall beside her, the girls bouncing on the sofa in the corner.

There was a flash of lightning outside, and Poppy exclaimed. "Oh!"

"What is it, Pops?" asked David.

"I just had the strangest picture," said Poppy. "Rose was in the rocking chair, just as she is now, but she was feeding a baby."

For a moment Rose didn't speak, as her mind filled with the picture Poppy's words described. "You said something before that I didn't really understand, Poppy. You said that everything was going to be fine?"

Poppy nodded. "Sometimes I just get a feeling, or I see something. It doesn't happen often. Mostly when I'm in church…"

David glanced out of the door. "Looks like the rain has eased off a bit. We should probably make a run for the house."

The girls tumbled through the front door, laughing. "We'll go upstairs now," said Poppy. "Don't worry, we'll dry our hair before we go to bed."

David nodded. "We won't be far behind you."

He guided Rose into the kitchen, taking a towel from the rail on the front of the oven. "Let me dry your hair a little."

Rose stood while he used the towel on her hair. He put the towel down, and wrapped his arms round her from behind, his cheek against her still-damp hair.

He moved his hand to rest gently on Rose's stomach. "I had the most amazing feeling when Poppy talked about her picture."

She leaned back against him. "I know what you mean."

She put her hand over his for a moment, then turned in his arms. "We'll just have to see what happens."

David nodded. "Anyway, it's time we got some sleep. You'll be all right, won't you?"

"I'm fine," Rose reassured him. They walked up the stairs, and David gave Rose a soft goodnight kiss as always.

Rose closed the bedroom door, and walked straight over to the chest of drawers. She took out the small box that the doctor had given her, and pushed the pills out of their foil one by one, gathering them in her hand.

She crossed the hall to the bathroom, and flushed the pills down the toilet, then went back to her room, screwing up the box and pushing it to the bottom of the wastebasket.

She changed for bed, lying down and pulling the covers over her. As she drifted off, she realised she hadn't asked Poppy whether her baby was a girl or a boy...

***

They drove to church the next morning, and Rose smiled shyly as the vicar asked her and David to stand while he read their banns and prayed for them. When the service finished, they went outside and watched the stalls for the fete being set up.

"We can get some lunch in a bit," said David, pointing at a stall where a young couple were starting to cook sausages on a gas barbecue.

"Look," said Lily. "What's that?"

A tall man was walking through the churchyard carrying a clipboard with a small yellow plastic duck tied to the top.

He came over to them. "Can I interest you in the duck race?"

"Real ducks?" asked Lily eagerly.

He shook his head. "Sadly, no. These little chaps."

He indicated the duck on his clipboard. "We number them, and let them go at the top of the stream. Whichever one reaches the bridge first wins. They're a pound a time."

David grinned. "I think we can manage a duck each."

He fished in his pocket, bringing out four pound coins. "Do we get to pick our numbers?"

"Well, you're the first, so the field's open."

David ran his finger down the clipboard. "I think I'll have… eleven."

Rose smiled. "In that case, mine's eighteen."

The girls whispered to one another. "Five, and fourteen," said Poppy.

"OK then. The race is at three, don't miss the start."

He moved on to another group, and David glanced back at the barbecue. "I think we can get some lunch now."

They ate as they walked, and Lily stopped at a stall displaying the work of local artists. "Look, isn't that your house, Poppy?"

David picked up the picture. "That's not bad, actually."

He glanced at the back. "Fifty pounds. Well, it's in a good cause."

He took out his wallet and paid for the picture. The stallholder carefully wrapped it, tying it with string.

"I'll carry it," volunteered Poppy.

Their next stop was the tombola, and Lily flashed a grin at Poppy as her ticket matched the number on a big teddy bear. "Think we can find somewhere in your room for him."

After they'd made the rounds of the stalls, David glanced at his watch. "Nearly three – we'd better make our way to the starting line."

They walked through the small patch of woodland to the stream, where the vicar stood. A young woman knelt by the stream, the crowd of plastic ducks kept from floating downstream by the thin plank she held across the water, and people stood along the bank, ready to watch the progress of their ducks.

The vicar smiled at David. "We're ready."

He nodded to the young woman. "Let them go."

She lifted the plank, and the ducks started their journey downstream.

Lily pointed excitedly. "There's one of ours."

She ran towards the bridge, taking off her shoes and splashing into the shallows. "Come on, number five."

Some of the ducks got snagged on twigs or rocks, while others drifted into still eddies at the edge, but Lily's stayed in the centre of the stream, bobbing and sometimes submerging in the moving current.

"Come on, you can do it," she chanted. "Yay!"

She glanced at the man with the clipboard, and he nodded. "The winner is... Miss Lily Middleton."

"Oh, well done," the vicar said to David. "I hope you're not rushing off anywhere?"

"We didn't have any plans," said David. "Why?"

The vicar grinned. "The prize for the duck race is for the winner and their family to stay on and share in the barbecue we put on for everyone who's helped with the fete."

"That sounds lovely," said Rose, joining them with Lily, who was still holding her slightly damp plastic duck.

"Feel free to stroll around for a while," said the vicar. "Once we've taken all the stalls down and cleared away, we'll be gathering on the back lawn."

Poppy joined them, still carrying the picture they'd bought. "I'll put this and the bear in the car," she suggested.

"Sure," said David, handing her the keys. "We'll just be walking around."

Finally the churchyard was restored to its normal appearance, and people began to drift towards the grassy area at the back. David spotted the vicar talking to a middle-aged man, and the vicar waved, beckoning him over.

"David, I'd like you to meet Peter Goodchild – he's been generous enough to sponsor our fete for the last few years."

Peter shook David's hand. "Great to finally meet you, David. Of course I've seen you around, and that gorgeous car of yours, and Philip Lewis occasionally mentions you when we play golf."

He grinned. "I understand congratulations are in order."

David nodded. "Rose and I will be married in three weeks, then we're off to India for our honeymoon."

Peter nodded. "I'm sure you'll have a marvellous time."

He glanced over at the people gathering at a long wooden table. "Right. I'd better get started – perhaps Arthur didn't mention that I do the barbecuing. By all means go over and find a seat."

David returned to Rose and the girls. "OK, let's go and sit down."

They found themselves next to the young couple who'd been running the hot dog stall, and Rose listened as the conversation ranged over various topics of village life. Poppy and Lily attacked the salad with enthusiasm, and snagged barbecued chicken legs as a plate passed down the table.

The sun began to drop toward the horizon, though it was still pleasantly warm, and people gradually began to drift away, making their farewells.

Peter came over to the table, still in his apron. "There are still a few bits and pieces left to cook. What can I offer you? A piece of steak for you, David, and a couple more burgers for the girls?"

"Yes please," piped Lily.

He went back to the barbecue, and David nudged Lily, grinning. "It's not every day a millionaire asks what you want him to cook for you."

Peter returned with a plate. "OK, here we go. Steak, burgers, and there was another chicken leg."

"Thanks," smiled Rose.

When they'd finished their meal, it was beginning to go dark, and David went to thank the vicar. "This has been a really great day."

As he walked back to the car to meet Rose and the girls, he saw Peter packing up the barbecue. Peter raised his hand in acknowledgement, then returned to what he was doing.

When they arrived home, Poppy said, "Can we find somewhere for the picture?"

David nodded. "I think I know where the picture hooks are."

He went out, returning with a hammer and a small brass hook. "Where did you have in mind?"

"Over the living room fireplace?" suggested Rose.

Poppy nodded. "Good idea."

They went through to the living room, and David held the hook while Rose stood at a distance. "Left a bit, maybe a little higher – there."

David carefully tapped in the nails, then unwrapped the picture and guided the cord onto the hook, straightening it and stepping back to stand by Rose. "It looks good, doesn't it."

She put her arm round his shoulders. "Perfect."

"Cool," said Lily. She turned to Poppy. "Come on, Pops, let's find somewhere for that bear, too."

"Then it's bedtime," smiled Rose. "Come down and say goodnight when you're ready."

The girls headed for the stairs, the bear between them, trying to come up with a name.

David smiled. "We can sit for a while."

He moved towards the sofa, drawing Rose with him, and she suppressed a squeal as he pulled her into his lap, grinning.

"Back to work tomorrow," he said with a hint of regret.

Rose nodded. "The time will fly, you'll see. There's still quite a lot to arrange, but I know how I'm going to tackle it all."

"Don't wear yourself out. As long as you and the girls are there, and the vicar can get as far as 'I now declare', everything else is optional," grinned David.

Rose chuckled. "Good point. But I think we can manage a little more than that."

The girls trooped back in, ready for bed. "We decided on 'Mr Bear'," Lily informed them.

David nodded. "That about covers it." He accepted a kiss on the cheek from her, then from Poppy.

"Night, darlings," said Rose. "See you in the morning."

When they were gone, Rose settled more comfortably in David's arms. "Everyone in the village seems really nice."

He nodded. "I could happily spend the rest of my life here with you. Only..."

"What?" queried Rose, curious.

David shook his head. "Nothing. I just wonder if there isn't an adventure waiting for us around the corner somewhere."

Rose smiled. "Maybe Poppy will tell us," she said thoughtfully.

David nodded, suppressing a yawn. "Sorry, darling, I think I need to call it a day too."

He grinned mischievously, and stood up, scooping Rose into his arms. She tightened her grip on him and closed her eyes as he carried her up the stairs, setting her back on her feet at the door of her room.

"Have to practice," he said, his eyes twinkling. "Only a few weeks before I bring you through the front door with that other ring on your finger."

"Which we haven't got yet," reminded Rose with a smile.

He grinned. "One for Saturday, then."

She lifted her face up for a kiss. "Night, darling."

"Night, my love."

***

As Rose had predicted, the week passed quickly, and Poppy's lists started to have more items crossed through than not. On Saturday they all went into town, finding wedding rings in the jeweller's, and stopping for lunch in their favourite café.

Their banns were read again on Sunday, and lunch was a picnic on the lawn by the summer house. The next evening, Rose and David took the vicar up on his offer, and they returned from the vicarage with a page of notes in Rose's neat handwriting.

"These are really good questions," said David thoughtfully. "We can talk about them on those long warm evenings on the verandah when we're in India."

"You know where we're staying?" queried Rose.

David nodded. "That place I mentioned was free, and we have it all to ourselves."

He grinned. "That'll give you an introduction to life over there – I booked it for three weeks, and it comes with a full-time housekeeper, who does the cooking, and her husband is the caretaker and also the driver for all our excursions."

"It sounds expensive," said Rose.

David shook his head. "Not really. The most expensive part of our trip is the air tickets."

He grinned. "I have a surprise for you there, too. We have quite a long stopover on the way, so I booked us a hotel in the airport so we could get some sleep. It's quite a place."

***

When Saturday came around again, David and Rose sat with the girls round the kitchen table after breakfast.

"Only a week to go," said David, smiling at Rose. "What haven't we done yet?"

"Well," said Rose, "On Thursday the girls get their dresses, and I have my final fitting. Then that evening is the rehearsal, and on Friday afternoon the girls and I are going down to decorate the church."

David nodded. "I almost forgot. This Monday evening my best man is coming round – I can't believe you haven't met Chris yet. Then on Friday I'm going to stay with him, and I've asked his brother to come up here to drive the car. John'll pick your Mum up on the way here."

"OK," said Rose. "And Alice's father is dropping her off here too."

David grinned. "I think that gets all the key players where they're supposed to be."

He pulled out his organiser and made a note. "Must remember to confirm the flights on Saturday."

"And then you'll be gone for a whole month," said Lily.

Rose nodded. "Mum will make sure you and Poppy get packed up and back to school OK."

"Talking of packing," said David, "I've got a list from the last time Poppy and I went, of things we'll need. We should take a look through it and see if there's anything you want to add, Rose, then I can go into town one lunchtime and pick up anything we haven't got."

He passed Rose the list, and she scanned down it. "There seem to be quite a few medicines and things like that."

David nodded. "We hardly needed any of them last time, but you never know when they'll come in handy."

He grinned. "Are you beginning to feel like an explorer going to unknown lands...?"

***

When David came home from work on Monday evening he had Chris with him. "Chris, this is Rose, and her sister Lily."

Chris smiled. "Great to meet you two at last."

"How do you know David?" Rose asked as they walked toward the house.

"We were at university together," Chris replied. "We've kept in touch since then – though lately David's been a bit slow at answering emails."

"I think that's mainly my fault," apologised Rose. "It's all been a bit of a whirlwind since we met at the beginning of the summer."

"Don't worry," Chris said, shaking his head and grinning. "It's great that he's got someone – he worked non-stop all the way through university and the same since he got the job at Lewis's. We wondered when he'd find time."

They reached the kitchen, and Poppy put down the spoon she was using to stir a pan. "Hi, Chris," she said, hugging him.

"Hi, Pops. They've got you tied to the stove, then?"

Poppy grinned. "My two stepsisters –" she indicated Rose and Lily – "are terribly cruel, they beat me and make me do all the work."

Rose chuckled. "At least she didn't call us *ugly* stepsisters, Lily."

Poppy waved at the table. "Sit down, dinner will only be a minute."

"I'll open a bottle of wine for us," said David.

They sat down, and Poppy brought plates of spaghetti to the table and a large bowl of bolognese sauce. "Dig in."

"So, Chris, you know how everything's supposed to go, right?" asked Rose when they'd finished eating.

He nodded. "Friday, I pick David up from work and take him to my place. We'll probably go out for a drink, but I promise –" he held up his hand solemnly – "that nothing crazy is going to happen to him."

"Then on Saturday morning we drive to the church, and I try to stop him from fretting when you're just a little late."

Rose grinned. "Bound to happen."

"You arrive, the vicar asks who has the rings, I pat my pockets pretending to have forgotten them."

Poppy elbowed him playfully in the ribs. "Better not."

"Then it's 'You may kiss the bride', and back here for speeches and the party."

Rose grinned. "That about sums it up. Then when David and I have driven off –"

"With the obligatory tin cans trailing," said Chris.

"– you take Mum back to her house with Lily and Poppy."

"Gotcha."

Chris stood up. "Well, I'll leave you to it – I'll see you on Thursday for the rehearsal, right?"

David nodded. "Seven o'clock. You know where the church is?"

Chris grinned. "Of course. I have to get you there on time, remember?"

David walked to the door with him, and they heard the sound of Chris's car going down the drive.

"He seems nice," Rose said when David came back into the kitchen.

David nodded. "He likes to sound as though he's not taking things too seriously, but when it comes down to it he's as solid as a rock."

He glanced at Poppy. "Thanks for cooking, Pops. Rose and I can clear up, if you and Lily want to do something upstairs."

Poppy grinned. "Actually there is something we need to do, but it's a surprise."

She and Lily went up the stairs, whispering to one another, and Rose shook her head, smiling. "I wonder what they're plotting."

David nodded. "It's bound to be something for the wedding – and knowing those two, it'll be worth the wait."

He started the water running in the sink. "Right, let's tackle this lot, and we'll still have time to sit in the lounge for a while."

***

Thursday came, and when David had left for work, Rose said, "OK, girls, we should get going. We have a few things to do in town, then we're meeting Alice for lunch before we go to the dress shop, right?"

Poppy nodded. "One o'clock, at the café."

When they arrived at the café, Alice was waiting outside for them. She hugged Poppy and Lily, then hesitated. Rose smiled, and gave her a big hug. "Hi, Alice. It's good to see you. I can't wait to see all of you in your dresses."

They found a table, and ordered their usual paninis. "Milkshakes all round?" asked Rose.

Poppy nodded. "You like banana, don't you, Alice?"

Alice nodded. "I don't mind chocolate if they don't have it, though."

When they'd finished lunch, they walked down to the dress shop in the precinct. Sarah came to meet them as Rose pushed open the door.

"Come on in," she said, smiling. "You must be Alice, right? The ticklish one?"

Alice gave an embarrassed grin. "They weren't supposed to tell you."

"Anyway, your dresses are here and they look pretty good to me. Ready to try them?"

Rose sat down as Sarah shepherded the girls to the back of the shop. They returned a few minutes later, and she smiled. "Wow, look at you three."

Poppy grinned. "This is just how I imagined us."

Sarah nodded. "Now, if you three want to stay as you are for a minute, Rose can put her dress on, and we can see how you all look together."

She took Rose to the changing room, and brought out the dress. "Tell me if it seems a little tight anywhere?"

She helped Rose put the dress on, and Rose took a few steps. "No, it's fantastic."

Sarah nodded. "And the train falls just right."

They returned to the girls, and Poppy said, "You look even more amazing than you did before."

"Come and stand either side," suggested Sarah. "Alice and Poppy this side, and Lily here."

They moved into position, and she nodded. "Your heights are just different enough, and I know the photographer will be thanking his stars that you picked him."

She glanced at Rose. "I'd really like a couple of shots for my album, if that'd be all right."

"Of course," smiled Rose. "I'll make sure we get copies for you."

She looked at the girls. "OK, we'd better change back – you can carry your dresses to the car."

She turned back to Sarah. "It's OK if I take mine with me, right?"

"Certainly – just make sure you hang it somewhere that David won't come across it by accident."

They drove back home, and carried their dresses upstairs. "I'll put mine at the back of David's wardrobe," said Rose.

"Can you put ours with them?" asked Lily. "They're all supposed to be a surprise, right?"

Rose nodded. "Of course."

At about six, David arrived back from work. "Sorry I'm a bit late – a few loose ends still to tie up before we go away."

He held up a bag. "I brought fish and chips, so we don't have to cook."

They sat down to eat, and Lily squeezed the ketchup a little too enthusiastically, catching Poppy's sleeve. "Good job we weren't still wearing our dresses, Pops."

Poppy grinned. "I'll change my top before we go out."

When they'd finished eating, David glanced at his watch. "We should get going."

Poppy dashed upstairs to change, coming back down in a white t-shirt with an Indian flag. "I got this at the airport coming back last time."

They drove to the church, parking next to Chris's car, and walked up the path. "Next time you come up here we'll be holding your train," Lily whispered to Rose.

The vicar was standing at the front of the church with Chris. "We're just waiting for your mother now, aren't we, Rose?"

She nodded. Just then the church door opened again and Rose's mother came in. "Sorry I'm a little late – Charles got held up at work."

At the mention of her brother's name, Rose glanced at David, who shot her a reassuring smile.

"So, Mrs Middleton," the vicar said. "You're giving Rose away, is that right?"

She nodded. "I'll walk beside her down the aisle, then step to the left a little, until you ask the question."

The vicar nodded. "That sounds perfect. Shall we walk through it?"

David and Chris took their positions at the front of the church, while the girls walked with Rose's mother to the door.

Rose took her place at the top of the aisle, her mother beside her, and the three girls behind them. Lily held her hands in front of her as though holding Rose's train, and Alice giggled. "You look like you're riding a horse."

"OK," said the vicar, "start your walk."

Rose paced slowly down the aisle, resisting the temptation to look back, and glanced at David when she drew level with him.

"Now you hand your bouquet to Lily," the vicar instructed. Rose turned, pretending to pass over the flowers, and Lily grinned.

They walked through the rest of the ceremony, and the signing of the register. "That all seems fine," said the vicar. "Let me just have a word with David and Rose by themselves for a moment, if that's OK?"

He led them to the vestry. "Now," he said, "Saturday's only two days away. Is there anything you want to ask, and are you both still OK with everything that's happening?"

He paused. "If you do have any uncertainty, please, don't ignore it. It's a big decision for both of you, and if you decide you need more time, that's more important than all the arrangements you've made, even though they're perhaps what's uppermost in your minds at the moment."

Rose shook her head. "Probably most couples say this, but David and I are absolutely certain that this is… meant, I suppose is the only way to put it."

She paused. "Actually, it's a couple of things Poppy said that really make me sure."

She tried to explain, searching for words to describe Poppy's moments of insight, and the vicar nodded thoughtfully. "It's reassuring to know that someone – forgive me, not the first person I'd have thought of – is open to some of the more mysterious ways in which God works."

He smiled. "Then everything's OK. Let's get you back to your family before they start to feel anxious."

They returned from the vestry, and Rose smiled reassuringly at the girls. "Right, we're done. Mum, can you drop Alice back at home, and we'll see you both at David's first thing on Saturday morning."

Her mother nodded. "No problem, dear."

"David, I'll see you at the office at about five o'clock," said Chris.

Poppy grinned. "Someone should say, synchronise watches."

They thanked the vicar, and walked out to the car park. The girls hugged, then Alice got into the car with Rose's mother. "Bye, then."

Chris glanced at Rose. "I'll see you on Saturday morning, then. You'll be the one in white, right?"

She rolled her eyes. "David told me you were a comedian."

"Wait till you hear the speech," he grinned, throwing her a wink.

They watched him drive away, then David said, "OK, time we were getting back too."

When they reached to the house, Poppy and Lily went upstairs to get ready for bed, then returned to get their goodnight kisses. Rose hugged them, feeling tears pricking at her eyes. "You two are the best," she said.

David smiled, seeing the emotion in her face. "Hey, there," he said softly, touching her cheek.

Rose nodded. "I'm fine."

She took a deep breath. "OK, girls, up you go."

When the girls were in their room, David walked up the stairs with Rose. "I'll come in tomorrow morning before I leave for work."

She smiled. "Just make sure you don't accidentally look in the wardrobe."

David shook his head. "The look on my face when I see you walk down the aisle has got to be real – I wouldn't spoil that for anything in the world."

Rose's eyes filled again. "David, I love you."

He nodded, bending to kiss her eyelids. "I love you."

***

David opened the door, briefcase in hand, and walked over to stand by the bed. "Morning, Sleeping Beauty."

Rose opened her eyes. "Morning, darling. Is it that time already?"

He nodded. "So I'll see you tomorrow. You can ring me before you go to bed if you want – I don't care if that's bending the rules a bit."

He bent down to kiss her, and she lifted her head, trying to keep her lips against his as he straightened again.

"Tomorrow," he promised, taking one last look over his shoulder as he left, closing the door.

Rose and the girls spent the morning finishing the wedding favours for each table, then after lunch the caterers arrived to set up the marquee on the lawn.

"We'll leave you to it," Rose told the girl in charge. "We'll be down at the church if you need anything."

When they arrived at the church, the florist had already dropped off all the arrangements, and they carefully tied the bows to the ends of the pews, then positioned the larger sprays on either side of the altar and at the entrance.

"When's your bouquet coming?" asked Lily.

"The florist will bring it in the morning, with your flowers," Rose reassured her. "Right, I think we're done here."

When they arrived back at the house, the marquee was up, and the tables and chairs were set out. "It looks fantastic," said Poppy. "And there's the board for the seating plan."

The girl from the catering firm came over. "That's everything for today. We'll be back in the morning to lay the tables and get ready to serve lunch."

The van drove away, and Rose grinned at the girls. "Come on, let's take a look."

They went into the marquee, and Rose sat down at the top table, Poppy and Lily beside her. "I think I can imagine how it'll look when everyone's here," said Poppy.

Rose glanced at the empty seat next to her. "And my husband will be with me."

Lily looked solemn. "That sounds like a serious word."

Rose nodded. "I suppose in a way, it is."

She grinned. "Come on. I made sure we could have fish finger sandwiches for tea."

"Yay!" said Lily.

When they'd eaten, Poppy said, "Why don't we have a game of Scrabble, Lily? It's the last time we'll get to play with Rose until next half term."

The two girls played against Rose, doing their best to come up with wedding-related words. "OK," said Rose. "I'll let you have 'church', and 'flower'. But 'plane' is pushing it a bit – it ought to be 'aeroplane'."

"OK," grinned Lily. "We'll stick to the rules."

In the end, the girls won easily, and Rose held up her hands. "I give in. Time we went to bed, anyway – it'll be a long day tomorrow, remember."

Poppy nodded. "You have to give us double hugs, though, seeing as David isn't here."

Again Rose blinked back tears. "Thanks so much for helping today, you two."

She wrapped her arms round both of them. "I'm going to miss you."

She released them reluctantly. "See you in the morning."

The girls went upstairs, and Rose walked through to the kitchen, sitting at the table with her phone.

She pressed the key to dial David's number, and listened to it ringing.

"Hi, darling," came his voice at the other end.

Rose breathed out, realising how much she'd missed him. "Are you OK?" she asked.

"Fine," came the answer. "We're just having something to eat in the pub near Chris's house. He's stuck to his promise, no dropping me in the middle of nowhere to find my own way back. You?"

"Yes, I'm fine," said Rose. "The church is finished, and the marquee's up here, it looks great."

"Good. So the girls are in bed?"

"Mm-hm. And I'm heading that way myself in a minute."

There was a pause at the other end of the line. "I miss you, darling. But tomorrow night we'll be together. And then, 'til death us do part'."

Rose tried to answer, but the words wouldn't come. Finally she managed through her tears, "Can't wait. I'll see you tomorrow."

She smiled, recalling Chris's words the previous day. "I'll be the one in white, remember."

She could tell he was smiling too. "I'll remember. Love you."

"Love you."

Rose ended the call, and sat for a moment holding the phone. Then she turned out the kitchen light and climbed the stairs to her room.

As she opened the door, she stopped. On the bed was a small package, wrapped in ribbon, and a note in David's characteristic flowing hand, obviously written with his special fountain pen.

She shook her head, smiling, and picked up the note.

"Darling, just a little something to help you have sweet dreams. D."

Rose forced herself to wait until she'd changed for bed before looking at the package. She undid the bow, and as she unfolded the white handkerchief inside, she caught an unmistakeable hint of David's aftershave.

She lay down, pulling the covers over her and clutching the handkerchief to her face, and finally she gave way to her emotions, wetting the cotton with her tears.

***

Rose woke in the morning with all three girls bouncing on her bed. "OK, OK," she protested good-naturedly. "I'm awake."

She sat up. "First things first, breakfast. We need to have plenty to eat, the photographer's bound to take hours."

She grinned. "I know. We can make waffles."

"Yay!" said Lily. "Honey and golden syrup."

"And maple syrup, and chocolate sauce," added Poppy.

"I like black treacle," said Alice plaintively.

"We have that too," laughed Rose. "Come on, down the stairs with you."

When they'd finished breakfast, Rose said, "Right, time for a shower."

"We all went in while you were still asleep," said Poppy.

Rose smiled. "OK, just me then. Lily, can I borrow some of your cream to do my legs?"

"Sure – it's in the bathroom cupboard."

Rose went upstairs and showered, using the cream on her legs. When she came down, the girls were whispering over a piece of paper, which Poppy pushed hastily into her pocket.

"OK," said Rose. "We'd better think about getting changed."

There was a knock at the door, and Rose opened it to see the florist's van. "Your bouquet, and the bridesmaids' flowers," said the girl.

"Thanks," grinned Rose. "I'd almost forgotten in the excitement."

She took the tray into the kitchen, and Lily leaned over to look. "The bouquet's gorgeous."

Rose nodded. "Right, let's get you into your dresses."

A few minutes later the girls were standing in Rose's room, looking almost ready. "Can we help you with your dress?" asked Alice.

"I think I'll need you," grinned Rose. "It seemed much easier with Sarah there."

Finally she was in her dress, and Poppy said, "Do you still want your hair the way we talked about?"

"Please, darling."

Rose sat down in front of the mirror, and Poppy carefully arranged her hair, pinning it in place.

"Just right," she said. "Now, Lily, Alice, let me do yours. I'll need the flowers…"

When Chris's brother arrived, Rose and the girls were just coming down the stairs.

"Perfect timing," grinned Rose.

"You look stunning," her mother said. "And the girls are amazing – the different flowers to suit their hair."

Rose nodded. "We should go, shouldn't we?"

They went outside, and John held the car door for Rose's mother to get into the passenger seat. The three bridesmaids got into the back, and Rose joined them. "Good job the car has these fold-down seats," she grinned.

When they arrived at the church, Rose draped her train over her arm as they walked up the path. They went through the door, and Rose caught the eye of the organist as they entered. He waited till they were in position, then the unmistakeable notes of the wedding march rang out.

Rose took a deep breath, and stepped forward, the girls holding the train of her dress. Her mother slipped her arm through Rose's, and looked sideways for a moment, smiling. "This is it."

Rose saw David turn to look over his shoulder, and as her eyes drank in the expression on his face, she remembered his words the previous morning.

She matched her pace to the music, and reached the front just as the last flourish of the organ faded. She remembered to turn, handing her bouquet to Lily.

"Dearly beloved…" began the vicar, and Rose smiled at David, hearing the words she'd anticipated for so long.

At "Who gives this woman," Rose's mother stepped forward. "I do." The vicar nodded, and she smiled, taking her seat.

"…by the giving and receiving of rings." Chris looked at Rose, his eyes dancing, and hesitated just long enough to make Rose's eyes flash in response, before pulling the small box from his pocket.

"I now declare…"

At the vicar's words, Rose was certain she heard a whispered "Yay!" from behind her.

"You may now kiss the bride." David leaned over, and Rose saw tears in his eyes as his lips touched hers.

They took their seats, and the vicar stepped forward. "Before I say a few words, could we have our Bible reading?"

John walked up to the lectern, opening the heavy Bible and running his finger down the page until he found the place.

"I saw the Holy City, the new Jerusalem, coming down out of heaven from God, prepared as a bride beautifully dressed for her husband. And I heard a loud voice from the throne saying, "Look! God's dwelling place is now among the people, and he will dwell with them. They will be his people, and God himself will be with them and be their God. He will wipe every tear from their eyes. There will be no more death or mourning or crying or pain, for the old order of things has passed away."

"Thank you," said the vicar as John returned to his place. He turned to the congregation. "Perhaps it will seem strange to many of you to hear a city compared to a bride…"

He spoke briefly, ending with a reading from a psalm, and put down his notes with a smile. "Before we finish, one of the bridal party has asked if she can say a few words."

Rose glanced behind her, not entirely surprised as Poppy left her seat and made her way to the front.

Poppy smiled at everyone. "I remember when I first saw Rose. I got back from school for half term, and she was standing next to David at the top of our drive."

She paused. "I knew straight away that they were meant for each other. When she and Lily came to us that other day –" she hesitated, but continued – "it was as though they were coming home."

She took a piece of paper from her pocket. "I know this poem is David's really, but I hope he won't mind if I read it to you all – it says everything we all feel about Rose."

She took a deep breath, and read:

"Tyger! Tyger! burning bright, In the forests of the night,
What immortal hand or eye, Could frame thy fearful symmetry?
In what distant deeps or skies, Burnt the fire of thine eyes?
On what wings dare he aspire? What the hand dare seize the fire?"

She continued to the end of the poem, then folded up the paper and returned to her seat.

"Thank you, Poppy," said the vicar. "We'll move to the signing of the register now. Please, everyone, enjoy the anthem Rose and David have chosen, while the wedding party goes through into the vestry."

The organ started to play, and David offered Rose his hand to help her up. They went through to the vestry, and Rose took her seat in front of the register while David stood behind her. He reached inside his jacket, taking out his fountain pen.

Rose took the pen from his hand with a smile, and took a deep breath, starting to sign her name. "Rose..."

She glanced at David, and nodded. "... Stuart."

She exchanged places with him, and he added his signature below hers.

Chris and his brother signed as witnesses, and the vicar blotted the page, then carefully parted the certificate from the book along the perforations, handing it to David.

David slid the paper into his jacket pocket, and took Rose's hand. "Shall we?"

They made their way out to the churchyard, and submitted patiently to the photographer. Finally he nodded. "More pictures at the house."

David made sure that Poppy and Lily were in John's car with Rose's mother, then helped Rose into the roadster, taking his place next to her.

Chris got behind the wheel. "Ready, Mr and Mrs Stuart?" he grinned.

They arrived back at the house, and Rose leaned on David's arm as she got out of the car.

They took their seats at the top table, and Poppy and Lily joined them with Rose's mother and Chris.

"It seems strange not having your Mum and Dad here," Rose said quietly to David.

He nodded. "We can talk them through the video when we see them. Look, there's John with the camera."

Rose glanced across the marquee, seeing John panning the camera across the assembled guests. "He looks like he knows what he's doing, anyway."

There was the sound of a fork tapping on a wine glass, and the Reverend Wood got up from his seat. "Let's pause a moment to give thanks for our meal. Father of the heavenly lights, you give all good gifts, and we thank you for this special day, for Rose and David, and for the food we're about to enjoy. Amen."

The caterers began to move among the tables, and Rose smiled her thanks as a young woman in a white apron put a plate in front of her.

"Wine?" offered David.

Rose nodded. "Please."

He poured for her, and she took a sip. "Mm, this is pretty good – sort of spicy?"

The caterers had done a superb job, and the meal proceeded smoothly through dessert, to cheese and biscuits, and on to coffee. Rose glanced across at her mother. "You ready for your speech, Mum?"

Her mother got to her feet. "Good afternoon, everyone. Thank you so much for being here on Rose and David's special day."

She paused. "Of course it's sad that Jack couldn't be here, but I know he'd have been delighted that Rose has found someone she's obviously deeply in love with, and who I know will do his very best to make her happy."

She raised her glass. "David and Rose."

The guests echoed the toast, and she sat down, looking relieved.

"Thanks, Mum," whispered Rose. "It means a lot to hear you say that."

Chris stood up next, and Rose wondered what embarrassing incidents and anecdotes about David he was planning to relate.

He began to speak, and Rose realised that though he'd clearly gone to a lot of effort to make his speech entertaining, hilarious in places, underneath his words was a solid affection and regard for David that no-one could have missed.

He ended with another toast. "To the bride and groom."

David got to his feet, nodding his thanks to Chris. "It's great to see everyone here today. There are so many people to thank, and if I don't mention you by name, please don't think you're forgotten.

"First of all, Rose's mother Elizabeth. I can't thank her enough for the wonderful young woman who's become my bride today. Chris and John, for all their help – Chris, I've said it before and I'll say it again, you've been a rock for me."

David grinned. "And I couldn't possibly finish without mentioning our bridesmaids, Poppy, Lily and Alice. Girls, thank you so much for supporting Rose."

He pulled a piece of paper from his pocket. "I have another reason to thank Poppy. As she's already shared with you one of the poems that has meant a lot to all of us since Rose and I first met, I have the opportunity to read another piece which has been close to my heart over the last few days and weeks."

Without glancing at the sheet of paper in his hand, he began to speak. "She walks in beauty, like the night of cloudless climes and starry skies, and all that's best of dark and bright, meets in her aspect and her eyes…"

As he ended the last line, the marquee was hushed, and he looked up. "So, friends, on behalf of my wife and I –" he glanced at Rose, seeing her smile at his words – "I want to thank you again for being with us today. Please enjoy the rest of our celebration."

He sat down, and Rose put her hand on his. "Well done, darling."

David smiled. "I think this is the point where we circulate among our guests."

As they moved from table to table, Rose noticed John following their progress with the camera.

She nudged David. "That'll be great – your Mum and Dad will see all the guests, and we can tell them about the ones they don't know."

They were just finishing their circuit of the marquee when the caterers started to bring in the buffet. "Perfect timing," grinned David.

Rose glanced at the trays of sandwiches. "I think I'm ready for something else to eat now."

David nodded. "We can always get room service if –"

He stopped, a guilty look on his face. "Wups."

Rose chuckled. "I don't think it matters if I know a little bit of your plan now. So we're not flying tonight?"

David shook his head. "I booked us into a place not all that far from here, I thought we'd probably be pretty tired after the day."

"Perfect," nodded Rose.

"I'll go and fill us a plate each," said David. "Any particular preference?"

Rose grinned. "We picked smoked salmon, didn't we? And some of that soft cheese, and a bit of salad."

He returned after a few minutes with heaped plates, and they sat and watched as the guests helped themselves.

"I almost forgot," said Rose when she'd nearly emptied her plate. "We have to cut the cake."

"I think we can let people carry on eating, the ones who want to take photos will see us," said David.

He took Rose's arm as they walked to the table holding the cake, and picked up the silver knife. Rose put her hand on his, and they posed for a moment with the knife resting on the cake, while the cameras flashed. Then David glanced at Rose and pressed down, making a clean cut.

Poppy and Lily appeared from among the guests. "We'll make sure everyone gets a piece," Poppy said, taking the knife from his hand.

Shortly they were circulating with neatly-wrapped slices of cake, and David smiled at Rose. "There's nothing those two won't be able to do if they set their mind to it. I can't wait to hear what they get up to at school."

She nodded, looking thoughtful. "I'm going to miss them."

David sighed. "You're right."

He brightened. "Still, it'll only be two weeks to half term when we get back."

There was a brief noise of feedback, then Chris's voice came over the loudspeaker. "It's time for the evening's entertainment to get started, so if we could have David and Rose for the first dance please?"

Rose glanced at David. "I'm not exactly much of a dancer."

He chuckled. "Fortunately that's not what everyone's expecting."

The music started, the sound of the flute haunting, and Rose looked at David, her eyes already filling with tears. "I hope you've got plenty of hankies."

David led Rose to the space that had been cleared in the centre of the marquee, taking her in his arms. She rested her head on his shoulder, not caring if everyone saw her tears as she swayed gently to the music.

Finally the track faded into silence, and Rose smiled shyly as Chris started the applause. "Rose and David, everyone."

As they walked off the floor, the DJ cued a more upbeat track, and Rose grinned as here and there across the marquee, reluctant partners were urged to their feet and encouraged to the dance floor.

"It's OK if we slip away soon, isn't it?" she asked David.

He nodded. "We'll just make sure your Mum and the girls, and the really close friends, know we're off."

Just then Poppy appeared, her face betraying her emotions. "You're going now, aren't you."

Rose reached out to hug her. "I should have guessed you'd know."

"I'll find Lily and your Mum," Poppy said, slipping away again.

David shook his head. "That's one special gift she has."

Poppy reappeared, Lily in tow. "Your Mum's waiting outside."

They made their way to the exit from the marquee, and found Chris standing with Rose's mother. "The car's all ready," said Chris. "I made sure all your luggage was packed."

He held out his hand. "Congratulations again."

For a moment David moved to take his hand, then grinned and wrapped his arms round his friend. "Thanks, Chris."

He turned to Rose's Mum, taking both her hands in his. "Mrs Middleton – Elizabeth – again, thanks so much for everything."

She nodded. "I know you'll take care of Rose."

"What about us?" said Lily insistently, tugging on David's sleeve.

David grinned. "Be careful what you ask for."

He wrapped his arms around Lily and kissed her briefly but firmly on the lips. "See you soon, sister-in-law."

For once, Lily had no answer, stepping back with a mixture of surprise, pleasure, and sadness on her face.

David turned to Poppy. "Take care, Pops," he said, kissing her on the cheek. "We'll see you both at half term."

He opened Rose's door, and she got in, scooping her dress inside the car as David closed the door behind her.

David got behind the wheel and started the engine. He glanced at Rose. "One last thing you have to do."

She looked puzzled, then smiled. She turned to look back at the group of guests who'd come out of the marquee to watch them drive off, then tossed her bouquet high in the air.

"Oh, well done, Anne," they heard Lily say, as her friend looked with an air of happy bewilderment at the flowers in her hand.

David put the car in gear, revved the engine, and they moved off down the drive.

They drove for about half an hour, then David turned in past a low gatehouse, a single light showing in its windows. Sheep grazed on closely-cropped grass to either side, and in the distance Rose caught a glimpse of a ruined folly on a wooded hill.

She glanced across at David. "This doesn't look like just any old hotel."

He smiled. "Well, it's not just any old day."

The road curved, cresting a stone bridge over a small stream, and Rose gasped as the main building came into view. "It's practically a stately home."

David grinned. "It *is* a stately home. Former seat of the Baron of Denbigh, now open to guests."

He pulled up at the bottom of the massive stone steps. "Will you be OK walking up here?"

Rose chuckled. "If Keira Knightley can do it…"

David helped her out of the car, and she rested her arm on his as they walked up the steps, then in through the burnished brass doors.

As they approached the reception desk, a dark-suited man got up and walked round to them. "Mr and Mrs Stuart, of course, welcome. I'm the manager here. Please, if you'll give me the keys to your car, my staff will take care of your effects."

David passed across the keys, and Rose couldn't help feeling just a hint of satisfaction as the manager raised his eyebrows at the logo on the fob.

He snapped his fingers, and a young man hurried over to them. "Take care of Mr Stuart's car," instructed the manager.

He turned back to David. "Let me conduct you to your suite, and your luggage will arrive momentarily."

He led them up the sweeping stairs, and pushed open a set of double doors, stepping back to let them enter the room beyond.

Rose walked into the suite, turning slowly to look at the period furnishings, while David watched her from the door.

"You look perfect," he said, smiling.

The manager coughed discreetly. "Your luggage is here, Mr Stuart."

He made sure all their cases were taken through to the master bedroom, then withdrew, drawing the double doors closed behind him.

Rose smiled shyly at David. "We're on our own at last."

He returned her smile. "Shall we take a look around?"

"I think this would have been called the morning room," said Rose, looking at a writing table by the window, and the formal but still comfortable chairs grouped near the fireplace.

David nodded. "I can just imagine the Bennet sisters and their mother sitting here with their embroidery."

Through an arch to one side they could see the bedroom, and Rose grinned. "A real four-poster – I've always wanted to try one."

They walked through the arch, and David glanced across the room. Another doorway led to an en-suite bathroom, and he looked in. "One part of the facilities that's reassuringly modern, anyway."

He turned to Rose. "Do you want to freshen up while I bring the cases through?"

She nodded. When he returned, he could hear the sound of the shower, and shortly Rose emerged in a hotel bathrobe. "Your turn."

She sat on the bed, watching him, and David felt a moment of self-consciousness as he bent down to take off his shoes. Rose smiled reassuringly, and he continued undressing, putting his morning suit on a hanger and making a neat pile of the rest of his clothes on the chair by the bed.

Rose reached out to run a finger down his forearm. "Did you scratch yourself?"

David nodded. "I was checking the car yesterday, there's a bracket that's a little rough. I'll file it down when we get back."

He walked across to the bathroom. "I won't be long."

When he came out of the shower, Rose was in bed, the covers pulled over her, only the lamp on the bedside table illuminating the room.

She smiled. "I left some room for you."

David paused, fixing the moment in his mind. Then he slid under the covers beside her, his eyes not leaving hers.

He reached out to touch her face, and felt her eyelashes on his fingertips as she blinked. She turned her head slightly, her breath warm on his palm as her lips touched his skin, then looked into his eyes again. "Kiss me."

As their lips met, David reached out to her, his fingers barely touching her skin, and she smiled. "I won't break," she whispered. She closed her eyes as he caressed her gently.

His lips followed his touch, and she felt something awaken in her, a flame she'd known was there waiting but had kept to the glow of a promise. "Darling..."

***

When she woke, David was still sleeping, and she propped herself on one elbow to look at his face. His expression was utterly peaceful, reminding her of paintings she'd seen of medieval saints.

He opened his eyes, turning his head to look at her. "Naked and unashamed," he quoted, and she returned his smile, leaning over to kiss him. "Good job there weren't any apples in that fruit bowl the hotel left for us, then."

She stood and walked over to the bathroom, feeling totally at ease. When she returned, David was just putting the hotel phone down. "It seems almost sacrilegious to cover you up, but breakfast will be here in a minute."

She pulled on her robe. "I can always take it off again."

He grinned. "True."

There was a knock on the door. "Come in," called David.

The door opened, and a young woman entered pushing a trolley. "Would you like me to set things out on the table?"

David glanced at Rose. "No, thanks, that's fine. We'll serve ourselves."

She nodded, and slipped out, closing the door behind her.

David held Rose's chair for her as she sat down, and she glanced up at him with a smile.

"Now, what would you like to start with…?" he asked.

When they'd finished breakfast, David poured Rose another cup of coffee, and they moved to chairs in the wide bay window overlooking a formal garden.

Rose closed her eyes, the morning sun warm on her face. "This is such a lovely place, it's almost a shame we have to move on."

David smiled. "Our flight isn't till this afternoon, so we have a little time to enjoy it."

He got up from his chair. "Everything was such a blur yesterday, I forgot to give you your present."

Rose smiled. "Actually I have a little something for you, too. Can you bring me my bag?"

When David returned, he handed Rose her bag. She took out the small velvet-covered box, and passed it across to David. "Hope you like them."

He opened the box, and laughed softly, shaking his head. "I'm going to start suspecting you of having Poppy's gift if you're not careful."

Rose's face showed pleasure and puzzlement. "How's that?"

David handed her a small package. "Open it – you'll see."

She carefully tore off the paper, and opened the small box. "Oh!"

Inside nestled a pair of earrings, gold and silver, their pendants set with tiny ovals of lapis lazuli, the blue flecked with tiny glints of gold.

Rose nodded, smiling. "So we'll match, then."

David grinned. "I didn't tell you we were going to the High Commissioner's reception, did I? It's at the old Maharajah's palace."

"Wow," said Rose. "It sounds like a different world."

She finished her coffee. "How about a walk? It's such a lovely day."

David watched as she dressed. "I never really understood before, what it meant by 'two shall become one', but I'm beginning to get the idea."

He pulled on his own clothes, and they walked out onto the paved area overlooking the garden. Across the manicured lawns was an area of woodland, and Rose said, "Shall we head over there? It'll be nice and cool."

Hand in hand they walked to the edge of the trees. "The girls won't be waiting to sprinkle magic dust on us this time," grinned Rose.

"I can still be a lion," said David. He pretended a fierce expression, growling, and scooped Rose off her feet, carrying her into the woods. "Any last words before I eat you up?"

"Yes," said Rose.

"Go on then."

"Just 'yes', she grinned. "If you were a lion, I'd want you to eat me."

David shook his head, smiling. He set her back on her feet and they walked deeper into the wood, the air cooler and smelling faintly of pine needles.

"Look," pointed Rose, "there's a little clearing."

They walked back out into the sunlight, and Rose suppressed a squeal as David tumbled her to the ground, pinning her down on the grass with his body. He kissed her gently. "I didn't hurt you, did I?"

She shook her head. "I don't think you could."

He held her for a while, one arm under her head, the other around her waist, and Rose closed her eyes. "There's nowhere else I'd rather be."

Finally David sighed. "I suppose we'd better get back. We have to be at the airport a couple of hours before the flight."

He brightened. "But I think there's somewhere we can get a decent lunch."

Rose shook her head, smiling. "We didn't finish breakfast all that long ago."

When they got back to their suite, David said, "There's still plenty of time for you to have a shower if you want one."

She grinned. "Wash my back for me?"

***

They pulled up in the airport car park, and Rose said, "We aren't leaving the car here the whole time, are we?"

David shook his head. "Chris will pick it up, and he'll come and fetch us when we get back."

He fetched a trolley, and piled their luggage on. "Right – let's find the check-in."

He pushed the trolley to the check-in desk for first class, and smiled at the young woman behind the desk, putting their tickets and passports on the counter.

She glanced through the documents. "Ah, Mr Stuart, one of the tickets is in a different name to the passport?"

David nodded. "Copy of our marriage certificate in the back there."

She looked up smiling. "In that case, congratulations. You're flying through to Kolkata?"

"That's right."

She tapped keys. "I should tell you that if you're connecting with a domestic flight, the facilities at Kolkata are a little basic."

David nodded again. "I've travelled that way before. My parents live in the north of West Bengal, they've not met Rose yet."

She smiled. "Well, that's all the paperwork done."

Their cases vanished out of sight on the conveyor belt. "I'd suggest you go through security straight away, there can be a bit of a queue."

David took the documents she held out. "Thank you, you've been very helpful."

Rose glanced across the concourse. "It's that way for security, isn't it."

They were quickly through the checks, and Rose looked at the array of luxuries on offer as they walked through the duty free shop. "Anything you particularly fancy?" asked David.

Rose shook her head. "Don't think so. I'm sure there'll be much more interesting things when we get to India."

They emerged into the food court, and David pointed to a sign over in the far corner. "I thought we could try that place."

They found a table, and Rose looked at the menu, grinning. "Did you know they had paninis?"

David chuckled. "I might have had a quick look on the web site. Ham and cheese?"

He went to the counter, returning with a tray. "They'll bring our food in a minute. I got you coffee, but only a single espresso – I thought you might like to sleep for a while on the first leg of the journey, to try and avoid the jetlag."

A waiter arrived with their paninis, and Rose took a bite. "Mm, this is good."

As she was picking up the last crumbs from her plate with a finger, David glanced at the screen showing departure information. "Looks like they're ready to board us."

They walked the length of the concourse, and a smiling stewardess checked their boarding cards at the gate. "First class is up those stairs," she indicated.

They climbed the stairs and went along a short corridor to where the gate met the curve of the aircraft. Another stewardess looked at their cards. "Ah, Mr and Mrs Stuart. Please, let me take you to your suite."

Rose glanced at David as they followed her. "You really did push the boat out."

The stewardess opened the door. "Please, make yourselves comfortable. We'll be taking off shortly, but once we're airborne please feel free to press the call button if there's anything you need."

She closed the door behind her, and David gestured to the window seat. "I guess you'll want a view, darling?"

Rose sat down. "Wow, this seat is amazing."

David nodded. "And it folds down flat so you can sleep. The connecting flight from Dubai to Kolkata isn't quite so special, but we'll still have plenty of space."

The engines started to spool up, and David took his own seat, glancing across to make sure Rose had fastened her seat belt. They watched the safety video, then the plane started to taxi towards the runway.

There was a pause, then Rose glanced at David with a trace of fear in her eyes as the engines rose to a scream, the acceleration pushing her back into the seat. "Darling?"

He reached out and grasped her hand tightly, his eyes on her face. As the plane lifted into the air, she closed her eyes for a few moments, then turned to look at him. "I'm OK now…"

There was a quiet chime, and David unfastened his seatbelt, going over to Rose and wrapping his arms around her. "I'm sorry, darling, I didn't think to ask if flying bothered you."

Rose shook her head. "It's fine."

She smiled. "Now, let's see if we can figure this seat out, and I'll take your advice, try and sleep for a while."

David reclined the seat for her, and she turned on her side. He carefully laid the blanket over her, and kissed her hair. "Sweet dreams."

He returned to his seat, deciding to read for a while, and took out the novel he'd picked up at the airport, a romance set in America at the time of the Wall Street crash in the nineteen-thirties.

After a couple of hours, Rose stirred, opening her eyes. "Where are we?"

David glanced at the map display. "Somewhere over southern Iraq."

Rose sat up and looked out of the window. "Wow, what an amazing view. Come and look."

David perched on the seat beside her. Below, snow-covered mountains reflected the sun in an almost painful glare.

"Look," pointed Rose, "you can even see cars moving on the roads."

Here and there, the sun glinted off a moving dot, and David nodded. "I can hardly believe we can see them from this altitude."

There was a tap at the door, and David opened it to find the stewardess outside with a trolley. "Would you like some refreshments?"

"Please," David smiled.

The stewardess brought in a tray and put it down on the table. "We'll be serving dinner a couple of hours before we land."

The door closed, and David lifted the cloth covering the tray. "Mm," he said. "I think you'll like this, Rose."

He handed her a bowl, and she smiled. "I love iced fruit."

She shivered. "Although with all that snow outside, I somehow feel a little chilly."

"It'll be warm enough when we get to India," David promised.

He took a spoonful of fruit, and closed his eyes. "Surely it doesn't get any better than this."

When they'd finished eating, David said, "Do you want to nap again?"

Rose shook her head. "Do you think two could fit into these seats?" she asked hopefully. "It would be nice to have a cuddle."

"Definitely," said David, shifting over to make room for her. She curled up next to him, closing her eyes. "Perfect."

"What would you like to talk about?" asked David.

Rose thought for a moment. "Tell me more about where we're going."

"Well," said David, "I told you that my parents live near the Air Force base – the runway is only about half a mile from the house, but there isn't too much noise.

"Their house is in a village – Dad got to know one of the families there really well when he used to fly out there – and they have a piece of land. You saw some of the trees when we spoke to them on the computer, remember."

He paused. "The area is really lush – being near the mountains, there's plenty of water – and there are wildlife reserves all around, so we'll be able to see elephants, and rhino, and all sorts of birds.

"The place where we're staying is further east, and closer to the mountains – not far away is the most beautiful picnic spot in the world bar none, and I'm sure the couple who are looking after us will be able to arrange to take us out there and cook us a meal. We'll need a four-by-four and a driver as well to get there, of course."

Rose shook her head, smiling. "Three people to take the two of us for a picnic. It reminds me of that Jack Vettriano painting, the couple dancing on the sand in the rain while the butler and the maid hold umbrellas for them."

David grinned. "If you want to dance, my love, then dance we shall. I can guarantee there won't be any rain, though."

He continued. "There are quite a few interesting places we can go – there's an old fort, ruined now, where the British used to keep political prisoners. There's the Maharajah's palace, where we're going for the reception. Oh, and there's the vulture sanctuary."

Rose looked puzzled. "Why do vultures need a sanctuary? I thought they were everywhere in India."

David shook his head, and Rose saw his expression become sad. "They're under threat because of a drug the farmers use to treat the cattle – when the cattle die and the vultures eat them, the drug kills the birds. They're trying to ban it, but in the meantime the only way to conserve the birds is to keep them in captivity and give them safe meat."

Rose nodded. "I'm glad they're trying to help them. We should go and look."

She thought for a moment. "It all sounds quite rural. Are there towns nearby? I'm not sure how well I'd handle a big city, but it'd be nice to get at least an idea of what things are like when there are a lot of people about."

David grinned. "Admit it, you want to go shopping."

Rose looked sheepish. "But we did promise Lily something special to wear," she said, a teasing glint in her eye.

"Of course we'll go into town," David said, smiling.

He looked thoughtful. "I wonder if there'll be any weddings in the village while we're there. That's another experience it would be a pity for you to miss."

Rose nodded. "I bet they're pretty different to ours," she said.

David chuckled. "You don't know the half of it," he said.

Rose shifted position slightly. "Think I could doze for a while now. You don't mind, do you?"

David shook his head. "I think I could nap for a while myself."

The plane forged on through the darkening sky as they slept wrapped in each other's arms, and below them the lights of cities and towns gave way to the glow of campfires in the desert.

The soft chime sounded again, and David took a deep breath. "Think that means it's nearly time for dinner."

Rose opened her eyes, blinking. "Mm."

"You can have a shower if you like," offered David. "You'll feel fresher."

Rose smiled. "I'd like that. Is there anything this plane doesn't have?"

She opened the door, glancing to either side. "No-one seems to be about."

When she returned from the shower, David was glancing through the selection of films on the screen. "I thought we could watch something for the last part of the flight."

Rose looked at the screen. "How about Pocahontas?" she said. "The music's nice."

"OK."

There was a tap on the door. "Dinner," grinned David. "Did you decide what you wanted from the menu?"

As they sat down to eat, David clicked the control to start the film, and they watched as John Smith found himself falling in love with the young woman from a world so alien to his own.

"I've always wondered what it must be like to marry someone from such a different background," mused Rose.

Finally the credits rolled, and David flicked back to the map. "We're practically there."

The stewardess returned briefly to clear their dinner things and make sure the seats were upright, and Rose sat down, tightening her seat belt.

David glanced across. "Will you be OK?"

She nodded. "As long as you hold my hand…"

***

They got off the plane, and Rose looked round in awe at the airport. "It's absolutely huge."

David grinned "Not huge enough, apparently. See out there, where they're building? That's the *new* airport, about four times the size."

He glanced at the signs. "Ah, the hotel's that way. You did put a change of clothes in your hand luggage, didn't you?"

Rose nodded. "My cotton dress, I thought it'd be cooler for when we finally arrive."

They walked along the concourse, Rose glancing aside at the glittering shops. "Look," she said, "aren't those toy camels cute?"

David grinned. "Small, medium, or large?"

He went into the shop, returning with a small carrier bag. Rose looked at the coins in his hand. "They give you change in local currency?"

"More souvenirs," smiled David. "We can give them to Lily and Pops, maybe put a couple in when we wrap presents for people."

They reached the hotel, and David checked them in. Rose looked at the buttons in the lift. "Wow – how high are we going?"

"All the way to the top," grinned David. "And you have to close your eyes."

Rose obeyed, and when the lift stopped David took her hand, leading her out into what she sensed was an open space.

"OK, you can look now," he said.

Rose opened her eyes and gasped. They stood in a large marble-floored atrium, with a fountain in the centre and exotic plants here and there. Floor to ceiling windows looked out over the sea, and through double doors at the other end she could see another room, with more deep windows.

She wrapped her arms around David. "This is wonderful - you're really spoiling me."

They walked through into the lounge, and Rose stood gazing out across the water while David took their things into the bedroom.

After a few moments she followed, looking into the bathroom. "I'm definitely looking forward to trying the jacuzzi."

David grinned, putting his arms around her from behind and kissing her hair. "The bed looks worth a try, too. You tired?"

She turned in his arms, smiling. "Not really. But what's that got to do with it...?"

***

The next morning after breakfast they checked out, Rose taking a last look at the stunning view of the islands in the bay, and headed for their next flight.

David glanced at Rose in her cotton dress and sandals. "You look perfect."

She smiled. "I'm already a little nervous about meeting your parents. I remember what the girl at the airport said about Kolkata – I hope I'm not too frazzled when we finally arrive."

"You'll be fine," reassured David.

They boarded the plane, and settled into their seats in first class. Soon they were airborne again, and Rose looked out of the window. "We're crossing a coast," she said. "Will that be India?"

David nodded. "We fly across pretty much the whole width of the country. I'm afraid the route doesn't take us near the mountains this time, but going back we're flying via Delhi, so you'll see them then."

"Have you ever been to Everest?" Rose asked. "You know, the base camp or anything?"

David shook his head. "I've never visited Nepal, though you're right, it's hardly any distance at all from where we'll be."

He looked thoughtful. "Maybe when we come back with the girls we can take a trip – I'm sure they'd love to see Kathmandu."

Rose nodded. "I think I'll shut my eyes for a while," she said. "The next meal's lunch, isn't it?"

David grinned. "I think we're doing pretty well with the time zones, actually."

He took out his book, his thoughts soon transported half a world away.

***

Rose touched David's arm. "I think we're coming in to land."

He opened his eyes. "Mm. Are you OK, darling?"

"I'm fine," she reassured him. "I'm getting used to it."

When they were on the ground, the plan taxied over to the gate and the passengers began to disembark. As they walked up the sloping corridor, David took a deep breath, and Rose tried to identify the emotion on his face.

"I love the smell," he said. "I've never been quite sure what it actually is — probably the heat, and people, and cooking, and a touch of diesel fumes. But it gets me every time I step off the plane."

Rose took his hand, smiling "I'm glad we could come."

They queued for immigration, and Rose couldn't help staring a little at the impressive turban and beard of the Sikh gentleman behind the desk.

Once their passports had been inspected and their visas stamped, David found a trolley and retrieved their cases. He grinned at Rose. "Ready? It's just a short walk from here to the domestic terminal."

She nodded. "Sure."

They walked out into the sunlight, David pushing the trolley, and Rose looked around. "It doesn't seem as chaotic as I expected."

David nodded. "That's another reason I chose this route."

As they walked, Rose glanced across the road. "Oh, look, David, there are two of the sisters."

David looked across at the two women in their distinctive white saris with blue edging. "Well spotted."

They reached the domestic terminal, and David negotiated the queue for the luggage scanner, then took their cases to the check-in for their flight.

"Will it be like a budget airline back home?" asked Rose. "Those are always a bit of a maul."

David shook his head. "It surprised me at first, but no – the internal carriers here are absolutely fantastic. You'll see."

They went through security again, Rose smiling at the green-clad girl who was in charge of the women-only line.

When they reached the departure area, Rose looked around at the metal chairs, already filled with people reading or dozing under their newspapers. A stray cat wandered through the door from the outside, ignored by the soldiers guarding the gate, and there was a small shop selling sandwiches wrapped in plastic.

Rose glanced at David. "The girl at the airport was right, it does look a bit basic. Not that I'm complaining – it's amazing to even be here at all."

He nodded. "Come with me – I know where we can get a seat."

Rose followed him up a flight of stairs. Along a short corridor was another lounge, almost deserted, and to one side a stall displaying sweets and bottled drinks.

"Have a seat," indicated David. "I'll get us a couple of things."

Rose sat down, and he returned with a tall tube of crisps and two bottles of lemonade. "It's probably time we took our malaria tablets."

Rose made a face as she washed the bitter pill down with a mouthful of lemonade. "Yuck."

David glanced at the departure board. "I think that's us."

A small queue formed at the gate, and they joined it. Rose blinked as one of the attendants touched her arm. "Please, madam, sir, to the front."

They walked down a ramp to the tarmac, the other passengers following, and a bus took them out to the waiting plane. "Did they do that because we're Westerners?" whispered Rose.

David nodded. "I still haven't got my head round it. They don't seem to bear any ill will on account of the colonial days, and they're incredibly proud of their democracy and their independence, but then they go and do something like that."

He smiled. "Of course, some of it may just be pragmatic – we are tourists, after all."

They climbed the steps to the plane, and Rose smiled at the stewardesses in their pencil skirts and crisp white blouses. When they reached the cabin, a steward greeted them. "Sir, madam, would you like to sit in the seats by the emergency exit? There's more room."

David nodded. "Thank you."

The doors were closed and the plane started to taxi. The intercom came to life, and Rose was surprised to hear an Australian accent.

"This is your first officer speaking. On behalf of Captain Sharma I'd like to welcome you to our flight today. We're expecting to depart from Kolkata promptly, and our flight time will be just over an hour. Weather at our destination is good, temperature on the ground about twenty degrees. We hope you enjoy your flight with us."

The intercom clicked off, and the cabin staff ran through the safety drill, then took their own seats for takeoff.

When the plane was in the air, a stewardess pushed her trolley through the cabin and stopped by David's seat. "Your meals, sir, madam."

She put trays in front of them. "What would you like to drink?"

David glanced at Rose. "Coffee?"

She shook her head. "Another cold drink would be nice."

"Two Cokes, then, please," David requested.

The stewardess served their drinks, then moved on.

"Did you arrange that before we got on?" asked Rose.

David nodded. "You can select your meal when you book the tickets – the web site is great. Easier than the international flights, in fact."

He opened the box on his tray. "Hope it's not too spicy for you."

Rose grinned. "Are you kidding?"

She took a bite of her sandwich. "Mm, it's good – it does have a kick to it, though."

It seemed only a short time before the plane was descending again, and Rose looked out of the window. "There are fighter planes on the tarmac?"

"That's right – the airport here is military as well as civil. Suggest you don't take any pictures."

They got off the plane, this time walking to the terminal building, and Rose watched as their luggage moved past them on a trolley pulled by a small tractor.

David again found a trolley, and retrieved their cases from the carousel, piling them up.

"Right," he said. "Mum and Dad should be waiting for us outside the barrier. It won't be hard to spot them – did you notice we haven't seen another white face since we left Kolkata?"

Rose linked her arm through his for reassurance as they walked toward the gap in the barrier, hoping David's parents wouldn't see the gesture as too possessive.

Suddenly David smiled and waved. "There they are."

He pushed the trolley out onto the pavement, and Rose smiled shyly as David's parents spotted them through the crowd.

"You made it," smiled David's mother. She stepped quickly forward to embrace Rose. "Hello, darling. It's wonderful to finally meet you for real."

David's father waited his turn to hug her. "We're so glad you decided to come."

Rose nodded. "Thank you for picking us up, Mr Stuart."

David's mother waved her hand. "Please, we're Rachel and Mark."

Mark took over pushing the trolley. "Our vehicle's waiting just across there."

Rose had heard a baby's first experience of the world described as 'booming, buzzing confusion', and as they drove from the airport into the nearest town, she decided the phrase fitted her impressions perfectly. People were everywhere, and so were goats, chickens, cows, vehicles of all shapes and sizes.

The first time a lorry appeared to be driving straight towards them, only to veer aside into a gap in the traffic, Rose flinched, but she soon realised that the drivers had amazing judgement, and their driving was simply not hampered by the conservative rules she was used to on Western roads.

"We'll be out of the town soon," said Mark. He pointed. "Keep an eye out for kites scavenging, you can get a really close look at them."

Finally the road left the town and began to climb up the side of a steep gorge, the river moving slowly beneath them. Rose looked around, then exclaimed, "Oh! Monkeys!"

The monkeys – from infants to grey-haired adults – sat here and there by the side of the road. "People throw food to them," explained Rachel. "Because they represent Hanuman, it's a kind of religious observance. So of course they hang around waiting for vehicles to pass. But they won't bother us."

The road continued to wind its way upward, and here and there groups of people were repairing the surface. "Aren't there any machines?" asked Rose.

Mark nodded. "They do have them, but for a lot of the jobs it's simpler to employ people to do the work by hand. Labour's cheap here, and for many of them work guaranteed by the government is a kind of social security."

Rose watched a group of women in saris spreading tar on the surface of the road, then pushing stones from a bucket into the hot tar at regular intervals. She'd seen hundreds of yards of road with the patterned stones, and she was stunned at the sheer time and effort put in by these people on every inch, just so that she could pass by with hardly a backward glance.

David squeezed her hand. "There's a lot to take in, there are so many things that are different to the way we'd do them."

Rose nodded, leaning against his shoulder as they drove on.

Mark pointed ahead of them. "We're nearly at the junction. If you go left, the road takes you straight up into the mountains, to Darjeeling."

The name conjured up the fragrance of tea in Rose's mind. "And the other way?"

"We go straight on," said Rachel. "It's a long road cross-country to the east, but I promise it's worth it."

They reached the fork in the road, and Rose glanced left, wondering if sometime they'd have a chance to travel that way. Up ahead, she saw the graceful spans of a bridge across the gorge, and she asked, "Do we go across there?"

Mark nodded. "The Coronation Bridge – named for George the Sixth. You'll see the two lion statues at one end, the locals call it Tiger Bridge in their language because it's the nearest word they have."

David glanced at Rose, smiling. "Tiger, tiger," he said softly. Rose nodded, her fingers pressing his.

They crossed the bridge, and the road wound its way down the other side of the gorge then turned east, away from the river.

"It's about another four hours to the village from here," said Mark. "We thought you'd want to break your journey and travel on east tomorrow."

He grinned. "Anyway, we have a surprise for you."

They travelled on, and Rose drank in the sights and sounds – tea gardens, the railway running near the road and sometimes crossing it, bustling towns giving way again to neat fields bordered by raised grassy walkways.

She pointed to a group of white birds standing in a field. "What are those?"

"Egrets," replied Mark. "And you might see a bittern or two, they're harder to spot because they're brown."

At one point the road passed through a stretch of forest, and Rose pointed. "David, look at that, isn't it beautiful?"

The branch of a tree grew low over the road, festooned with orchids in full flower. "You can take a photo if you like," said Mark. He spoke to the driver, and they pulled in at the side of the road.

Rose took out her camera, and got several shots of the tree. "That's great."

They carried on, the road now very potholed in some places. "Now I see why we have a four-by-four," said Rose.

Rachel nodded. "The rains do a lot of damage to the roads. It's a vicious circle – in most places they never quite build the road base deep and strong enough, so the water takes material away, and they have to keep repairing the holes, so they never have the money to build better foundations."

They reached a stretch of smooth road, and the driver accelerated. "We're nearly there," said Mark.

They passed a piece of land enclosed by a fence, with a low building to one side and what looked like open huts made of palm thatch scattered around.

"That's the new restaurant," explained Rachel. "They really want to attract tourists, give them the facilities they want. There's certainly plenty to see."

Rose nodded. "David told me about the wildlife reserves and the vulture sanctuary."

Mark smiled. "They have a couple of chicks this year – they're delighted."

The driver turned off the road onto a gravelled track, slowing again. The track wound through stands of palm trees and past houses, mainly of concrete with corrugated iron roofs. Here and there a small car stood outside, and Rose looked puzzled.

"How do the cars survive the roads?" she asked.

Rachel nodded. "You may well ask – but they seem to have mastered the art of going round potholes, or even down into them slowly then out again. Certainly it takes an awfully long time to get anywhere compared to what we're used to."

In the distance there was a rumble, as if of thunder, and Rose glanced at David. "Thought you said no rain?"

He grinned. "That was one of the Air Force jets – we're nearly at the house."

Finally the track ended at a house which looked much like the ones they'd passed, though a little larger and with the shutters and ironwork painted in bright colours. Next to the house stood a low building with palm-thatched sides, a thin thread of smoke rising through an opening in the roof.

Mark nodded. "Sita's already preparing dinner."

They got out, and the driver carried the luggage to the verandah, then drove off, the tyres sending up a low cloud of dust as he disappeared into the distance.

Rachel smiled. "Right, let me show you where you'll be sleeping."

She opened a door leading from the verandah, and David and his father carried the luggage in.

"We'll give you two a while to land after all that bumping about," said Mark. "Come out when you're ready, we'll be under the trees at the back."

"If you want to freshen up, the easiest way is just to stick your head under the pump while someone works the handle," suggested Rachel, smiling.

David closed the door. "How are you doing, darling?"

Rose nodded. "Fine. I wouldn't mind just lying down for a minute, though."

She stretched out on the bed, and David joined her. "I'm afraid we'll need the mosquito net tonight," he said, pointing to hooks on the tall bedposts.

Rose grinned. "That's fine – it'll be a bit like when I slept in the tent with the girls, pretending to be the princess from Love's Labour's Lost."

David smiled. "It used to be traditional for a princess to have a sort of tent over her bed – a canopy to signify her importance."

Rose touched his shoulder. "That's very sweet, but really I'm just me."

David kissed her lightly. "You're still my princess."

Rose sat up. "I think I'm up to going out again now. Want to try the pump?"

He nodded. "Just be careful not to swallow any of the water – it's pretty clean, the well's deep, but I don't want to take any chances. Dad's brought plenty of bottled water for us."

They walked out to the yard, and David worked the handle while Rose splashed her face and arms, then he stuck his head under the spout, spluttering, while Rose returned the favour.

They found David's parents sitting behind the house. "Have a seat," Mark indicated. "Sita will bring tea, then our meal."

After a few moments a young woman appeared with a tray. She beamed at David and Rose, putting their cups down on the low table in front of them.

"Thank you," said Rose. "You're welcome," Sita replied with a warm smile.

She returned after a few moments with plates and bowls, and Mark lifted a lid. "Here's rice, and this other one is daal – they make it very runny here, so be careful. Then we have curried chicken, and vegetables."

"The chicken's on the bone," added Rachel, "so feel free to pick it up in your fingers."

David heaped rice onto Rose's plate. "Try to eat plenty – I always find the heat makes me really hungry."

When they'd finished eating, Mark seemed to be waiting for something, and he nodded as he heard the sound of an engine approaching. There was something strangely familiar about the sound, and Mark grinned. "Your surprise is here."

They walked back round to the front of the house, and Rose shaded her eyes to look along the track. "No!" she said incredulously as she caught sight of the approaching car.

"I did mention it," grinned David. "Dad, what have you done?"

The car stopped, and a large Indian gentleman in a khaki uniform, sporting an impressive handlebar moustache, opened the door. He stepped onto the running board then down to the ground.

"She's a beauty, isn't she," were his first words.

"I think our guests are speechless, Commander Sridhar," chuckled Mark. "Come on in, I'll get you a drink."

When they were again seated in the shade, the commander with a glass of whisky in his hand, he spoke.

"Mark told me how much effort you'd put into restoring your own car, so I knew you'd appreciate this one. It used to be the Maharajah's, you know."

Rose was about to ask him how the car came to be his now, but something made her hold back. "It is beautiful."

He smiled. "So, I want you to use it while you're here. I have a perfectly good jeep, my adjutant will get me around."

David nodded. "We're very grateful. I'll take good care of her."

Rose glanced at him, smiling.

"I'll drop you back at the base," said Mark, getting up.

"Is there anything else you need?" Rachel asked Rose and David.

Rose shook her head. "Probably time we went to bed, it's been a long journey."

She took Rachel's hand. "Thanks so much for all this."

Rachel smiled. "It's the least we could do."

They went back to their room, and David set the mosquito net up as Rose undressed.

"OK," he said, "climb in, and I'll make sure there are no gaps when I join you."

Finally they were both under the net, and Rose smiled. "We don't really even need the sheet over us, it's so warm."

David grinned. "You won't hear any argument from me – I can just look at you."

Rose raised her eyebrows. "I hope looking isn't all you're going to do…"

***

The air was cooler in the morning, and Rose put on jeans, then a jumper over her t-shirt, before going out onto the verandah. Sita was setting the things out for breakfast, and she paused, smiling and putting her hands together in an obvious gesture of respect.

Rose did her best to imitate the gesture in return as Rachel came round the corner. "I see you're picking things up," Rachel said.

Rose nodded. "I really want to get on with the people here – the last thing I want is to cause offence."

Rachel shook her head. "Don't worry. Just keep your eyes open, and ask if there's anything that doesn't make sense. Most of the people you'll meet are used to Westerners, and if you make an effort even with little things – like the greeting – they'll be absolutely delighted."

David appeared, suppressing a yawn. "Is breakfast ready yet?"

Rachel rolled her eyes. "Not even here a day and you're just the same," she teased.

Sita returned with a plate, and David's eyes lit up. "Mm, my favourite."

They sat down, and David explained to Rose. "It's a kind of deep fried bread, a bit like a cross between a waffle and a croissant. We put jam on them, Sita thinks we're mad, but it tastes great."

Rose followed his example and bit into one of the soft ovals. "Mm, they do taste good."

Sita brought coffee, and Rose sipped. "It's very milky."

"I can get her to make it black if you like," offered David.

Rose shook her head. "I'm determined not to just have things the way I'd usually prefer them – I'll try everything that comes, and if I don't like it I'll just have something else instead."

David grinned. "Very wise. There's one fruit that's very popular here, it's called jackfruit. It looks like a couple of hedgehogs stuck together and painted yellow. For some reason, I just can't stand the taste, it makes me queasy. But maybe you'll like it."

They finished their breakfast, and David walked over to the Rolls, finding Mark checking everything carefully. "Anything I need to know?"

Mark shook his head. "It's fine. Fortunately the road from here to Hathipota is fairly good, but then again this car was built specially to come to India in the last century, so I don't think you'll have any problems."

They walked back to the house. "You ready, Rose?" asked David.

She came out of their room. "Just finished shutting the cases."

David and Mark carried the luggage out to the car, and David opened the door for Rose to get into the passenger seat, then slid behind the wheel.

"Enjoy yourselves," said Mark.

"We'll see you in three weeks," said Rachel. "I'll make sure we arrange a couple of trips for you around here, too."

David pressed the starter, and the engine came to life. Rose turned and waved as they drove down the track, then settled in her seat as the house dropped from sight behind them.

"You'll be all right with the driving, won't you, darling?" she asked.

David nodded. "We won't be going very fast, and no-one will be able to miss us in the Maharajah's car."

They reached the main road, and David turned east again. "If you look carefully, it's clear enough today that you'll see the mountains in a while."

Rose watched the horizon carefully. "Oh! There they are."

She shook her head. "Now I see why they call this place the roof of the world."

They drove on, eventually reaching a fairly large town. David picked his way carefully through the streets, and Rose tried to smile at everyone who gave them a curious glance.

Finally they were on the open road again. "We head north for a while now," said David. The mountains seemed as distant as before, but the landscape on either side of the road became more undulating, the tea bushes still covering the bumps and dips in the ground.

They came to a T-junction, a concrete sign giving the place names to left and right.

"Left," said David, turning the wheel.

Rose looked concerned as the road petered out into what looked like a broad, dry river bed, its surface a light dusty grey. "Are we going the right way?"

David grinned. "Sure. We wouldn't be able to cross here in the rainy season, but right now it's fine. You remember the satellite photos we looked at, all those vertical grey lines where the water runs off the mountains? That's exactly where we are now."

He aimed the car towards a dip in the opposite bank, and soon they were back on the road. They passed the gated entrance to a tea garden, then David turned right onto a track. "Nearly there now."

The track led upward again, and Rose gasped as the foothills of the mountains came clearly into view. The steep slopes were covered in vegetation, and Rose smiled. "That must be the things we saw at the restaurant – balsam, and magnolia."

They reached a set of metal gates, beyond them a neat compound. In the centre, a wooden building stood on tall pillars, steps leading up to a balcony.

A man emerged from a low house at the edge of the compound, and quickly swung the gates open. He pressed his hands together in the gesture of respect.

"Sir, madam, welcome to Hathipota. I am Anit, my wife is Aditi, we'll be looking after you."

David opened the boot, and Anit picked up the two heaviest cases. "Please, I'll come back for the rest. Follow me."

He led them up the steps into the lodge, where a young woman was setting the table. The dining area was panelled from floor to ceiling in wood, and there were doors opening off it on all sides.

Anit opened the door at the far end. "This is the largest room, but of course you can choose – no-one else is here."

David glanced at Rose. "This one?"

She walked through into the room and looked out of the window at the mountains, then turned back to him. "It's perfect."

Anit put the cases down and went to fetch the rest, while David explored the room. Off to one side was a spacious en-suite, and tall wooden cupboards lined one wall. "No problem with where to put all our clothes."

Aditi stood at the open door. "Lunch is nearly ready. Please, come through when you like, I'll make coffee."

"Let's sit at the table, David," said Rose. "Then after lunch we can take our coffee out onto the balcony and decide what we want to do next."

Lunch was a similar meal to the one Sita had prepared for them the night before. "We can ask Aditi to do some different things if you like," said David.

He spoke to her in her own language, and her face lit up. She answered enthusiastically, nodding.

David turned back to Rose. "I love doing that," he grinned. "Mum told you how much they appreciate us even trying, didn't she."

Rose nodded. "So one thing we're definitely going to do is, you're going to start teaching me."

They went out onto the shaded balcony, and Rose stretched out in one of the reclining chairs. "We're finally here."

David sat opposite her, his chair angled slightly to look south down to the plains. The heat haze shimmered, and he smiled. "It's much cooler here – I can see why the colonial administrators all escaped to the mountains for the summer."

Rose smiled. "When did you say the High Commissioner's reception is?"

"At the end of the week. It's a bit of a drive south again, but nothing like as long as the journey here."

Rose closed her eyes. "I think today we should just relax. Maybe when it's a little cooler this evening we can go for a walk."

The next few days were idyllic, and they soon found a routine which suited them – getting up whenever they woke, rotis for breakfast, sharing a leisurely bath, then a walk before the day became too hot.

After lunch they would sit on the balcony reading, or writing postcards, or just watching the kites soaring on the thermals, the smaller birds swooping and darting at the insects that came to feed on the flowers in the compound.

David kept his promise to teach Rose some of the language, and Aditi always broke into a brilliant smile when Rose tried out a new word or phrase. At David's suggestion, Aditi varied the menu a little, and Rose began to know the names of her favourite spices and herbs.

After dinner, they would sit again for a while, watching the sun go down, then get ready for bed, David looking through the mosquito net at the dark silhouette of the mountains as he waited for Rose to join him.

One night they crept out to the balcony, and David smiled at Rose, glancing upwards. "Cloudless climes and starry skies," he quoted, as she leaned her head on his shoulder.

After lunch on the day of the reception, David said, "We should start getting ready."

He watched as Rose changed into her dress and carefully put in her new earrings. "You look amazing."

Rose smiled. "I'll help you with those cuff links, shall I?"

David buttoned up his shirt, then watched as Rose carefully put the cuff links in. "I think we're ready, then," he said, pulling on his jacket.

Anit and Aditi stood watching as the Rolls set off down the track, and Rose looked across at David. "We really should do something for them before we leave, they've gone out of their way to be helpful."

David nodded. "I'll see what I can think of."

They retraced their path along the road, crossing the river bed and turning south at the T-junction.

Just before the town, David turned off the road, and they passed between moss-covered stone pillars. "This must be the entrance to the Maharajah's estate," said Rose.

David nodded. "They've done a pretty good job of restoring the palace, but the grounds aren't really what they would have been in his day."

Ahead of them Rose saw a lake, and beyond it a broad-fronted building with a central dome. "He really liked arches, didn't he."

David drove into the portico covering the entrance, and handed the keys to a waiting attendant, then helped Rose out of the car. They walked up the steps to the entrance hall, and a tall man with greying hair excused himself from the group he was talking to and approached them.

"I'm Sandy MacDonald, the High Commissioner," he said, holding out his hand.

David shook it warmly. "David Stuart, and this is my wife Rose."

MacDonald nodded. "I saw you arrive – that's a fine car you have there."

David grinned. "Only on loan, I'm afraid – my father knows the commandant at the border airbase."

"Well, do enjoy the reception. I'm afraid I must circulate."

He moved off, and Rose smiled at David. "Well, at least we can say we met him."

David snagged a couple of glasses from a passing tray and handed one to Rose. "Cheers, darling."

As they sipped, they saw a young Indian woman making her way towards them. From her height and slim figure Rose would have taken her for a girl of Poppy's age, but her bearing was confident, and when she spoke her voice held an unmistakeable air of authority.

"Welcome to the palace," she said. "I'm Maya. It's lovely to have you as guests. I am curious, though, how you come to be driving my grandfather's car."

She touched Rose's arm reassuringly when she saw their startled expressions. "I'm sorry," she said, her eyes twinkling with laughter. "I should have explained, my grandfather was the last Maharajah, and I know the car only from photographs. It's quite unmistakeable."

David returned her smile. "Commander Sridhar very kindly gave us the use of the car for our honeymoon. But I'm not sure if he knows how it came to be one of the base commander's perquisites."

She nodded. "Please, let's sit down. It's an interesting story."

They found seats in a corner away from the press of people, and Maya spoke again. "Actually Grandfather had quite a number of cars – it was a passion of his. When his son, my uncle, went to England to study, my grandfather gave the then commander of the base that car in exchange for making sure my uncle had the chance to learn to fly."

She smiled. "I can see I'll have to visit your Commander Sridhar – history is important for us."

There was the sound of a gong, and Maya looked up. "That's the signal for dinner. Please, join me – I want to hear more about how you come to be here."

She grinned. "And though Sandy is a very good diplomat, he's not very good at making conversation."

They followed her in to the dining room, and Rose's eyes widened at the crystal and silverware. David held her chair as she sat, while the High Commissioner did the same for Maya.

After the meal, they lingered over coffee, but David finally sighed. "We should be getting back."

Maya nodded. "I'm really glad we met. Please, visit again before you leave."

"We'll do our best," David promised.

A uniformed attendant brought the car, and David opened the door for Rose as always. They drove back through the estate, the lights from the palace reflecting on the surface of the lake.

By the time they reached the lodge, Rose was asleep, her head resting on David's shoulder. She stirred as he switched off the engine. "Are we home?"

David smiled, walking round to help her from the car. "Home from home, anyway."

She leaned on his arm as they climbed the steps up to the lodge. "Do you think we could give the girls a call tomorrow? It'd be nice to speak to them."

"Of course."

They slept in late the next morning, and David asked Aditi to make them omelettes. "I don't know if this is a late breakfast or an early lunch," he smiled.

They had a quiet day, and after supper David glanced at the clock on the wall. "I think we can call the girls now."

"They won't be in class or anything?" asked Rose.

David shook his head. "Pretty sure they have free time now."

He took out his mobile and dialled, putting it on speaker.

Poppy's familiar voice came from the phone, her excitement obvious. "Hi!"

They heard her call to Lily. "It's David and Rose – come quick."

"Hi, you two," came Lily's voice. "How's it going?"

"We're having a wonderful time," said Rose. "The High Commissioner's reception last night, and we met the Maharajah's granddaughter."

"Wow," said Lily. "Have you seen elephants yet? Or tigers?"

"There was an elephant working in the forest when we drove past one place," said Rose. "But we haven't been to the wildlife reserve yet. And sorry – no tigers so far either."

"OK," said Lily. "What else are you planning?"

"Mostly we're just relaxing, walking. Next week we're going on a picnic, then the week after that back to David's parents. They'll take us shopping, and to see the elephants. That's when we'll see a tiger if we ever will – the elephants take us into the jungle and the tigers don't know we're there."

"How are you two?" asked David.

"We're fine," said Poppy. "Lily's settling in great, and we're rehearsing already for the Christmas concert."

"Can't wait to hear that," grinned David. "OK, we'd better go – you can call us if you need to, remember, Pops."

"Will do," she promised. "Bye, then."

"Bye, darlings," said Rose.

David ended the call. "They sound fine."

Rose nodded. "I knew they'd be OK."

She yawned. "I think I'm still catching up after the excitement yesterday…"

***

The day of the picnic came round more quickly than Rose had expected, and after breakfast a large four-by-four arrived, Anit helping the driver to load everything they'd need onto the roof.

He tapped on the door of their room. "We can go now if you're ready."

Rose followed David down the steps, and they got into the back of the vehicle, Anit and Aditi in the front next to the driver.

They set off, and soon reached one of the grey watercourses, this time with water flowing down it in shallow rivulets. Instead of driving across the river bed as Rose had assumed they would, the driver turned upstream, splashing through the water for a while before guiding the vehicle to one side. The terrain rose, the river bed now rocky, and finally the driver stopped at the point where the water flowed from the first real rise of the foothills.

"This is it," said David. He helped Rose out of the vehicle, and she looked around at the spot they'd picked. Green slopes rose on either side, and in the centre the river trickled around rocks, making pools. Looking back the way they'd come, Rose could see the river bed widen. "Would that all really be full of water in the rains?"

David nodded. "So, where would you like to sit while Aditi and Anit are cooking?"

Rose selected a slightly higher spot not too far away, and Anit brought chairs, and a coolbox with bottles of lemonade.

They sat down, and David opened a bottle, passing it to Rose. "I'll have some if you don't want the whole bottle."

She drank, then got to her feet. "I think I'd like to paddle for a bit, if that's safe?"

David nodded. "Of course."

Rose picked her way down to the water, and took off her sandals, dipping her feet in the water. "It's lovely and cool."

David joined her, sitting on a nearby rock, and watched as Rose swirled her fingers in a rocky pool. "Look, there are tadpoles," she said.

Smoke rose from the fire that Anit had made to cook on, and David closed his eyes. "Didn't I tell you that this was the most perfect picnic spot in the world…"

Aditi took her time preparing lunch, and it was the middle of the afternoon before they sat down near the cooking fire to eat. Rose looked at her plate. "It's printed to look like banana leaves," she said. "I suppose that's what they would have used before."

David nodded. "If we do find there's a wedding in the village when we go back, you'll see a lot of the traditional ways of doing things."

Finally the sun began to set, and Anit and Aditi started to pack things up. "They're in no hurry," said David. "We can go for a walk if you want."

He offered Rose his hand as they picked their way up the other side of the gorge and followed a narrow path further into the rocks. Soon they were out of sight of the vehicle, and Rose leaned against a boulder, smiling at David.

"I don't think I've had a proper kiss today," she teased him.

He looked repentant. "Then I'll have to do something about that straight away."

He trapped her against the rock with his arms, and Rose smiled. "Remember that time in the tree house, when you were being a lion, and you ate up the girls but you were still hungry?"

David nodded. "And at the hotel, when you said if I was a lion you'd want me to eat you."

He growled quietly, and Rose closed her eyes. Their lips met, and she wrapped her arms around him with an urgency she hadn't expected. "They'll wait for us, won't they...?"

***

Finally it was their last day at Hathipota, and when the car was packed, David called Anit and Aditi to the dining room. "Rose and I really want to thank you for everything you've done. We'll definitely be back next summer with the rest of our family to stay again, the whole six weeks."

Anit smiled broadly. "That'll be no problem."

Aditi spoke in her own language, and Rose grinned, replying slowly but fluently.

"We'd better get going then," said David. As they drove off, he explained to Rose. "I couldn't think what we could give them, then I realised that knowing they had a definite booking for the lodge in high season next year was probably the thing that would make the biggest difference."

Rose nodded. "Lily and Pops will love this place, all the places to explore, and the birds, and that picnic spot. What did you say the place was called?"

"Chunia," said David. "And the tea garden behind it is Paskawa."

When they finally reached the village, Rachel and Mark were waiting at the point where the track ran over a small bridge.

"We guessed you'd be along around now," grinned Mark, "so we thought we'd wait and get a lift."

"Hop in," smiled David.

They drove the short distance to the house, and David parked the car on the area of grass outside. "I suppose Commander Sridhar will be back for his car soon."

"Don't forget to tell your Mum and Dad what we found out," reminded Rose.

David nodded. "We have a story to tell the commander that I think he'll like – and someone who wants to meet him."

"How mysterious," chuckled Rachel. "We thought you were going off for a quiet honeymoon retreat, and here you are with all these surprises."

"We did have a lovely time," said Rose. "And we've promised the couple at the lodge that we'll all go next summer – there's plenty of space."

Mark nodded. "Anyway, your room is ready for you, and we've lined up something for you to do practically every day."

David grinned. "No lazing about any more, is that it? I think we'll cope."

The next day was the elephant excursion round the wildlife reserve, and when they returned Rose was adamant that just for a moment in the distance she'd caught a glimpse of a black and orange shape disappearing into the forest. "I wasn't quick enough with my camera, though."

"Well, there are certainly tigers in the reserve," said Mark. "So I think you can count that one."

That evening Commander Sridhar came round, and when he heard the tale of their meeting with Maya he grinned so broadly Rose thought his face would split.

"I'll get the regimental historian to meet her and put a full account down in writing," he promised. "You two have done me a huge favour – what can I do in return?"

David shook his head. "More than letting us drive your amazing car for three weeks?"

The commander was still grinning as he drove off, turning back to wave at them.

The following day they drove to the vulture sanctuary, and Rose looked at the untidy bundles of fluff and feathers that were the vulture chicks. "Poor things," she said, "I bet they can't wait to have their proper plumage – a bit like the ugly duckling."

The next morning David came back in from the verandah and found Rose sitting on the bed.

"Are you OK?" he asked. "Has something happened?"

She didn't speak at first, but a shy smile spread across her face.

"Actually it's something that hasn't happened," she said. "David, I think I'm pregnant."

He scooped her into his arms, hugging her tightly, then caught himself, putting her down on the bed gingerly. "Oops, didn't mean to be so rough. Are you going to – that is, can we still fly back?"

She shook her head, laughing softly. "Don't worry, silly. Everything's fine. I think we might have to do some very different packing for our trip back here next summer, though."

"Can we tell Mum and Dad?" asked David.

Rose thought for a moment. "Let's keep it to ourselves for the time being."

She grinned. "I can't wait to see Poppy's face when we tell her."

David sat down slowly. "The summer house... you in the rocking chair..."

It was his turn to shake his head. "What was it the vicar said about God moving in mysterious ways?"

At the end of the week Mark and Rachel drove them back to the airport, David trying not to glance anxiously at Rose every time they bumped over a pothole.

As they flew back to Delhi, Rose looked out of the window at the mountains. "I'm glad you chose this route for the journey back."

In the distance she saw a small silver dart, a private jet heading back the way they'd come. As they approached the airport, Rose leaned closer to the window, trying to see some of the landmarks. "I think that's the Red Fort," she pointed.

By the time they reached Dubai, Rose was starting to flag. "I'm really looking forward to that first class suite."

She was still sleeping when they crossed the English coast, the white cliffs easily visible, and David hesitated before gently touching her shoulder. "We'll be landing in a few minutes."

Chris was waiting for them in the arrivals hall. "You two look great," he said. "Especially you, Rose. You've really got some colour in your cheeks."

She smiled, throwing David a knowing look. "Travel must be good for me."

They walked to the car, and Rose grinned as David helped her in. "We know another horse from this stable, don't we, darling."

When they turned into David's drive, Chris said, "I have a surprise for you, too."

The front door of the house opened, and Poppy and Lily burst out, running to hug David as he got out of the car, then tearing round to the other side to wrap their arms around Rose.

"Rose's Mum got them special permission to come home from school for the weekend," explained Chris.

He glanced at his car. "I'll leave you to it, then."

"Thanks so much, Chris," said Rose, kissing him on the cheek. "We'll be in touch."

They watched him drive off, then Rose put her arms around the girls' shoulders. "It's so good to see you – what a fantastic surprise."

"Why don't I make us a drink and we can go and sit in the summer house," suggested David. "We can unpack later."

He grinned. "And yes, Lily, we did bring you both something back to wear."

"Cool," grinned Lily. "Now we can go out for a curry again."

The girls went into the summer house while David went to the kitchen. When he came out, Poppy and Lily were sitting in their usual place on the sofa, while Rose sat in the rocking chair.

She moved her hand unconsciously to rest on her stomach, and Poppy's mouth dropped open. "Rose? Are you, I mean…"

Rose nodded, and Lily looked at her sister with an expression more of awe than anything else.

David stood behind Rose's chair, his hands on her shoulders. "So you two are going to have a little niece or nephew."

"That makes us…"

"Aunts," Lily finished Poppy's sentence. She grinned. "So we need to learn to knit, Pops."

Over the next few weeks, Rose began to notice her bump, and by the time the girls came home again for Christmas, she found she was having to move around a little more slowly.

Poppy came down one morning before the New Year to find David and Rose sitting at the kitchen table, papers spread out in front of them. "What are you doing?" she asked casually.

David looked up. "Hi, Pops. Well, the market's up for a change, and Rose and I are looking at the best way to reinvest."

He grinned. "After all, we have to make sure you two – and the little one – have a decent trust fund for college."

Poppy sat down slowly, glancing at the papers. She was silent for a while, then said, "If I told you I had a really strong feeling about this, would you listen?"

Rose put her hand on Poppy's, tears springing into her eyes. "Darling... You were right about everything turning out OK, and what you said in the summer house that time was the reason I'm going to have this baby. Of course we'll listen."

Poppy paused for a moment. "I don't know much about shares and things, but is gold something you can invest in?"

David nodded. "Particularly if there's uncertainty in the economy."

He looked at the papers again. "But if anything, the markets are up."

Poppy shook her head. "I just keep seeing gold."

David looked at Rose. "I'm prepared to take the chance."

Rose nodded. "OK."

David shuffled the papers into a pile. "I'll make the calls this afternoon. There's a broker I know – he's in India, in fact, he handled all the financial side of things when Mum and Dad moved out there."

He grinned at Poppy. "And I'll keep a little bit back so you and Lily can even wear some of your own investment."

She wrapped her arms around him. "Thanks, David. I know this is the right thing to do."